THE SAVAGE DAWN

THE VAMPIRE WORLD SAGA BOOK 3

PT HYLTON
JONATHAN BENECKE

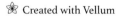

WHAT CAME BEFORE

ALEX GODDARD is the captain of the Ground Mission Team, an elite task force that supplies the ship *New Haven* with resources recovered from the vampire-infested Earth's surface.

The people of *New Haven* recently learned of the existence of another city, Agartha. Built into the side of a mountain, Agartha is protected one hundred intelligent vampires, led by JADEN.

DANIEL FLEMING, *New Haven*'s charismatic leader, believes in Resettlement. He tasks former GMT member FIREFLY with leading the effort to bring humans back to the surface of Earth.

But when Alex and the GMT stand up to Fleming, he sets a plan in motion to have them eliminated. After Fleming's people sabotage the GMT away ship, Alex and her team find themselves trapped in the ancient city of Denver. They set out on a desperate race against sunset, attempting to make it to Agartha before the Feral vampires come out. Jaden and his team rescue them, helping them battle the last few miles to Agartha after sundown.

Meanwhile, the first night of Resettlement does not go as planned. Firefly and his three hundred Resettlers are quickly killed by MARK and AARON, intelligent vampires with a grudge against Jaden. But the Resettlers soon arise, reborn as vampires under the complete control of their new masters.

Back on *New Haven*, Alex's allies CB, BRIAN, and JESSICA go on the run, hoping to escape Fleming's wrath. They are desperate and alone, all their friends gone, dead, or imprisoned.

In Agartha, Alex and Jaden plan their next move, hoping to find a way to take down Fleming, unaware of the new vampire army threatening humanity's existence.

PROLOGUE

Isaiah Craig glared at the guard through the bars of his cell. He'd been in this prison for nearly a month now, and in that time, he'd had almost no contact with the outside world, beyond the dozen guards who cycled in and out throughout the day. And it wasn't like the guards were chatty.

He still found it shocking how quickly his life had changed. A month ago, he'd been a general, tasked with overseeing both the badges and the Ground Mission Team. Law enforcement and the military had both reported to him. He'd probably been the most powerful person in *New Haven* who didn't sit on the City Council.

And then Fleming had come along, blown up that Council, taken control of the city and arrested Craig.

So where did that leave Craig? Could he still refer to himself as a general when he didn't even have freedom to leave the room?

He looked again at the guard outside and frowned. The man had reported to Craig not that long ago. Craig had been his boss's, boss's, boss. Now the guard didn't even deign to look at him.

Where was CB? Where was Kurtz? These two men had been his captains for years, his loyal seconds-in-command. Why would they allow him to sit in prison? Wouldn't they fight to get him out? Craig could only think of one reason they wouldn't: to protect their people. As different as CB and Kurtz were in many ways, they had one important thing in common: they cared more for the lives of the people who reported to them than they did for their own.

The video monitor in the corner flashed to life and the guard took a step forward. "All right, let's hear what the man has to say."

Craig scowled. The only times these monitors were used were during Fleming's city-wide announcements. He had mixed feelings about being forced to watch these. On the one hand, the sight of Fleming's smug face called up a righteous fury inside of Craig that he could barely suppress. On the other hand, these announcements were his only source of information about the city beyond these bars. As skewed as Fleming's perspectives were, it was through an announcement that Craig had learned that Alex was alive. Fleming had said that she was helping with the Resettlement efforts, but from the uncomfortable look on Alex's face, Craig got the idea that wasn't the truth.

Fleming's face filled the screen. ""Hello, my fellow citizens. Today I'm coming to you with some truly exciting news. We've had a rough go of it lately. I've asked for sacrifices from each and every one of you. My engineering crews have dismantled nonessential systems, and we've all felt the impact of that in our lives. The first thing I want to say this morning is, thank you. Thank you for believing in my vision for the future. Thank you for helping to make this day possible."

"Get to the point," Craig muttered.

The guard shot him a look. "Shut up, Craig."

Fleming continued, "Before we continue, I do have one piece of disturbing news to report. Despite the overwhelming support for our mission, there are still a few people who haven't been able to see our vision. They like their lives the way they are. They enjoy the privileged lifestyle aboard this ship that is the result of the hard work of the majority, and they don't want to give that up. One of those people is Colonel Arnold Brickman. Colonel Brickman took action against our city today, storming the badge headquarters in an attempt to free General Craig, presumably so the general could help him stage a military coup. Colonel Brickman failed, and he was injured by a heroic badge, but he remains at large."

There was more to Fleming's speech. Words about important matters like Resettlement and the state of the city. But Isaiah Craig was hardly listening. He'd already heard the one thing he needed to know. The thing that gave him hope. The thing that made him think that, as bleak as everything had been for the last month, maybe the good guys still had a chance.

CB was alive, and he was fighting Fleming.

1
___

"I'M DONE LOSING," Alex said. "I'm going to go after Fleming, and I'm going to win. And if you are really interested in protecting humanity, you're going to help me. It's time to save *New Haven*."

Jaden sat back in his seat and crossed his arms, a slight smile playing on his lips. "Wow, sounds serious. How are you gonna start?"

Alex pushed away the mild annoyance she felt at Jaden's casual response. They were sitting in a small meeting room in Agartha. It had only been hours since their harrowing battle with Ferals on the road to Agartha. Jaden and his vampires had saved their lives after George drove them out so they could strike the moment the sun went down. They'd made it, but at great cost. One of Jaden's vampires had been killed in the rescue.

Alex was still buzzing with adrenaline, and she didn't want to wait for that feeling to go away. She wanted to use it. To put that razor-keen edge she felt herself balancing on in her hand and slit Fleming's throat with it.

"George is going to give us the parts we need to fix our

downed ship," she said. "Then, at first light, me and my team are heading back to Denver. Once we have the ship repaired, we'll fly up to *New Haven* and take the city from Fleming."

"Huh." Jaden scratched at his chin. He was silent for a long moment. Then he leaned forward and looked her in the eyes. "You ever see a deer?"

Alex nearly laughed at the non sequitur. "A deer?"

"Yes, a deer. Four-legged mammal. Males have a rack of antlers. Generally brown."

"Yes, Jaden, I have seen a deer. Damn things are everywhere."

"Well, back in the pre-infestation days, deer hunting used to be a popular pastime. But deer are dumb creatures. Skittish, yet prone to freezing when faced with danger. There were so many ways to kill them that humans came up with rules and limits. You could only kill them at certain times and in certain ways."

Alex opened her mouth, but no sound came out. She was so flummoxed by this strange line of thought that she didn't know how to respond.

"My point is, if you're not careful, you'll be the deer. You're so focused on Fleming, you're frozen. Staring at him. You don't see that you've left your human scent at every point along the road between here and Denver, and that Ferals will be waiting in every shadow for a shot at you. You don't see that this trail is putting my city in danger."

"I'm very sorry about that, but we'll be out of your hair really quick. Give us what we need, and—"

He held up a hand, cutting her off. "You also don't see that your team has just been through a traumatic battle. They need rest. You leave here without letting them get some sleep, you'll be lucky if you make it to Denver without accidentally shooting each other. Not to mention how easily Fleming will put your little team out of commission when you get home. If you're serious about this, if you really want to take out Fleming, you need to stop talking and start listening."

The vampire did have a point, not that she was about to admit it. Underneath the waning adrenaline, she felt a deep well of exhaustion screaming to be filled with sleep. If she were being honest, she wasn't in ideal fighting condition. After a long day of driving to Denver, fixing the ship, and flying to *New Haven*, she'd be crashing. Her team would be just as bad, if not worse.

She looked down at the table. Asking for help had never been her strong suit, and she found herself unable to look the vampire in the eyes as she spoke. "What do you suggest?"

"I suggest you let me do my part. You said you wanted me to help save humanity."

"I'm listening."

"Tonight, we rest. We grieve for the fallen. Then, tomorrow at dusk, I take some vampires to Denver. The Ferals won't bother us, and we can have the ship back here by morning. Meanwhile, you and your team can start working on a plan other than 'fly to *New Haven* and take out their defenses with six people.' How's that sound?"

Alex considered that. "I don't know. Losing a whole day? I don't think we can spare it."

Jaden smiled his knowing smile once again. "Let me ask you a question. Who put you in charge of *New Haven*?"

"Do you have to be in charge to do the right thing?" There was an edge to her voice.

"So that's another way of saying no one put you in charge of *New Haven*. Got it." That infuriating smile still played on his lips. "But someone did put you in charge of the Ground Mission Team."

"What's your point?"

"I see it in your eyes. You want so badly to be a great leader. I've met a few of those in my time, and a whole lot of bad ones. But my advice is to focus on the things you're actually in charge of, for now. See to your team. Make sure they're at their best. Then figure out how to help *New Haven*. I'll let you get to it."

With that, Jaden stood up and walked out.

Alex sat for another moment, trying to gather herself. Every conversation with Jaden left her a bit confused. He had a way of seeing the world that felt both true and absolutely absurd at the same time. She had to admit that he had a point. If she truly wanted to help *New Haven*, she was going to have to be smart about this.

She got up and walked to the room where the team was waiting, eating off of trays that the vampires had brought them.

The moment she walked in, Ed pointed at his brother. "Patrick is planning how to kill the vampires who saved us."

Patrick immediately responded, "I am not!" He paused. "Well, not exactly. I just thought it was an interesting exercise. To think about how I'd do it. You know, if I had to." He paused again as Alex took a seat among the team. "Shotgun blast to the head, if you're wondering. I don't care how fast they are. I guarantee I could get off a shot before they—"

"Can we not, right now?" Alex said. "They saved our lives, like, two hours ago. At least wait a full day before plotting their murders."

Despite the ridiculousness of the situation, a smile crept onto Alex's face. Patrick and Ed could be total idiots, but she loved them. Besides, she didn't have much room to judge.

She'd gotten into a fistfight with Jaden's friend, Robert, only hours after the first time they'd saved the GMT.

"What's the plan?" Chuck asked, his forehead scrunched in worry. Unlike the Barton brothers, Chuck tended to consider the possibilities of every situation carefully. It was a quality that made Alex believe he'd be a good leader someday, but it also made him prone to living inside his own head.

"Jaden and his vamps are going to recover the away ship from Denver tomorrow night," she told them. "We should have it back thirty hours from now."

"Then we fly up to *New Haven* and shoot somebody?" Ed asked hopefully.

Alex chuckled. "Honestly, that was my first thought, too. But I think we need to be smarter about this. We need a solid plan for when we reach *New Haven*."

"*If* we reach *New Haven*," Owl interjected.

Wesley tilted his head and looked questioningly at the pilot. "What do you mean?"

"If Fleming wants to keep away from us, all he has to do is fly *New Haven* in the southern hemisphere. No way we could reach it with the away ship. It's designed for shorter-range flights."

Alex considered that. "I don't believe that'll happen. Fleming thinks we're dead. He'll want to fly close to Fort Stearns for Resettlement. Besides, he'll want to recover the abandoned away ship."

"Could be you're right," Owl allowed. "I'm just saying it's going to be hard to find *New Haven* if they don't want to be found."

"Noted," Alex said. "Let's see if George will start working on intercepting their radio communications to Fort Stearns. And let's all work on a plan."

The heads around the table bobbed up and down in nods.

Though none of them said it, they were all thinking it. Fleming had made his move against the GMT, and that meant their friends still on *New Haven* had to be square in his sights, as well. CB, Brian, and Jessica were in serious trouble.

"YOU KNOW WHAT'S FUNNY?" Mark asked as he paced in front of the line of newborn vampires. "They actually think they're safe."

Firefly felt a droplet of blood hanging off his chin, a remnant of his recent death. Part of him wanted to reach up and wipe it away, but another part of him was afraid to try. What if he found he couldn't do it without his masters' permission?

Only an hour ago, everything had been so hopeful. They'd been the Resettlers, paving the way for the future of humanity. Two intelligent vampires named Mark and Aaron had ended that. They'd used the chaos of Ferals attacking Fort Stearns to do much more damage than Firefly would have believed possible. They didn't just kill the Resettlers; they brought them back to life and enslaved them.

"You thought you were safe, too," Mark continued. "You thought your guns and your walls would save you. You lasted, what, twenty minutes?"

Firefly looked up and down the line of men and women, all standing at attention. Some of them were shaking. A few were crying. But all of them had the same shocked, hollow expression in their eyes. Not that it was surprising. They'd all just been through something very traumatic: their own deaths.

A wave of nausea washed over him. These people had been his responsibility, and he'd failed them in the most profound way imaginable.

Mark stopped in front of Firefly and gave him a crooked smile. "Agartha has walls and guns, too. Bigger ones than you did. But we'll bring them down."

Agartha? Firefly hadn't considered that this was just a warmup for Mark and Aaron. Now they wanted to move against Agartha?

Aaron stepped forward and stood next to Mark. "As you're going to figure out real soon, we need to move on this fast. In the next few hours, you're going to start feeling the hunger. But vampire hunger ain't like human hunger. It's not just in your stomach. You're going to feel it in your bones. Crawling across your skin. Every part of you is gonna be crying out for blood."

As Aaron spoke, Firefly realized he could feel it already. It was mild, like a light humming throughout his body.

Mark nodded. "And the only way we're going to satisfy that hunger is to take down Agartha. Then we can worry about *New Haven*."

Firefly felt a flush of anger. Mark had ordered him to reveal everything he knew about *New Haven*, and Firefly had been forced to comply. Not only had he let down his Resettlers, he'd let down his city.

Aaron stared at Firefly for a long moment. "Tell me what you're thinking."

Firefly started talking immediately, before he even consciously registered the question. "We can't take Agartha. Their city is built into the side of a mountain. And they have one hundred vampires."

Aaron burst out laughing. He put a hand on Firefly's shoulders. "You goddamn idiot. We have *three* hundred vampires."

A chill went through Firefly. That was why they'd come here and turned the Resettlers, instead of just feeding off of them. They'd wanted an army.

"Point is," Mark said, "that hunger is only going to grow stronger. If we don't feed in a few weeks, every one of us will go Feral. But we're going to make sure that doesn't happen. We might be your masters, but you've gotta start believing we have your best interests at heart. We want you to feed."

"Enough jawing," Aaron announced. "We leave for Agartha in five minutes. Get your weapons." He looked at Firefly. "You follow us."

As the newly turned vampires hurried to gather their weapons, Firefly followed Mark and Aaron outside into the night. Though the attack had been in full swing when he'd last been out there, seeing the prison yard was still a shock. With his improved vampire sight, he could see everything perfectly, even though every light had been torn down and destroyed. The yard was filled with what had to be hundreds of Ferals. They slammed into buildings, smashing supplies. Firefly realized they were being driven wild by the residual scent of humans, a pungent, honeysuckle smell that Firefly felt arousing his own hunger.

To his left, a group of five Ferals fought over a spot of blood-soaked ground, battling for the best position from which to lap at the dirt.

The Ferals ignored Mark, Aaron, and Firefly as they passed among them. Firefly's shoulder even brushed up against one, but it didn't react.

Mark shook his head. "These poor bastards will be holed up here for months, unable to ignore the lingering scent of the humans. This place will have a thousand Ferals and not a damn thing to feed any of them." He turned to Firefly. "Before we go, we wanted to have a little chat with you."

Firefly said nothing. His eyes were fixed on a guard tower on top of the wall. One of its sides had been ripped off and it stood empty. He wondered what had happened to the man who'd been stationed up there. Had he been turned, or had he fed a Feral?

"As you've already figured out, you can't disobey our orders," Mark said. "It's best if you don't even try. It won't work and it'll just stoke your hunger."

"If I can't disobey, then why are we even having this conversation?" Firefly asked.

Aaron glared at him. "Because we'd prefer you to proactively help us, rather than just obey orders. Once we take Agartha, there will be leadership positions available. If you want one of them, now's the time to get on board."

Mark nodded. "We're going to take Agartha, but it won't be easy. We'll start by taking out the rail guns mounted around the city. Then we'll take out their nightly patrols. Then we have to figure out a way past the doors. Point is, there will be a lot of moving pieces. We need a few people we can trust to actively help us figure things out."

Firefly opened his mouth to speak, but Mark held up a hand.

"Don't answer now. Think about it on the way to Agartha. We'll be there by morning."

Firefly felt his mouth click shut.

He took another look around Fort Stearns. All of this destruction was his responsibility. He'd let down so many people. All because of the fantasy that he was Garrett Eldred, the great leader. But he wasn't. Not really. He was

Firefly, the warrior. If he wanted to help his people, he needed to embrace that fact.

He thought about what Mark had just said.

"How are we going to get to Agartha by morning?" he asked.

Aaron grinned. "You're a vampire now. That means you're fast as hell and you don't get tired. We're going to run."

2

Sarah fixed her gaze on Fleming as he paced back and forth from one end of his office to the other. The man was making her nervous.

He was always full of energy, and yes, sometimes he expressed that energy by pacing. But even in his most fidgety moments, Fleming displayed an air of excitement and confidence. It was as if he were moving because the ideas and optimism inside of him couldn't be contained behind a desk. It was part of what she loved about him, part of what had led her to take a bullet for him.

But this was something different. He wasn't pacing out of excitement.

"Colonel Brickman," he muttered. "Jessica. Brian. Three of the greatest minds in *New Haven*. And all of them disappeared. Probably off sowing discontent in my city."

Colonel Kurtz glanced at Sarah, and she saw the unease she felt mirrored in his eyes. He'd just betrayed CB, one of his oldest friends, for Fleming. It had to be disconcerting to see him like this, in what should have been a moment of triumph. "We'll find them, sir. We're on a ship. There's a limited number of places to hide."

"Yes," Fleming agreed, "and Jessica knows every one of them." He ran a hand through his unkempt hair, then he turned toward Kurtz. "I want your best men guarding this building. No one gets in or out without your guys checking them and making a record of it."

Kurtz nodded.

Sarah drew a deep breath. She knew speaking meant risking getting her head bitten off, but she had to try to calm him down. "Sir, let's not let this minor problem cloud an otherwise beautiful sky. We did it. *You* did it. Resettlement is real. When morning comes and we re-establish contact with Fort Stearns, the people aren't going to care about three fugitives. As much as the people love CB, he's yesterday. You're tomorrow."

Fleming nodded slowly. "You're right. Still, I'm not going to underestimate them again. CB has access to half the weapons on this ship—"

"Had access," Kurtz corrected. "We deactivated his security card two hours ago."

"Fine, but who knows what he might have stockpiled somewhere? And with Brian on his side, they might not need our weapons. That guy could probably make a cannon out of an old pair of socks and a doorknob." He turned to Kurtz. "It's time for us to activate the faceless GMT."

Kurtz was silent for a moment, then he nodded. "I'll make it happen."

Sarah looked back and forth between the two men. Clearly, they knew something she didn't. "What's the faceless GMT?"

Fleming turned to her and smiled, a bit of that old confidence back now. "I'm sorry, Sarah, I didn't mean to hide anything from you. I wanted to keep this from Garrett, though. He has strange loyalties to the GMT."

"Okay," Sarah said slowly.

Fleming leaned back against his desk and crossed his arms. "One problem we've had from the beginning is that people love the GMT. They're heroes of an almost mythical level. For a while, I tried to use that to my advantage, like when I brought Alex on my citywide announcement. But I realized I've been going about this the wrong way. We need the GMT, but we don't want the people idolizing them."

"How do we do that?" Sarah asked.

Fleming nodded to Kurtz. "Tell her."

"Fleming asked me to form a new GMT," the colonel said, "but to do it in secret. There are thirty-six of them, and we cycle them in and out."

"So, no one gets to be the face of the GMT," Sarah said, starting to get it.

"No one but me," Fleming chuckled. "Tell her the rest."

"Your 'no one gets to be the face' comment is righter than you know. They'll wear masks and go by call signs, referring to each other simply by a number, reassigned on each mission. They won't even know each other's names."

"Damn," Sarah muttered. She wasn't sure if the plan was brilliant or crazy.

"The GMT was always meant to be a tool," Fleming said, thoughtfully, "nothing more. Now they can selflessly serve their city. The way it was meant to be."

The rest remained unspoken, but Sarah understood. If the people of *New Haven* wanted a hero to look up to, Fleming would make sure his was the only face they had to see.

IN THE VENTILATION ducts far below the surface of *New Haven*, everything echoed. Even though Jessica had assured them that the chances of anyone overhearing their conversations were infinitesimal, CB still found the reverberation of his own voice disconcerting. He spoke quietly when he had to speak at all.

"Hold still. I'm almost done." Brian had finished cleaning the wound in CB's shoulder and was now redressing it. "How's that feel?"

"Like I got shot in the arm." In truth, the bullet had only grazed him. He had full movement and the pain was minimal. He hoped that as soon as Brian stopped fussing over the injury, he'd be able to forget about it altogether.

"So, what's next?" Jessica asked. "As much as I'd enjoy living down in these tunnels for the rest of my life with you two boys, they're going to find us eventually. There's only so much real estate on this ship."

CB pulled his shirt back on, wincing as the cloth grazed his wound. "Now, we figure out how to take back *New Haven*."

He saw weariness in his friends' eyes. He could relate. Even though he'd only been on the run for twelve hours, it felt like he hadn't slept in days. But he also knew they couldn't rest. Fleming certainly wouldn't. The man had already started the campaign to publicly discredit CB with his citywide announcement, and he wouldn't ease off until he found them and eliminated them.

"We're fighting a two-front battle here," CB said. "We need to take the city back from Fleming, but we also need to figure out how to combat the lies he's spreading. It won't do much good to take down Fleming if the people consider us traitors. We need a way to get the word out."

Jessica thought about that for a moment. "I know where

the communication lines run underneath the agricultural sector."

CB turned toward Brian. "Think you could find a way to splice us in? Hack our way to a citywide broadcast of our own?"

Brian scratched his chin. "It's possible. Without access to my equipment in the lab, it'll be tough. I might be able to pull it off."

CB put a hand on his shoulder. "You're in the GMT now, son. We don't try; we get it done." He turned to Jessica. "You two head to the agriculture sector and see what kind of magic you can make happen."

"What about you?" Jessica asked.

"While you two are fighting the information war, I'll be working on the other one. I'm going to find the weapon that just might give us a chance."

3

FIREFLY RACED ACROSS THE SNOW, aware of the cold air rushing past him, but not feeling its bite.

When he'd woken in Fort Stearns to his new life as a vampire, he'd been confused, disgusted, and terrified. Now, he felt something else: wonder.

He'd been sprinting for hours, yet he felt no fatigue. Despite the effort, he wasn't sweating. There was a heavy deadness in his chest where his heart should have been pounding, yet a cold strength emanated from every muscle. He felt invincible.

It was nearly sunrise. He knew it even though the eastern sky was still dark. There was a smell in the air that almost burned if he sniffed too deeply, and it was growing more powerful by the moment.

What a strange new life, to be able to smell the approaching sunrise.

"Here!" Mark called. "Hold up."

Firefly felt himself stop running before his brain had even processed the command. He looked around and realized they were nearly at Agartha. He'd been so deep in the experience and the new sensations that he hadn't noticed.

The three hundred vampires around him halted, and Mark and Aaron conferred for a moment. Though they were thirty yards away and speaking at almost a whisper, Firefly had no trouble hearing every word they spoke.

"We'd better hole up for the day," Aaron said. "How do we approach this thing tomorrow night?"

Mark sighed, his eyes fixed on the distant entrance to the city. "It's not going to be quick or easy. We have to be patient if we want to get this done."

"Heh," Aaron chuckled. "We waited one hundred fifty years in the snow. Patience, I can do."

Mark nodded absently. "We'll need to take out the automated rail guns first. That'll make them nervous. If all of them go offline at once, hopefully they'll think it's a system malfunction of some kind. We'll have snipers waiting outside every entrance to the city. Jaden will send a few of his idiot disciples out to check on the guns. When that happens, our snipers take them down."

Aaron glanced at him. "You think that'll work? They're not going to send all one hundred vamps out one at a time for us to headshot, like it's a video game."

Now, Mark turned toward Aaron. "You played video games back in the day?"

Aaron grinned. "*Call of Duty* was my game. X-Box."

Mark grimaced. "I was more of a *Destiny* guy. PlayStation."

"Heh, of course you were. My friends and I would have kicked your ass so hard in COD. Then we would have put another bullet in your head, two seconds after you respawned."

"Can we focus on the task at hand?" He paused a moment. "You and your squad of twelve-year-olds wouldn't have lasted five minutes in a *Destiny* run."

Firefly listened to the odd conversation, wondering what they were talking about. He didn't understand the context, but it seemed trivial compared with the attack they'd just been discussing.

His stomach twisted at the thought of what was to come. He and the other Resettlers were going to be forced to attack Agartha, and there was nothing he could do to stop it. He'd be made to fight, forced to kill. He'd caused so many deaths already. How many more would he add to that toll tomorrow night?

Mark continued in his near-whisper. "Eventually it's going to come to a straight-up fight. We already have Jaden's vamps outnumbered three to one. Our goal with the snipers is to increase those odds even more. Then, when they send out the rest of the vamps, we stomp them. How's that sound to you, Firefly?"

He said the words in the same quiet voice, his eyes still fixed on Aaron.

Firefly was so surprised that he stood there frozen, unable to answer.

"That's right, I know you're listening," Mark said, turning to look at him. "Get over here. Now."

To Firefly's surprise, his body didn't immediately obey as it had to other orders. He remained standing where he was.

Mark grimaced. "I gave you an order. Get over here!"

Still, Firefly remained frozen.

A slow smile crept across Aaron's face. "Ah, I see what's happening. Firefly, get over here!"

This time, Firefly immediately obeyed, moving to Aaron's side as quickly as his feet could get him there.

Aaron nudged Mark. "I turned him."

Mark scratched his chin. "Hmm. I hadn't thought of that. We need to remedy this situation. We can't have half following you and half following me." He raised his voice and addressed the former Resettlers. "Listen up. When Mark gives you an order, I want you to follow it as if it came from me."

"Let's see if it worked," Aaron said. "Show me one of yours."

Mark pointed to a tall, thin man who couldn't have been more than twenty.

"You!" Aaron shouted to the thin man. "Shoot the guy next to you."

The young man immediately drew his pistol, turned to the wide-eyed man standing next to him, and fired.

The man who'd been shot cried out in pain and clutched his stomach where the bullet had entered.

"What'd you do that for?" Mark said, the annoyance clear in his voice. "This is our army."

"Relax, he shot him in the stomach. He'll be fine."

"Okay, we've proved we can assign master powers to each other. Your turn. Tell your people to obey me."

Aaron just grinned. "I don't know. Not sure I want to share my army with a loser who games on a PlayStation."

Mark took a step toward him. "You want this army to have only one leader, we can decide that right now. I'll kill you so fast you won't even realize you're dead till you've been in hell for five minutes."

Aaron held up a hand. "Chill, I'm just busting your balls." Then, in a louder voice, "Same as what he said. Any order Mark gives is the same as if it came from me." He turned to Mark. "Happy?"

"I'll be happy when Jaden is captured, and we have a

nice supply of human necks to feed on. For now, let's get our people into place. Then we'll have them burrow under the snow for the night."

Firefly stood next to them, waiting for his orders, the knowledge of what he'd be forced to do tomorrow night eating away at his heart, even as the growing hunger reverberated in his bones.

ALEX MANAGED four hours of sleep in the cramped quarters they'd provided her before she gave up and left her room. She spotted Ed leaning against the wall, looking bored.

"You couldn't sleep either?" she asked.

He shook his head. "Everyone says me and my brother are so similar, but Patrick could sleep in a war zone. Me, not so much. I have a hard time turning off my brain."

"I can relate," Alex said. "I'm headed to the transport area to see how George's preparations are coming. Want to come?"

Ed shrugged and fell into step alongside her.

When they reached the transport area, Alex was unsurprised to find Owl harassing George as he prepared vehicles for that night's journey to Denver. They were standing on an eighteen-wheeled vehicle with a wide, flat area on the back of it.

"The thing you've got to remember is, you're dealing with a piece of precision machinery," she said insistently. "Forgive me if I'm a little concerned about a bunch of superstrong vampires manhandling it onto...whatever the hell this is."

George continued organizing supplies, not looking at her as he answered, "It's a flatbed truck."

"Okay, fine." She took a step closer to him. "The point is, if one of those undead weirdos squeezes a little too hard and bends the hull, we're talking major performance issues. I've already lost one ship in these mountains. If I lose another—"

George's eyes brightened as he spotted Alex. "Captain Goddard!"

"How's it going, George?"

"Excellent." He glanced at Owl. "Owl has been a great help, but we're pretty much done here, so if you need her for anything else..."

Alex chuckled. "Are you driving him crazy, Owl?"

George blushed. "I didn't mean—"

"Of course, you did," Alex said with a smile. "Believe me, I can relate."

Owl's brow creased as she frowned. "I'll gladly bother every engineer in this mountain, if it means getting my ship back safely."

Alex crossed her arms. Something about Jaden's plan had been bothering her since she woke. "George, I'm having second thoughts."

George looked at her warily. "About what?"

"Waiting."

Now both George and Owl were staring at her in surprise.

"Look, we all know Fleming's going to try to get that ship back," she pointed out. "With the way he's running low on resources, there's no way he lets a whole ship just rot down here. He's going to send a team down to get it."

"Does he even have a team?" Owl asked.

Alex hadn't considered that, but the answer came to her immediately. "Of course, he does. He'd been planning to strand us on the surface for a while. It wasn't a split-second decision. So of course, he's going to have people ready to replace us."

"A shadow GMT?" Owl said softly. "Is that even possible? How would he recruit them without word getting back to CB?"

Alex shrugged. "This is Fleming we're talking about. Even his shady plans have shady plans." She turned to George. "We can't risk losing that ship. It's our only way back home. You get that, right? We have to get the ship ourselves. Now."

For a moment, she thought he was going to give in to her demand. Then his face hardened. "You want me to list all the reasons that's not going to happen? Or should I just mention the only one that matters?"

"Start with the one."

"Jaden said they're going tonight. So that's what's going to happen."

Alex's face flushed with annoyance. "You sound like some of the people back on *New Haven*. Instead of using logic, you just give in to whatever the great leader says. Is that the way it is here?"

"Of course not. But we don't disregard his orders without discussing it with him, either."

Alex took a deep breath, calming herself. This man had risked his life to save her and her team. "Look, I appreciate everything you've done for us. At the same time, if we want to get our ship, I don't see why you'd stop us."

"Or how," Ed interjected.

George turned toward the Barton brother, the annoyance clear on his face. "I have Jaden and his undead warriors."

Ed grinned. "At night you do. During the day all you

have is a bunch of sleepy vampires. And sleepy vampires are sort of our specialty."

Alex shot him a look. "That's enough, Ed." Her voice was firm, but she hoped he spotted the smile in her eyes. She liked that he always jumped in to defend her, even when her position was wrong-headed. "George, I'm not saying we disregard Jaden's orders. Just give us the recharged batteries and the parts we need, let us use this vehicle, and we'll head up to Denver. Jaden and his buddies are welcome to join us when they wake up. By then, Owl should have the ship fixed, and we'll be out of your hair."

"Actually, I don't think it's going to be that easy," Owl said, sheepishly.

Alex raised an eyebrow. "Explain."

"We don't know what exactly is wrong with the ship," Owl said. "It's going to take time to diagnose the problem and fix it. I don't want to get caught out after dark again."

"So, we just give Fleming the opportunity to take the ship?"

"Why would he be in a rush?" Owl said. "Even if he is, they won't be expecting the batteries to be missing. I think the chances of his team successfully flying it home today are slim."

Alex had to admit that Owl had a point. Risking her team again by driving all that way was reckless. If they so much as popped a tire, they'd be in the same situation that they'd been in the previous night. Besides, the team did still need rest.

Her instincts made her want to be proactive, to always be in motion. At least this time, she'd have to find a way to silence that voice.

Maybe it was time to truly start trusting Jaden.

"Okay, we'll follow Jaden's plan," Alex said. "In the meantime, is there a gym in this mountain? I feel the sudden need to punch something."

4
_____

"YOU TOLD THEM, RIGHT?" Fleming asked Kurtz.

The colonel nodded. "They were ordered let us know as soon as they made contact."

Sarah sank further into her seat, hoping Fleming would forget she was there. They'd been trying to contact Fort Stearns for over an hour. _New Haven_ was circling the area above the settlement, and they were well within the radio's range. With each passing moment, the horrible feeling in Sarah's stomach grew stronger.

No one was answering. No one.

That meant either Fleming's theory that there was something wrong with the communications system was correct or...

No. She wouldn't think about the alternative. Not until she absolutely had to.

Fleming sat down on his seat for what had to be the fifteenth time in the last hour. He'd sit for a few minutes, grow antsy, stand back up, and then start pacing. "I have a dark theory we need to discuss."

Sarah looked up sharply, surprised. She never imagined he'd admit defeat so quickly.

"I hate to say it," he continued, "but we have to consider the possibility that CB is behind this problem."

Sarah was so surprised that she couldn't keep herself from responding. "I'm sorry. Did you say CB?"

He laughed, running a hand through his unkempt hair. "Well. it makes sense, doesn't it? He's on the run, and he's got two geniuses with him. They figured out some way to disrupt the radio signal."

Kurtz and Sarah exchanged a nervous glance. He looked as skeptical about that possibility as she felt.

"I suppose it's possible," Kurtz said after a moment.

Fleming stared at him, not blinking. "Possible? It's a lot more than possible. See, this is why CB got the jump on you before you could shoot him. You underestimate his cunning."

Kurtz cleared his throat. "It's not that, sir. It's just I don't see what motivation CB would have to disrupt our communication."

Fleming's eyes widened. "His motivation? What has been his motivation all along? To make sure Resettlement fails. He doesn't care how many people die in the process."

Sarah wasn't sure that was true. As much as she considered him a fool, she had to admit he was an ideological fool. He wouldn't want people hurt unnecessarily.

The radio on Fleming's desk chirped, and the tension that had been hanging in the air suddenly disappeared. A relieved smile crossed Fleming's lips. "Finally."

He punched a button on the radio. "Captain Eldred! Is that you?"

There was a long pause, and then a female voice

answered, "Uh, no, sir. You asked me to let you know when the GMT was ready for departure."

Fleming's smile fell. "All right. Send them out. It's time for the faceless GMT's first mission."

Sarah looked up sharply. "You're sending them to Fort Stearns, sir? If something happened to the Resettlers... I'm not saying it did, but if it did, do we really want to send our new GMT to the same place?"

"Relax, Sarah. It's the middle of the day. They'll be fine."

JESSICA AND BRIAN sat amidst a vast network of pipes. They were in the underbelly of *New Haven*, directly beneath the agricultural sector. Brian tapped furiously at his touchpad as Jessica watched in silence.

It hadn't taken long for her to splice into the fiber-optic network. The tricky part was hacking into the communications system. Brian had been working on that for twenty minutes, occasionally muttering about how this really wasn't his area of expertise, as he dug deeper and deeper into the code.

For someone who wasn't an expert in this area, he certainly was making a lot of progress.

"So, how'd you learn to do this?" Jessica asked softly as he worked.

"Huh?" He looked up, his focus broken.

"I was just asking where you learned this hacking stuff."

He shrugged. "I did some coding as a kid. One of my teachers thought it was important for the well-rounded scientific mind, or some such nonsense. I did okay at it, but I never came close to mastering the skills needed for this type of thing. I'm sort of figuring it out as I go."

Jessica nodded. "I understand. Don't feel bad if you can't get us in there."

Brian blinked hard. "Oh, I'm already in. Didn't I tell you? Sorry, I thought I did." He looked back at the tablet. "I'm just looking for that bit of footage you wanted, and we'll be good to go."

Jessica stifled a laugh. Brian McElroy was once again exceeding her expectations.

People sometimes called her a genius, and she supposed that was true. Brian couldn't hold a conversation about engineering like George from Agartha—he wasn't really the collaborative sort—but when left to his own devices, he operated at a whole different level.

"It shouldn't be long," he said absently as his fingers flew. "Just another... There! Got it."

"Geez, already?"

Brian grinned. "Yep. I guess that means it's the Jessica show now. Ready for your big debut?"

That made the director of engineering pause. She'd assumed this was going to take at least another hour, which would have given her another hour to mentally prepare. "I still don't understand why it has to be me," she grumbled.

Brian didn't even look up from his tablet. "You know why. People already know CB's going against Fleming, and they need to see someone who's not GMT, so it doesn't look like a straight up military coup. I can't do it because... Well, I'm me. I'd freeze up the second the camera came on. Besides, I technically work for the GMT, too. You ready?"

"What? No, I need to—"

"Best to rip this thing off like a bandage." He pulled a tiny camera out of his bag, attached it to the tablet, and pointed it at Jessica. "We're going in five, four, three, two..."

Jessica took a deep breath to steady her nerves and

forced the panicked look from her face. Brian pointed at her, indicating they were live. Though they couldn't see it down here, she knew that her face was appearing on screens all throughout *New Haven*.

Brian had hacked her into the ship-wide broadcast system; now it was up to her to use this opportunity to its utmost.

"Hello, people," she started lamely. She swallowed hard. This was much more difficult than Fleming made it look. "My name is Jessica Bowen, and I'm the director of engineering. As of today, I'm also a fugitive from Fleming and his badges."

She paused. Brian gave her an enthusiastic thumbs up, indicating she was doing fine.

She continued, "Those of you who know me are aware that I am a careful person. I'm a scientist. I look at possible outcomes and likely scenarios before taking any important action. I would never have made the decision to go against our leaders, if I had any other choice. In this case, I do not. Fleming is a murderer. He killed every other member of our City Council, so that he'd be the only one standing. Then, he hoped you'd believe his implausible lie that it was an accident.

"I don't have proof of his actions in killing the Council, but I do have proof of another murder he tried to commit. Brian, if you would?"

Brian tapped the screen, and video footage from the Hub began to play throughout the city.

"This took place yesterday morning. Fleming told you Captain Brickman was injured while attempting to break General Craig out of jail. As you can see here, that was not the case."

The footage showed Fleming, CB, and Kurtz walking

down a hallway, CB clearly unarmed, then Kurtz pulling a gun and pointing it at CB. It showed CB defending himself and disarming Kurtz, then other badges running in and firing on CB.

"Fleming attempted to kill CB because he disagreed with his agenda," Jessica said. "In Fleming's world, disagreement is unacceptable. Alex Goddard took a similar position, and Fleming arranged to have her, and the entire GMT, stranded on the surface. They spent last night down there, and I'm sorry to say it seems almost impossible that they survived. Fleming only cares about his own glory, not the lives of the people of *New Haven*."

Brian tapped the screen as the footage of the Hub ended. He made a circular motion with his finger, which Jessica understood as him telling her to wrap it up. It wouldn't take Fleming's people too long to trace where the comm system had been hacked, and they needed to be gone before that happened. But before they left, there was one more thing Jessica needed to say.

"I'm counting on every man and woman on *New Haven* to take a stand. When the time comes, you'll know. Help us take control of the ship from Fleming and help us protect every life onboard." She looked at Brian awkwardly. "That's all. Shut it down."

With that, screens around the ship went black.

5

THE FACELESS GMT'S first mission began as they landed the transport at Fort Stearns in the mid-morning. The cargo door opened, and six figures stepped out, all clad in black. With the body armor, their black face masks, and their silent demeanor, it was difficult to even tell which of the team members were male and which were female.

They simply looked like cold, efficient warriors, nearly indistinguishable from each other, just as Fleming had designed it.

The leader of the newly formed team—known only to his team as One—surveyed the ruins of Fort Stearns with surprise. He'd expected to find a settlement of three hundred people, perhaps some of them nursing wounds from their first night on the surface. Maybe a little wiser from the eye-opening experience of being so close to vampires at night, but more prepared for the journey of Resettlement ahead of them. Instead, he found utter destruction.

It was clear that no one had survived the night.

The realization was like a punch in the stomach to One.

He was a true believer in Fleming's cause, and to see that it had failed so completely was devastating. He couldn't see the faces of his teammates, but from the way they silently stared at the yard around them, he felt sure they were having similar reactions.

"What the hell do we do now?" Three asked.

"We do our jobs," One replied grimly. "We check for survivors."

They made their way to the nearest building, following One's lead. As they were approaching the entrance, Four called, "Wait. Check this out."

One looked where his teammate was pointing and saw a five-foot-tall, seven-foot-wide hole in the building.

"My God," Five said, staring at the hole. "What could have done this?"

No one answered, but they knew. They all knew. The same things that had done all of this.

Vampires.

They all stood in the light just outside the hole, peering inward. It took a moment for One's eyes to adjust to the darkness, but when it did, he took an involuntary step backwards. Something was staring out at him.

The strange, severe lines of its face were unlike anything he'd ever seen. He felt dizzy just looking at the inhuman creature.

Then he realized the creature wasn't alone. Slowly, his right hand went up to his helmet, and his finger found the switch. His headlamp turned on, bathing the interior of the building with light.

Dozens and dozens of pairs of eyes stared back at him. There may have been one hundred vampires jammed together body to body under just the narrow beam of his light. How many were there throughout the rest of the building? How many were there in this settlement?

Three turned toward him. "One, maybe you're going in there to check for survivors, but I sure as hell—"

A hand snaked out of the darkness with inhuman speed. Long, smoking fingers coiled around Three's ankle. He let out a soft yelp of surprise as a vampire pulled him into the building.

One watched in terrified horror as the vampires converged on Three. Ten vampires fell on him, tearing at his body with claws and teeth, devouring the blood that seeped and sprayed from his wounds. All around them, vampires fought, jockeying for position, all desperate to get a taste of this fresh victim's blood.

The rest of the team jumped back, shouts and screams erupting from their mask-covered mouths as they watched their teammate being devoured.

If there was any consolation, it was that Three only struggled for a few moments before his body went still. Which one of the dozens of injuries had killed him was anybody's guess, but at least he was dead.

Unlike One, who stood frozen, unable to turn his head-lamp away from the carnage.

"What do we do?" Five asked, her voice panicked. So far, the team had been relatively calm, at least considering what they'd just witnessed, but One realized that it was shock, rather than bravery, that kept them from screaming and running away. Three had been yanked into the building and killed so quickly that none of them even had a chance to consider what they might be able to do to save him.

One drew a deep breath. He needed to pull it together. Like so many great warriors before him, he was the field commander of the GMT. Like CB. Like Alex. Maybe it was his first day on the job, but he still needed to live up to that lofty legacy.

Even in the areas through the hole not illuminated by his headlamp, One could see ripples of movement in the darkness. The ground shook as vampires throughout the building began to howl.

One thought fast. "We need to bring this damn building down. Shine a little sunlight on these sons of bitches. Six, do it."

Six swung the backpack containing the explosives off his back and began rifling through it. As One watched, Six fumbled with the explosives, clearly rattled. Finally, he brought out five high-powered grenades. "These oughta do the trick."

He pulled the pins and tossed them into the darkness in quick succession.

One stared at the hole in the building. He hadn't received the explosives training Six had. Now that he thought about it, he wasn't sure exactly what explosives training his demolitions "expert" had received. He'd never even met the man until that morning. The faceless GMT had been prepared individually, to protect their identities.

Still, tossing six high-powered grenades so close to the team seemed perhaps a bit foolish—

The first grenade exploded, tearing into the group of vampires closest to the hole. Vampiric screams filled the air, as did the clangs of the other, unexploded grenades knocking around in the building. Three vampires were blown out the hole in the wall by the explosion. They instantly burst into flames as the sunlight touched their skin. Pieces of other vampires shot out of the hole, too. An arm whizzed by One, catching fire as it flew.

Then the rest of the grenades exploded, and chaos

erupted with it. A powerful, concussive wave slammed into One's chest, knocking him onto his ass.

For a moment, he just lay there, struggling to catch the wind that had been knocked out of him. Then he sat up and looked around, and he nearly lost his breath again.

Six had been the closest to the building, and he was clearly dead, the blast and the shrapnel having left him in a mangled heap.

Three was near Six and was equally dead. Half his right arm was missing, and the strange angles of his remaining limbs suggested that his bones weren't holding him together in the way they should be.

A scream to his left made One turn. He saw another team member—Two, he thought, though it was so hard to tell for sure with these damn masks—clutching her leg where a piece of rebar was sticking through both sides, having pierced clean through the thigh.

But at least Two was alive. One wasn't so sure about the remaining teammates, Five and Four. He struggled to his feet and stumbled toward where they lay. Pulling off his glove, he felt their necks, first Five and then Four, but found neither had a pulse.

The weight of the moment almost crushed him. His first mission, and four of his five teammates were dead.

Then another thought struck him: Four was their pilot.

After a moment, he remembered the bit of pilot training he'd received. He was meant to be the backup pilot. It was up to him to get them back to *New Haven*.

As he struggled to his feet, something in the shadows of what remained of the building caught his eye. He slowly crept forward, his still-engaged headlamp illuminating the shadows in the rubble. He saw a crowd of vampires huddled together in the darkness, their flesh shredded from the shrapnel. But as he silently watched, they began to heal. Their hideous skin mended itself before his eyes.

A shudder passed through One, and he realized the rest of his life would be dedicated to forgetting this moment.

"GET THAT HANGAR DOOR OPEN," Sarah growled to the tech sitting at the console.

He jammed the button, and the outer airlock door opened. Sarah turned and marched into the hangar, waiting for the ship.

They already knew it was bad. One had radioed in and told them to have medical staff ready. Beyond that, he hadn't been coherent. She just hoped he could dock the ship safely, so that she'd be able to appraise the situation fully before Fleming arrived.

She watched through the reinforced glass of the inner airlock door as the away ship approached. It was coming at *New Haven* at an odd angle, and it was tilted about twenty degrees toward starboard. The pilot over-corrected, and the ship approached tilting ten degrees port.

Sarah clenched her fists, not even daring to breathe as the ship entered the hangar. It set down with a thud, and Sarah flinched. Thank God Owl wasn't here to see this shameful display.

As soon as the outer airlock doors closed, the inner doors opened, and technicians raced toward the ship.

The cargo door opened, and One shambled down the ramp. He was carrying something in his arms. It took Sarah a moment to realize it was one of his teammates. The woman's mask had been removed, and her face was pale. A long piece of rebar protruded from both sides of her thigh.

Sarah marched up the ramp, meeting One halfway as the medical staff took the injured teammate from his arms. "What happened?" she shouted.

"They're dead," he said absently. "They're all dead."

She looked past him and saw two bodies lying in the cargo hold, their features still covered by their black attire. "Holy hell, tell me you didn't bring back your dead."

The medical staff had already started the emergency protocol for GMT members who may have been compromised. Rather than taking them back to the locker room, they tore off One's clothes right there so they could check for bites immediately. Two others had the injured woman on a gurney and were stripping off her clothes as well.

The rest of the medical staff surged into the cargo hold and went to work, checking the bodies. Just because these team members were dead, didn't mean they'd necessarily stay that way. The techs needed to be sure the corpses hadn't been bitten.

Just then, at the worst possible moment, Fleming arrived.

He ran to the ship, his eyes fixed on One.

"Sir," Sarah said, trying to intercept him, "I was just about to determine—"

But Fleming blew past her and ran to One, grabbing him by his bare shoulders. "What the hell happened?"

"They're all dead," One repeated.

Fleming squeezed his shoulders and shook him hard. "What is the status of Fort Stearns?"

One looked up slowly, as if just realizing who was speaking to him. "I just told you. They're all dead. The Resettlers are dead. My team is dead. Fort Stearns is destroyed, and there are hundreds of vampires living in the ruins." His head tilted a little, his eyes invisible behind that eerie mask. "Did you know, sir? Did you know you were killing all those people?"

"Killing? What are you—"

"No one could have survived a night with those monsters. Did you know what would happen?"

Fleming turned to the nearest medical person, a young woman named Brook. "This man is delusional. Sedate him."

"Sir," Sarah tried, but that was as far as she got before he whirled toward her.

"He has clearly lost his mind." The usual control in Fleming's demeanor was gone, and there was a wildness in his eyes. "The GMT didn't do their jobs. There's no way they searched the entire settlement already. They just got spooked when they saw some vampires and decided to come home."

Sarah glanced at the mangled bodies in the cargo hold. *Spooked* wasn't the word she would have used to describe them.

Fleming's eyes filled with anger and he looked up suddenly. "We were sabotaged. That's the only explanation. CB wasn't the only traitor. Maybe Firefly was in on it. Maybe he let the vampires in."

Sarah was so surprised that she didn't know how to respond. It seemed rather unlikely to her that Firefly would have willingly let vampires in to kill him and his Resettlers.

Fleming was losing his grip, Sarah realized. He'd believed in Resettlement so completely that he was unable to accept its failure.

"Firefly might have had accomplices among the Resettlers. There could be others." He paused a moment. "No one is to leave the GMT facility until further notice. We need to make sure these people aren't carrying a contaminant that could spread to the rest of the ship."

It wasn't clear if the contaminant he was referring to was vampirism or betrayal.

"Sarah, come with me to CB's office." With that, he stormed off, leaving the GMT support and medical staff staring at Sarah in confusion.

She clenched her fists, hoping it would stop her hands from shaking before anyone noticed. If Fleming lost it now, the entire city was in serious trouble. She had to calm him down and help him see reality, however terrible that reality might be. He'd done so much for her. Now it was time for her to repay the favor.

"Do as he says," she told everyone. "No one leaves the facility until further notice."

She hurried out of the hangar to CB's office.

When she arrived, she found Kurtz and Fleming both there, waiting.

"We need to call up the next six members of the GMT," Fleming was saying. "Have them suit up and get ready for action."

Kurtz nodded. "Smart move, staffing the new GMT with thirty-six members. That way, when something like this happens, sad as it is, we're not out of commission. We can slide the next group of soldiers in with no waiting. What's the mission? Back down to Fort Stearns?"

Fleming shook his head. "We need them to track down CB, Brian, and Jessica. As long as they're out there, sowing discontent, we're all in danger. While the GMT's hunting them down, I'll do a broadcast."

Sarah looked at him, surprised. "Are you sure you're up for that?"

"After Jessica's broadcast earlier? How can I not respond?" His expression softened a little. "Look, I'm sorry about before, in the hangar. I know I lost my cool. But I'm good now. I need to remind the people that CB is a terrorist. I'll tell them about how he sabotaged Resettlement. What Jessica showed them was real, but there was a very good reason behind it. That's what they need to hear."

"Okay," Sarah said. "I'll call down and have them start preparing for the broadcast."

"And I'll get the new GMT geared up," Kurtz said. "Anything else they need to know?"

"Yes," Fleming said. "Tell them I expect them to find CB, Jessica, and Brian before the day is out. And tell them I don't expect the fugitives to be brought in alive."

6

IT WAS late afternoon before Alex convinced George to allow her and the team outside Agartha. It was far too late in the day for the trip to Denver, and they had promised Jaden they would leave that journey to him and his vampires. But they hadn't made any such promises about heading out to salvage what they could of the rover that had been destroyed in the previous night's battle.

So it was that Alex, Chuck, Ed, Patrick, Owl and Wesley passed through the doors of Agartha and out into the cold, driving a borrowed truck.

It wasn't so much that they needed the rover parts immediately. Jaden and his team could easily grab them on their way back from Agartha. But Alex needed to be doing *something*. Being cooped up in a strange city while *New Haven* needed her was driving her absolutely crazy. She knew some of her team felt the same way.

Others were content to explore their new surroundings.

"I'm telling you, man," Ed said, "from what I saw, Agartha women have *New Haven* women beat hands down."

He glanced nervously at Owl and Alex. "Present company excluded, of course. You ladies are super hot."

"Thank you for making this conversation even more uncomfortable," Owl said.

"All I'm saying is, we ate lunch in that cafeteria, and the women were gorgeous."

Patrick nodded. "Can you believe it? A whole city of women and they don't even know us. It's like starting over."

Alex tried to ignore the Barton brothers' conversation and stayed alert to their surroundings. Although there were probably Ferals hidden in the snow drifts around them, they were keeping to the center of the road that had been packed down by the Agartha transport the previous night. As long as they drove away from the snow banks, a Feral wouldn't be able to get to them without lunging well into the sunlight.

Ed was moving around well for a man who'd had his leg sliced open the previous night. There was a slight hitch in his step, and he grimaced occasionally, but he never once complained.

It took them about three minutes to drive the mile to where the rover had been destroyed.

Owl let out an anguished moan when she saw the ruined rover. "First the away ship. Then the backup ship. Now this. How much can one person handle?"

Wesley chuckled. "If it's any consolation, I'm pretty sure the rover didn't suffer."

Signs of the battle were strewn around them. Pieces ripped from the walls of the Agartha transport vehicle. Body parts of Ferals who'd fallen in the fight. Bits of the rover.

Thankfully, the remains of the rover were lying at the edge of the road, the heat from its motors having melted the snow around it. They were able to get to the rover without risking being within grabbing range of any vampires.

Owl knelt next to the rover while the rest of them waited anxiously. After a few minutes of poking around the wreckage, she looked up. "Well, it's not great, but it certainly could be worse. The batteries appear to be undamaged, and that's the most important part."

"That means we can get the ship working again?" Chuck asked, hopefully.

"It means we have a chance," Owl answered. "We still have the parts Fleming's crew sabotaged to deal with, but assuming George can repair those, at least we'll have the power we need."

"Crap," Patrick muttered. "So, you're telling me we have to count on Jaden and his team to recover the away ship. And then we have to count on his engineering team to fix it?"

"Putting our lives in the hands of a bunch of vampires does seem a little odd for the GMT," Ed agreed.

"That it does," Alex said, "but that's where we're at. It goes against instincts, but so does overthrowing the head of *New Haven*, and that's next on our to-do list."

CB, Brian, and Jessica made their way down the tunnel, deeper into the bowels of the ship. Fleming's voice came from Brian's tablet, reverberating off the metal walls and floor.

"Is that really necessary?" CB asked, the annoyance clear in his voice.

"Fleming's addressing the whole city," Brian pointed out, "and he's talking about us. Don't you want to hear what he's saying?"

"We *know* what he's saying. It's the first play in his playbook."

Jessica spoke in a low voice, doing a surprisingly passable Fleming impression. "CB, Brian, and Jessica are enemies of this city. Every bad thing that has ever happened is their fault, and definitely not mine. If we don't catch them soon, your wives and husbands won't sleep with you and your kids will turn ugly."

Brian chuckled. "Fine, I'll put it away." He slid the tablet into his pack. "It's going to be tough getting the people on our side after a message like that. And I certainly don't see how we're going to do it while hiding out down here."

"It'll be tough, but not impossible," CB countered. "Even though Kurtz betrayed me, I believe there are plenty of badges who will side with us when the time comes. I fought with a lot of those guys and gals back in the day. Some of them have GMT in their blood. Fathers. Mothers. Cousins. There's hardly a badge family that doesn't have someone who served in the GMT at some point."

"Engineering's the same way," Jessica said. "We have a lot of supporters there. I say our first step is contacting them. Once we have the few who I know are loyal, we can—"

CB held up a hand, cutting her off. He tilted his head, listening. He hadn't been sure of the noise the first time, but now it came again. The scuffle of a group of people moving through the tunnels. Trying to be quiet, but not fully succeeding.

If they were close enough for CB to hear their footsteps, they were also close enough to have heard Jessica's voice.

"Run," CB said, flatly. Then he turned and sprinted down the tunnel, hoping his friends would follow.

As soon as they started running, their pursuers gave up

any pretense of stealth and chased after them, their shouts and heavy footfalls echoing loudly through the metal corridors.

"Stop!" a voice behind them called.

CB ignored the voice and pushed hard, and Jessica and Brian did their best to keep up, but within a few minutes it became clear their pursuers were closing the gap. Brian wasn't exactly a frequent attendee at the gym, and his gasps could be heard over the other noises as he ran. Jessica was in slightly better shape, but she wasn't a runner, either.

Looking over his shoulder, he caught a glimpse of them racing down the long corridor: six headlamps illuminating the darkness.

"Jessica, we need a way out of here," CB called.

Jessica thought a moment. "I have an idea. Think you can hold them off for a minute or so?"

"I'll do my best."

"Good enough." With that, she led them down a smaller tunnel to their left.

The ceiling in the tunnel was only ten feet high, and CB could touch the walls with both hands if he stretched his arms out.

"Brian, you're with me," Jessica said. "CB, you buy us a minute or two. When I yell, you jump as high as you can."

"Jump?" CB asked. "Why should I jump? What are you planning?"

But Jessica and Brian had already taken off running down the corridor.

A moment later, six figures entered the tunnel. They were dressed head to toe in black, with masks covering their faces. Each of them held a baton. That made sense. You couldn't use a gun in these tunnels without risking damage to an essential system.

CB looked around and spotted a fire extinguisher on the wall of the tunnel. Not exactly the ideal weapon, but it would pack a wallop. He grabbed it and held it in front of him like a shield.

"Colonel Brickman," one of the masked men said, "stand down. By the authority of Director Fleming and the GMT, I'm placing you under arrest."

CB raised an eyebrow, suddenly understanding. "The GMT? Is that what you think you are?"

"Sir, let's not make this any harder than it has to be."

CB took a step forward. "I have to admit the new uniforms are intimidating. Won't help against the vampires, though." He scanned their faces, wishing he could see their eyes. "Look, you boys must have been badges before getting this new gig. That means you know me. You know General Craig. There's no way you believe the stories Fleming's telling about us."

There was a moment of silence, then the lead man said, "We have our orders. Surrender, or we will take you down hard."

CB smiled grimly. "You've been GMT what? A day? Guess it's time for your first real sparring session."

The faceless GMT members moved forward cautiously. If they did know CB, then they knew he was a formidable opponent. They'd be careful.

CB reminded himself he didn't need to take every one of these GMT imposters down; he just needed to hold them off for a couple minutes. He believed he could do that, especially if he made a strong first impression.

The masked man in front—the one CB assumed was the leader—surged forward, swinging his baton at CB's midsection. CB stepped to his left, easily avoiding the telegraphed attack. While the man was still in motion, CB swung the fire extinguisher, holding it by the hose. The canister slammed into the attacker's face with a metallic clang. The new GMT leader dropped to the ground, unconscious, his ruined nose spurting blood.

"Not a great first attack," CB said. "Who can do better?"

The others hesitated.

"Come on!" CB growled. "You want to call yourselves GMT, then you damn well better act like it! Obey your orders."

Finally, three of the them stepped forward, each holding a baton. They attacked in unison, the three of them shoulder to shoulder in the narrow tunnel.

CB felt a slight smile cross his face. They were fighting like this was a brawl at Tankards; nothing about this seemed like a coordinated assault. He stepped left and forward, effectively putting the leftmost attacker between him and the others. When the man raised his baton, CB threw a right-hand jab, catching him in the throat. CB snatched the baton from the attacker's suddenly loose grip and whirled around, dropping into a crouch and hitting the center man in the knee.

As the center man went down, CB brought up his left hand, swinging the fire extinguisher upward. The canister slammed into the man on the right's jaw, and he reeled backward.

"Seriously?" CB shouted. He was talking louder than he'd intended, unable to keep the anger out of his voice. "If you were any sort of team, you'd have me on the ground right now. You better hope to God you never go up against the real GMT. They would grind you into dust."

He turned his angry gaze toward the remaining two, but before they could make their move, Jessica shouted in the distance.

"Now, CB!"

He leaped into the air as high as he could, bringing his knees up, getting as much air as possible.

A flash of light shot through the tunnel a moment before CB's feet landed back on the ground. The remaining members of the faceless GMT went down.

CB was breathing hard, trying to figure out what had just happened, when Jessica and Brian came running back down the tunnel.

"Nice work," Jessica said.

CB stared down at the fallen attackers. Now that the fight was over and his anger was subsiding, he almost felt sorry for them. They'd been following Fleming's orders, same as CB would have in another time. "Thanks. Back at ya. What the hell did you do?"

"We found the transformer panel," Brian said. "Jessica had the idea of disabling the ground and overloading the circuit. Sent a burst of electricity through the metal tunnel. The range was limited, but it worked." He gestured to the fallen faceless GMT members. "Obviously."

"You science people don't mess around," CB said. He dropped to a crouch next to the attackers and felt each of their necks. "Looks like they survived, but we need to get out of here. Fleming could have three more teams just like them, for all we know. One thing I want to do first."

He reached into one of their packs and found what he was looking for. Standard-issue Kevlar rope and a radio. "Let's tie them up."

Once they'd bound the faceless GMT, Brian, Jessica, and CB made their way deeper into the bowels of the ship. Jessica said she knew a place they would be safe, and even the GMT wouldn't be able to find them.

"So that's our strategy?" Brian asked. "Hide until Fleming gets bored of ruling *New Haven* and gives up?"

"Not exactly," CB said. "I have a plan, but we need to rest and recuperate before putting it into action. Then we just need to find a way to take over the flight controls for a few hours."

Jessica and Brian exchanged a glance. "That won't be easy," Jessica said. "The controls were designed to be un-hackable. The only way to steer the ship is to get control of the flight deck itself."

"Okay, let's do that, then," CB said. When he saw the looks on their faces, he grinned. "Hey, nobody said over-throwing a dictator and taking control of a flying city was going to be easy. I'm counting on you geniuses to help me figure out how to bypass the flight control's security, avoid these masked killers, and take control of the flight deck without killing innocent people."

"Uh-huh," Jessica said. "And what are you going to be doing?"

"I'll be arming my secret weapon."

7

THE CAFETERIA in Agartha was quiet, as was the team sitting around the table. Their plates had long since been cleared and they'd run out of things to say.

Once again, they were waiting, and Alex hated it.

It was a few minutes before sundown. A few minutes until Jaden and his team would wake up and prepare for their journey to Denver to retrieve the disabled away ship. Assuming it was still there. At that point, Alex could either go to bed and most likely stare up at the ceiling until morning, or pace around Agartha and drive all the vampires who stayed behind nuts with her questions.

Ed leaned forward. "Heh."

"What's so funny?" Chuck asked.

"I was just thinking about CB. He's gotta be *pissed* right now. He's the only guy I know who hates waiting more than Alex."

Alex chuckled. "Very true."

Owl climbed from her seat and sat on the table. "CB probably thinks we're dead, right? I mean, that's gotta be what Fleming told everyone."

"Sure," Wesley agreed. "He probably gave one of his big speeches. You know the ones. Tragic accident. This loss will not be in vain. Resettlement must move forward."

Something clicked in Alex's mind, something that had been bothering her for the last couple of hours, but which she hadn't been able to put into conscious thought. "I don't know. If Fleming said we were dead, CB would insist on being on the team that came down to check out the landing site and recover the away ship."

Patrick shrugged. "So what? Maybe he was on that team."

Owl shook her head, catching on. "If CB'd been to the landing site, he would have seen the missing batteries and rover. He would have known exactly where we'd gone."

"And he would have been knocking on Agartha's doors twenty minutes later," Alex added. She thought a moment. "We need to get back to *New Haven* fast. CB's in trouble. What are the chances we can have the ship up and running tomorrow?"

"Hard to say until we see it," Owl replied. "Though we have to be realistic about this. Even if Jaden and his team get the ship and it's an easy repair, *New Haven* has a defensive system. It hasn't been used since the early days, but it's tested and operational. Fleming could shoot us out of the sky if he sees us coming."

Alex looked at the pilot. "I have to believe the people of *New Haven* won't let that happen. They've got to be fighting Fleming by now. We have friends up there. Brian. Jessica. CB. Who knows how many more? When the time comes, we have to trust they'll help get us inside."

Patrick sighed. "This is great and all, but we need a ship before we have to worry about any of that. Let's let the vampires do their thing, and then we'll worry about doing ours."

Chuck looked at him in surprise. "Wow, Patrick, that might be the wisest thing I've ever heard you say."

Patrick stared back at him earnestly for a moment, then opened his mouth and let out a tremendous burp.

Ed burst out in laughter at the apparently brilliant piece of comedy.

Alex's radio chirped and George's voice came through.

"Alex, you there?"

She scooped up the handheld radio and held it to her mouth. "Yeah, I'm here, George. What's up?"

"Remember how you wanted me to let you know when he woke up?"

"Yeah."

"He woke up."

Less than five minutes later, Alex stood in the hangar area just inside the door to the outside world. Though the vampires had only been awake a few minutes, they were already moving with purpose, every one of them knowing his or her job and doing it without being told.

Jaden stood near the front, huddled together with George and Robert, going over some final details. Alex shoe-horned in between George and Jaden.

"How many are you taking with you?" she asked.

Jaden shot her an annoyed glance. "Alex, you're going to have to trust—"

"I did trust you," she snapped. "I kept my team inside all day, when it was the last thing any of us wanted. All because you said you and your team could handle recovering the ship better. I think that's as much trust as anyone should be required to have, and I don't think a few details are too much to ask."

Robert chuckled. "Have I mentioned that I like her, Jaden? Maybe we should bring her along."

A spark of hope kindled in Alex's chest for just a moment.

"Sure, and have the smell of a human attracting every Feral within a hundred miles of here?" Jaden countered. "I don't think so." He turned to Alex. "I'm taking fourteen other vampires with me. We'll be using a ramming truck to clear the road and a flatbed big enough to carry the away ship. I'm confident we can get there and back in plenty of time. What I don't know is how long it will take us to load up the away ship, so I want to get moving ASAP."

Alex started at him blankly. "What's that?"

"What's what?"

"ASAP. You said you want to get moving ASAP."

Jaden looked at her a moment, confused. Then he burst out laughing. "I'm sorry. You don't use the term ASAP in *New Haven*?"

"Apparently not." Alex was far less amused by this conversation than he was.

"It's an acronym," George interjected. "It means 'as soon as possible.'"

"Ah." She glared at Jaden, who was still laughing.

"It was a pretty common one in the days before infestation," Jaden said with a chuckle. "I wonder why your people let it die off."

Alex frowned. "Yeah, well, I can't help you there. But I would appreciate it if you got ASAP out of here so I could have my ship back."

That set Jaden off laughing again, even harder than before. "I'm sorry, Alex," he managed between laughs. "You really are quite entertaining. I'll get your ship back here as soon as I can."

Alex allowed herself a slight smile. "Good luck out there. I'll see you ASAP."

Jaden let out one last laugh and clapped her on the shoulder. "Very good. That was almost correct."

———

FIREFLY WOKE IN TERROR, darkness and icy cold surrounding him. And something else pulsating through his very bones: hunger.

It took a moment before it all came back, and when it did, he wanted nothing more than to lie there under the snow until his mind left him and he went Feral. But he couldn't do that, because under the hunger was an even more urgent need: his masters were calling him.

His fingers tore through the snow like lightning-quick shovels, and he burst forth into the darkness of the evening. As he landed, he ran, racing toward his masters. He found them at the top of a frozen pile of Feral corpses, looking down on the gates of Agartha.

Mark glanced at him when he arrived. "Took you long enough. Next time we call you, be faster."

Firefly felt himself nod. From the moment he'd opened his eyes until he'd arrived at their side couldn't have been more than fifteen seconds. He didn't know how it would be possible to arrive any faster. Yet, they'd given him an order, and he would have to obey it, even if it meant pushing his body beyond the point of injury.

Aaron clapped him on the shoulder. "It's a big night. Are you ready?"

He answered honestly, the only way he could answer his masters. "I don't know."

Aaron chuckled. "Well, you'd better figure it out real

quick, because we're going to be fighting Jaden's vampires in a couple hours, and these dudes do not play."

Mark gestured toward the outer doors of Agartha. "Based on what we saw when we were living in the city, the patrols started about two hours after sundown. Maybe slightly earlier if Jaden and his disciples were headed out on a large supply run. Either way, we want to make sure we're ready to attack the moment one of them sticks their head out that door."

Aaron nodded. "We've got the snipers in position, but we need to make sure they're ready. And that everyone's in the ideal location."

Firefly nodded, not understanding what any of this had to do with him.

Mark grunted. "Okay, look, what we're trying to say here is that, even though we are incredibly powerful vampires, we don't have a lot of experience in the military arena. Aaron was a mechanic or something, right?"

"And as far as I can tell, Mark was just a nerd," Aaron replied.

Mark shot him a look. "Point is, we haven't done this sort of thing before. I guarantee Jaden has. That's why we need your expertise. You were a captain, right?"

Firefly nodded briskly, not much liking the use of *were* in that sentence.

Mark chuckled. "You want to call yourself a captain, or even a general, that's fine with us. As long as you do your job. Help us set up this attack so it'll get the job done. Coordinate the troops. Make this work."

Firefly wanted nothing more than to refuse, but he knew he had no choice. Still, maybe he could leverage this situation. Ask questions that would help him better plan the attack, thus fulfilling orders, but also gather information that could be used later.

"Of course. But why do you need me to coordinate the troops? Can't you just do that mental orders thing, like you did to wake me up and tell me to come here?"

Mark shrugged. "It doesn't work like that. We can send simple messages, like *danger* or *come*. But for something this complex, I have a feeling we're going to want an actual voice on the radio."

"Got it," Firefly said. His mind was already racing, knowing that this information could be used against them. If he could somehow get into a situation where Mark and Aaron were at a distance and a simple command wouldn't do, he might be able to—

"What that hell?" Aaron muttered. He squinted as he stared at the outer doors to Agartha.

Firefly followed his gaze and was surprised to see that the doors were opening.

"Well, isn't this interesting," Mark said. "Looks like this thing is going down a little sooner than we'd expected."

When the doors were halfway open, a heavily armored truck burst through the opening and sped down the snowy trail. A second truck, this one with a massive flatbed and a boom arm mounted on it, quickly followed.

Though the trucks were a good three hundred yards away, Firefly was surprised to see he could easily make out who was sitting in the cab of the first truck. Robert was driving and Jaden was riding in the passenger seat.

Mark must have seen the same thing Firefly did, because he said, "Oh, hell yeah. Let's light 'em up."

Aaron waited a moment before answering, "I don't think so."

Mark turned to his partner, clearly annoyed. "Are you

serious? We could surround those trucks and take them down in five minutes. We'll never have a better opportunity."

Aaron gestured toward the vehicles. "Those trucks are headed to pick up something. Something big. I don't know about you, but I'd like to know what that something is."

Mark thought about that a moment. "Fine. We follow them wherever they're going. We check out their prize. Then we take them out." He turned to Firefly. "Gather the troops. Let them know to follow, but at a distance. We're moving out."

8

THE TRUCK SPED along the disused road, its massive six-foot tires rumbling over the uneven terrain.

As much as he preferred to run on these nightly excursions, Jaden had to admit traveling by truck had a certain allure. If he closed his eyes, he could almost forget the world had gone to hell. Almost.

Robert kept his eyes on the road as he drove. "Remember this area in the old days?"

"Yeah," Jaden replied. He'd spent significant time in these mountains in the pre-infestation era. Back then, it had seemed civilization was crowding in, threatening to drive the last ounce of wildness from humanity. He'd assumed the wildness would continue diminishing. How wrong he'd been. A few short years after he'd had those thoughts, wildness had been all that was left. "Back in those days, there were far fewer potholes." He gestured toward the road ahead of them. "And fewer obstacles."

While they'd made great progress on their journey thus far, they'd seen far more Ferals than they usually would on this remote road. And all of them were moving toward

Agartha. One of them stood in the road as their truck approached, sniffing the air. It paused for a moment, then took off running toward the mountain city.

A few vampires had even jumped onto the truck, probably drawn by the lingering smell of George and the human mechanics who'd worked on it that day. Jaden and his vampires hadn't bothered engaging them; as soon as the Ferals realized that there were no humans aboard, they jumped off.

"You know, I feel sorry for them," Robert said, staring at the Ferals gathering on the road. "To think that there are real people trapped inside those creatures. I kinda wish we'd never met Aaron and Mark."

Jaden watched one of the Ferals flinch as it caught the smell of humans and trotted toward the trucks. "Their human minds are gone. They're no different than animals. It's just if they feed that their human minds will return. Then they'll realize what they've been through, and their horror will begin. For now, they're just creatures operating on instinct."

"Maybe so," Robert said. "Seems like a fine line."

They sat in silence for a few moments before Jaden spoke again. "The real problem is their immortality. If they would eventually die, humanity could start over. Maybe even make a world better than the old one. No countries. No preconceived prejudices. Enough resources to keep every human living in abundance for generations." He sighed. "Unfortunately, we're still prisoners of the sins of the past."

Robert looked at him like he wanted to say something, then he paused.

Jaden didn't press. He knew that most vampires didn't like talking about the past much, himself included. Instead, Robert brought up the future.

"So, is this how it's going to be from now on? We just live in a hole in a mountain for the rest of time?"

"You know it's not."

"Good. Because I could do another one hundred and fifty years. Probably even three hundred. But there's a limit to how long I can live like that. I want to keep the humans alive as much as you do, but at some point, we have to start thinking about the next adventure."

Jaden nodded, then gestured to the road beyond the windshield. "My friend, we are on our way to recover an aircraft for a city we didn't know still existed until a month ago. We made new friends, and there's a chance we'll get to see their city in the sky. We *are* on the next adventure."

Robert chuckled. "You know something? You're right. These recent events are what made me realize how stale things have gotten in Agartha."

Jaden couldn't disagree with that sentiment. "Tell you what. Let's get through tonight's adventure, and then we'll start planning the next one."

As the trucks reached the edges of the ruins that had once been a sprawling metropolis, the number of Ferals taking an interest in them began to grow. At first, a few dozen ran along beside the trucks, then that number grew to a hundred. Then two hundred.

Even more watched from a distance, their eyes peering out from behind rubble and through broken windows. It seemed that every Feral in Denver was agitated tonight, and hordes watched the truck of vampires, confused by the conflicting smells of lingering humanity and the undead occupants.

FIREFLY RAN.

He'd run before, of course. Plenty of times. He'd run for exercise and as a way to relieve stress. He'd run as part of his GMT training, often with CB close on his heels, barking at him to go faster. He'd ran during missions, both to fights and away from them.

But before last night, he'd never run like this. He ran like his body had been designed for this very purpose. His legs pushed hard, each step sending him surging forward through the cold Colorado night and sending a delicious rush of pleasure through him.

He must have been going thirty miles an hour, and he knew he could have ran faster if he'd needed to. But he had his orders. He was to follow the Agartha trucks at a distance, so that's what he did.

As he ran, he looked around, taking in the night. Even though it was full dark and there was only a sliver of moonlight, he felt like he took in more detail with every glance than he had in his entire human life.

It was strange; back when he was human, he'd thought of vampires as undead. Something less than alive. But that wasn't the way it felt now. Every fiber of his being practically vibrated with sensations. The air hummed with an electric buzz that he'd never noticed as a human. And the colors! Even in the darkness, he was noticing shades his human eyes had never seen.

But the unpleasant sensations were just as powerful as the pleasant ones. The hunger was growing stronger. He felt like he hadn't eaten in days, but when he thought about his favorite foods, his stomach turned. Picturing himself biting into an apple or sipping a cold beer was nearly enough to make him vomit.

His body knew what it wanted.

Firefly believed that when the time came, he'd be able to resist biting a human, even though it would require every bit of self-control he had in him. He wouldn't allow himself to hurt anyone else.

But it wasn't really his choice, was it?

He wasn't in control of his own body. Mark and Aaron were.

He'd considered circling back to Agartha and warning them about the vampires surrounding their city, but his mind had immediately rejected the treasonous thought. He'd thought about killing his fellow Resettlers and then himself, but his hand wouldn't even draw the weapon, knowing that his intention was to betray his masters.

His will was not his own, and as wondrous as some of the new sensations were, the horror of this knowledge outweighed everything else.

Firefly looked over his shoulder and saw the soldiers running behind him. They'd believed in him and followed him to Fort Stearns. Now they were following him again, and who knew if the results would be just as disastrous?

He was a slave, and so were they. As long as Mark and Aaron lived, Firefly would kill the people he loved and destroy everything he held dear on their slightest whim.

He needed to find a way out.

But for now, he ran.

9

———

ROBERT PULLED the truck to a stop about a block away from the location Owl had given them for the away ship. "Gee," he said, "do you think they can smell the human scent on the away ship?"

"I think that's a fair guess." Jaden's eyes scanned the massive horde of Ferals in front of them. The creatures filled the streets, standing shoulder to shoulder. Getting past them would be impossible without causing a serious distur-bance. And if they wanted to get to the away ship, they *had* to get past the Ferals.

"This is bad," Robert said. "If we set them off, we're in serious trouble."

Jaden nodded. Ferals generally left the vampires alone, but if they felt threatened, or if they felt a food source was in danger, they wouldn't hesitate to attack. And the way they were surrounding the away ship, they had to feel that it was a food source.

"Do they think there are humans on that ship?" Robert asked. "Or are they just hoping the humans will come back?"

Jaden considered that a moment. "I'm not sure their level of thought goes that deep. They smell a strong human scent, so they gather. The human smell means the potential for food."

"Ouch. This could get ugly."

Jaden turned and called into the back of the transport. "Igor, Natalie. I need you two to scout ahead. Find out if this is as bad as it looks."

"On it, Jaden," Igor answered.

The two vampires leaped out of the truck and scampered up the side of the nearest building. When they reached the top, they leaped to the next one. And then the next. They vaulted from building to building, high above the Ferals. Finally, they paused, watching the streets below.

Jaden followed their progress with his eyes. Even after all these years, he still occasionally marveled at the grace and beauty in the movements of his fellow vampires. He supposed it was like living with an exceptional piece of art. You might grow accustomed to it, but it still had the power to bowl you over now and again.

A few of the Ferals glanced up at the vampires on the building, clearly aware of their presence but not bothered by it.

A moment later, Igor and Natalie made their way back to the transport.

"They're packed in tight, all the way to the ship," Natalie reported. "They're all over the ship itself, too. If I hadn't known it was there, I might have thought they were standing on a hill or something. Not one inch of the damn thing is visible."

Jaden thought a moment, considering how best to proceed. They needed to get some of these Ferals out of here, but they needed to do it in a way that didn't cause a massive riot of the undead.

"I need you two to do something else." Jaden gave Igor and Natalie their instructions. They grabbed two sniper rifles out of the truck and went to work, climbing to their position near the top of a building east of the transport. Then they fired.

The first shot struck a Feral in the shoulder. It wasn't a killing blow, but it certainly got the attention of the Ferals gathered around the target. The next shot took a Feral's arm clean off.

By the third shot, Natalie and Igor had the Ferals' full attention. The undead horde surged toward the sound of the gunfire, and Natalie and Igor took the signal to get the hell out of there. They leaped down onto the street and took off running east, away from the ship and the transport.

The Feral horde raced after them. It wasn't long before the street was nearly clear.

Robert chuckled. "Wow, that actually worked."

Jaden nodded. "Let's take advantage of the moment."

The Ferals hadn't all followed Natalie and Igor, but the vast majority had. There was plenty of room for the truck to proceed.

Robert drove the truck forward slowly and carefully. When they reached the away ship, he turned off the vehicle. The flatbed truck rolled up beside them.

Robert nodded out the window. "Looks like we still have some work to do."

Jaden eyed the twenty-five Ferals who remained gathered around the away ship, apparently too enthralled by the human scents to be lured away by gunshots.

He turned to his team. "Let's do this quickly and quietly. Time's a factor here, so don't get fancy."

That was all he needed to say. The thirteen vampires emerged from their vehicles and drew their swords.

As they approached, one of the Ferals let out a grunt of rage and bared his teeth at them. Clearly, he wasn't about to give up his prize.

"On my mark," Jaden said, a sword in each hand. He scanned the area with his eyes, making sure each of his team members was in position. "Go."

They worked without speaking. Though the Ferals around the ship had them outnumbered two to one, they never stood a chance. Jaden's vampires moved with furious speed and an economy of motion that came from decades—in many cases, centuries—of working side by side.

In a matter of seconds, they'd removed the heads of every Feral within ten feet of the ship. The Ferals hadn't even had time to realize what was happening, let alone to fight back.

They barely paused before turning to the next task: loading the away ship onto their flatbed. Two of the vampires cleared the Ferals' bodies away while the rest rigged the ship to the boom arm. They did their best to work silently, but the boom arm and the chain they'd used to secure the ship produced clangs and whines that attracted more Ferals back to the ship.

So far, the Ferals who'd gathered were leaving them alone, but Jaden wasn't about to take any chances. They needed to get out of there as quickly as possible.

It took them a little over half an hour to get the ship loaded on the flatbed. Jaden eyed the road and saw that there was still plenty of room for the truck to pass through the gathering crowd of Ferals. They would have to move slowly with the ship on the flatbed, so they needed to get going soon.

After ensuring that his vampires were done securing the ship, Jaden said, "Let's move out."

Distant, angry howls came from the east side of the city. Apparently, Natalie and Igor were still leading the Ferals on their merry chase. Jaden would have to trust them to eventually shake the horde and meet up with them back in Agartha.

Jaden motioned for the flatbed to start moving, while the rest of them climbed into the transport.

As the flatbed began to creep down the street, a Feral leaped onto the back. It paused for a moment, then bent down to gnaw on one of the straps.

Jaden nodded at a vampire named Akono, who hopped onto the flatbed and lashed out, knocking the Feral to the road. He hopped down after the Feral and slashed his sword through its neck. Its head tumbled to the road.

For a tense moment, the Ferals in the area froze, their eyes fixed on the head on the pavement.

Jaden waited, sword in hand, to see if they would attack.

The moment passed and the Ferals returned to their confused wandering.

Robert exhaled with relief. "Okay, let's get—"

Something on a distant building caught Jaden's eye. "Everybody down!"

A gunshot split the air.

A vampire named Leslie was climbing onto the transport truck. A bullet fired by a distant weapon hit her and her arm was blown off at the elbow.

She cried out in pain and surprise.

The vampires hit the deck, and Jaden stared at the spot where he'd seen the distant reflection of the scope, his mind reeling as he tried to figure out who could possibly be attacking them.

FIREFLY STOPPED RUNNING as he reached the edge of Denver. He looked over his shoulder and saw exactly what he'd expected to see: three hundred new vampires and two dickheads.

Mark and Aaron slowed to a halt on either side of him.

"Good call," Aaron said. "Let's stop for a moment and figure out how we want to attack this thing."

Mark glanced at Firefly. "You were a field commander back in your human days, albeit an unsuccessful one. Tell us what you think. How would you approach this?"

Firefly didn't want to answer, but once again his new vampire instincts overrode his human desires. "We've got them outnumbered three hundred to less than twenty. They're more experienced, so we'll probably take some casualties, but there's no doubt that we'll win."

"I don't disagree," Mark replied after a moment. "Still, we don't want to make the same mistake you and your buddies did at Fort Stearns. Overconfidence can be a killer."

Firefly had just about had it with this vampire's smug comments, but he knew better than to ever try to make a move against his master.

"You gotta respect a vampire as old as Jaden," Aaron agreed. "Besides, we want to take him alive. That makes things more complicated." He thought a moment. "Here's what we do. We track them into the city to figure out where they're headed, but we don't get too close. Shouldn't be too hard to blend in, with all the Ferals running around. Then we set up snipers around their perimeter. We kill as many of them as we can from range, then we swoop in and overwhelm Jaden with our numbers."

Firefly felt himself nod. Seemed like a sensible plan.

Mark glared at him. "Don't just nod. Make it happen."

After briefing the vampires, Firefly started into the city. He felt an odd chill as the buildings rose around him. It took him a few minutes to realize what it was: a remnant from the instincts he'd developed as a member of the GMT. In those days, being out at night in the mountains would have been crazy, but being in the city? Surrounded by hundreds of thousands of Ferals? It would have been unthinkable.

Now he was walking through a city filled with the creatures.

With his vampiric eyesight, he could pick them out clearly, even far away and in the darkness. He saw them scurrying along the street, sniffing the ground. Others crawled along the sides of buildings, hunting for who knew what. Still others stood in the street, staring up at the sky as if watching for something to come down and save them from their pathetic fate.

"You smell them?" a voice beside him asked.

He turned and saw Shirley, her gaze fixed on the road ahead of them. In the preparations for Resettlement, Shirley had been his right-hand woman. Now, because of him and Fleming, she was a blood-sucking corpse.

It was odd looking at her, someone he'd known so well in life, as a vampire. There was a strange deadness in her eyes, but also an electricity in the way the tiny muscles of her face twitched occasionally. It was as if she were dead, but still more alive than she'd been as a human.

He wondered what he looked like. If he saw himself in a mirror, would he recognize his own face? He knew there were old legends that vampires' reflections couldn't be seen in a mirror, but he also knew that was as false as the thing about garlic. He almost wished it were true. His reflection was just about the last thing he wanted to see.

"I can smell them," he confirmed.

Her nose wrinkled slightly as she sniffed. "Outside of the city, it's subtle. Like old leather. But here..." She trailed off as she sniffed again.

Firefly knew exactly what she meant. The scent of the Ferals permeated the entire city; they smelled like rancid death. "I thought they smelled bad when I was a human."

She chuckled. "Yeah, maybe a heightened sense of smell isn't a blessing."

"Not today, it isn't," he agreed.

Shirley hesitated for a moment before continuing, "There's something else in their smell. It's like... They're on edge. Like they expect prey and are ready to pounce."

Firefly nodded. He felt it, too. Though the source of the feeling was difficult to identify. Was it really their smell, or was it something else? Something like that mental connection Alex had said that vampires shared?

Either way, he needed to stay focused on the task at hand. His masters demanded it.

They'd almost reached the center of downtown when a couple of vampires he'd sent ahead came running back to report they'd found Jaden's crew. Apparently, they were loading a ship onto a truck.

Firefly's stomach turned when he heard the news. That had to be the away ship. Did that mean the GMT was dead? But if so, how would Jaden know to come get the away ship? Was it possible that the team had made it to Agartha?

He pushed the thoughts away. There was work to do.

The snipers moved into place and Firefly joined two of them and a spotter, on a building with a view of the away ship's crash site. He could see Jaden and his vampires loading the ship onto the flatbed. The majority of the vampire army was hanging back, out of sight, their scent hopefully masked by the hordes of Ferals roaming the streets.

He eyed the other buildings they'd picked out, watching until all twenty snipers were in position. Then he lifted his radio and contacted Aaron. "We're ready."

"Good. Make sure they know not to kill Jaden. He's our ticket into Agartha."

"They know."

"Okay, then. Go when you're ready."

Firefly switched channels and addressed all the snipers. "All right. Everyone, select your marks. Maggie, you shoot Jaden in the leg. The rest of you pick another target. Everyone, confirm that you're ready."

He waited a few moments as the confirmations rolled in. Looking down at the crash site, he knew they'd have to act fast. Jaden and his team already had the away ship loaded onto the flatbed.

If his team were more experienced, this fight would be over quickly, but with this inexperienced crew, Firefly couldn't help but be concerned. But he also couldn't disobey his masters.

"Okay, all, fire on my mark. Three. Two."

Suddenly, the vampires on the ground began to move. They were diving for the pavement.

One of the snipers fired, and far below, a fifty-caliber round slammed into a female vampire's arm, severing it at the elbow.

"Damn it!" Firefly shouted. "Fire! Everyone, fire!"

The snipers all began shooting, but they were rattled, and Firefly imagined that had to affect their accuracy. A quick look through his binoculars showed two dead vampires in the cab of the transport truck, but no other injuries.

Jaden's team was in motion now, moving so fast that Firefly's eyes couldn't track them. Everything was happening so quickly, including Firefly's thoughts. They were racing through his head, but he was new to this vampire thing and he didn't know what to do with them.

All he knew was that they'd lost the element of surprise and Mark and Aaron were going to be pissed.

He saw movement out of the corner of his right eye and turned. Ferals were swarming up the building across the street.

"Shit!" He touched his radio and broadcast to the snipers. "The gunshots are attracting the Ferals. We need to get off these roofs."

He kept his eyes fixed on the building to his right as he spoke. The Ferals had reached the roof and were scampering over. There were three soldiers waiting: two snipers and a spotter with an automatic weapon. The spotter sprayed a wild burst of ammunition at the Ferals, taking down a few of them, but his inexperience was outclassed by their numbers. The Ferals quickly overtook all three of them, who appeared to be too shocked to fight back.

A pang of sorrow flashed through Firefly as he watched three of his Resettlers meet their end. So much for the immortal life of a vampire. These poor bastards had only lasted a day.

"Get to street level," he shouted into the radio. "Don't bother trying to shoot them, just get out of there. Remember, you're vampires, and you're as fast as they are."

A Feral hand reached over the rooftop and a body quickly followed. Firefly lifted his weapon, briefly considering ignoring his own orders and taking this creature down. But then he turned to the door and dashed into the building to join his army on the streets.

10

ALEX GAVE up her futile attempt to sleep after three hours of trying.

She'd probably managed two hours of real sleep before waking up in a panic, wondering where she was. At that point, her mind had come fully awake, and she'd known that getting back to sleep was a pointless endeavor.

Still, she'd given it her best effort. She'd laid in the uncomfortable cot for three hours, while thoughts of *New Haven* and the hell CB and her friends still onboard must be experiencing swirled through her mind. On the rare occasions when she successfully managed to push thoughts of *New Haven* away, the void was quickly filled with anger and regret that Jaden and his vampires were currently working to recover the away ship, while she lay in this dumb bed under a mountain.

When she finally gave up, she sat up with a sigh, left the small room Jaden had assigned her, and went for an aimless walk around the city, letting the corridors and her whim lead her.

She'd been walking for ten minutes, when she heard a

familiar sound that made her wandering mind snap to attention. It was a sound she'd recognize anywhere: the clashing of swords.

She stood stone-still for nearly a minute, listening to that sound. The rhythm of the clash—a few moments of frenzied clanging metal followed by a small break—made her realize it wasn't the sound of a battle that she heard. Someone was sparring.

Following the sounds, she eventually found herself outside of a room that she'd never seen before, but one in which she immediately felt comfortable. It was a training facility.

Two vampires, a male and a female, stood on the mat near the center of the large room, each holding a sword. The moment Alex entered the room, they disengaged their sparring and looked at her.

"Hello, I'm Alex Goddard."

They stared at her dumbly for a moment. Then the female vampire said, "We know. Jaden keeps us up to date on such things. The question is, what are you doing here?"

Alex gave a shrug. "I heard you sparring. Thought I'd come check it out."

The vampires exchanged a glance. The male cleared his throat. "This facility is designated for vampire use. That way, we can cut loose without worrying about accidentally hurting a human."

A slow smile crept across Alex's face. "Ah. I see."

"Good." The male vampire waited, clearly expecting her to leave.

Which made Alex want to stay, even more. "Thing is, I'm the captain of the Ground Mission Team. We're sort of an elite fighting force. We can go out in the sun, and everything. I thought I might like to see how you amateurs train."

The two vampires looked at her for a long moment, as if trying to figure out if she was joking or if she was an idiot.

Finally, the male shrugged. "You want to watch us work, fine. Just try not to distract us."

Alex nodded. "That, I can do. You won't hear a peep." She crossed her arms and leaned back against the wall.

Now that she was here, she realized how lucky she was. She'd faced many vampires—well, Ferals, mostly—but it had always been when her life was on the line. Her perspective had been skewed by the rush of battle frenzy. Now, she had the opportunity to observe two vampires sparring in a safe environment, where she could calmly analyze their skills.

This was a goldmine.

The vampires stood stone-still, their swords raised, staring at each other from across the mat. Then, as if prompted to begin by some imperceptible signal, they both sprang into action.

Alex watched, struggling to follow their lightning-quick movements. She wanted to find a weakness, something that could give her an edge against a vampire or a Feral, should she ever be in the unlucky position of facing one at night. After a few minutes, it became clear that finding a weakness was not going to be an easy proposition.

The vampires didn't seem to tire. After an hour, Alex still hadn't seen anything too useful. To defeat an enemy like these two, she would need to predict their actions, since they moved far too fast for her to just react. Their brutal strength could make any mistake a deadly one.

With sad resignation, she realized that these two were fighting at a level that she would never reach. Their technique was masterful, and both were incredible with their swords. Still, watching had made her think about how she might be able to survive a fight with a Feral. It would have the speed and strength of these two, but none of the skill. Feral attacks were fairly straightforward. If she could anticipate their moves, she could strike at the place where they would be in a moment, rather than where they were, presently.

But these intelligent vampires? She didn't see any way to beat them.

She was just about to give up when she saw something that gave her pause. The female lunged forward a bit too far, and the male dropped to his back and kicked upward, sending the female sailing through the air. She came down hard on the mat and quickly popped back up, her sword ready to parry the strike she knew was coming.

It wasn't the exchange itself that sparked Alex's imagination. She would never be able to pull off those types of moves against such a fast opponent. Yet, it had given her an idea. A kernel of an opening that she might be able to exploit at some point. She filed the idea away in that place in her mind reserved for things that needed to gestate.

She doubted there was much more she was going to learn from watching these vampires tonight, so she slipped away. The vampires were so engaged in their sparring session that they didn't seem to notice.

This time, she had a destination in mind. She didn't know if the Agartha cafeteria served at this time of night, but she aimed to find out.

She found the place nearly empty. The exception was one table, where the rest of the GMT sat.

Alex sauntered over, a knowing smile on her face. "Shouldn't you be resting?"

Ed looked up at her and chucked. "Shouldn't you?"

Alex slipped into the nearest empty chair. "Fair enough.

I just spent an hour watching two vamps sparring. They are some incredibly deadly creatures."

"Maybe," Patrick replied, "but we are pretty deadly creatures, too."

No one objected to that.

"Speaking of being deadly," Wesley said, "when do we get to go mess up Fleming and save the city?"

Alex looked at Owl. "That depends on how fast we can fix the ship."

Owl said, "The batteries are in good shape, and George and I are pretty sure we can make the new circuit board work. I'm hoping I can have the ship up and running a few hours after Jaden gets it here."

"That should be any time now, right?" Chuck asked. "Dawn is getting close."

Alex nodded. "I'll go check in with George, but let's start getting ready to move out. I want us rolling as soon as the ship is operational. *New Haven* needs us."

CB, Brian, and Jessica moved quickly through the maintenance tunnels, deep in the belly of *New Haven*. Brian held up a hand as they approached a tunnel opening that crossed paths with theirs. They stopped, and Brian held up his echolocation device and pointed it in the direction of the other tunnel.

After a moment, he said, "We're good."

The group started moving again, almost running now.

CB shook his head and chuckled as Brian held up the device and he caught a glimpse of the three-dimensional image of the tunnel around them on its screen. The stupid-looking thing had helped them avoid Fleming's faceless

GMT goons ever since the encounter with the group that Jessica had electrocuted.

It was hard not to marvel at the possibilities that existed in Brian's mind. He'd made the echolocation device as a side project in his spare time. For someone else, such a device might be the work of a lifetime.

Now, here they were attempting to overthrow a leader who would most likely kill them all. It would be a damn shame if someone as brilliant as Brian met his end in these tunnels. CB hoped that their one-in-a-million chance would pay off, but he knew the reality would almost certainly be different. The thought of losing these great people for a cause that was already lost made him sick.

He tried to push the thoughts from his mind. There was no time to go down that path. He needed to focus, and hope that his leadership and the brilliance of these two would be enough to pull this off.

Jessica stopped a bit further down the tunnel. "This is the place."

"Thank the sun," Brian muttered, a little short of breath. He sat down, resting his back against the tunnel wall. He looked pale, and a thin layer of sweat covered his face.

CB patted him on the arm. "Brian, you really need to get out of the lab more. A healthy body makes for a healthy mind."

Brian raised an eyebrow. "Okay, Colonel. If I live through the next twenty-four hours, I promise to take up the CB fitness routine. For now, keep your guilt trips, and let me rest a moment. I need to concentrate on hacking the system." He looked at Jessica. "Are you sure the Hub security lines run through here? We're under sanitation, right?"

Jessica was already working on removing an access panel from the tunnel ceiling. "Have a little faith. I'm more than just a pretty face. The security network room in the Hub is well protected, and the lines have a failsafe, so they would know if we tapped into them directly. But the backbone that they run on shares bandwidth with the agricultural systems. If we tap into the backbone here, we can access the Hub undetected."

Jessica finished unscrewing the access panel and bent down to place it on the floor.

CB tried not to stare as she worked. He'd been attracted to her for a long time, but seeing her like this, fighting for her life, facing near-certain death with such poise and brilliance, the attraction had grown into an ache inside him. He wanted her badly, both for her mind and her body. Why hadn't he done something about it before now?

If they made it through this, he vowed to correct that at the first opportunity.

"You *are* a lot more than just a pretty face," he said. "How do you keep track of every system on this ship?"

Jessica stuck her head into the opening and looked up. "This ship has to be one of the most amazing engineering feats humanity has ever created. How could you not want to know about every working piece? Now, give me a boost. I need to get up into the cable tray."

CB linked his fingers, creating a step. Jessica's foot slipped into it and he lifted, boosting her up into the ceiling.

She worked in silence for a few moments, then she re-emerged with a wire, which she hooked into a device attached to Brian's tablet. "Okay, you should be tapped into the network."

"Here we go," Brian said. He worked silently on his tablet for ten minutes, his fingers moving quickly for a few moments, then pausing for a minute or two, while he calculated his next step. Finally, he said, "Got it. We're in the system."

Jessica smiled widely. "Okay, that means you're up, CB. You ready for your acting debut?"

CB felt an unexpected knot of worry in his stomach. Leading a team into battle, he could do, but this? This was something else. It was a whole different type of subterfuge.

Brian pointed the camera at CB and manipulated the picture for a moment. "Ready on this end. CB?"

The colonel took a deep breath and then nodded. It was show time.

THE MOOD in Daniel Fleming's office was tense. Sarah and Fleming were alone, but there were two guards outside the door. There was no way that any unwanted visitors were getting into this room.

Sarah sat on her chair, not daring to relax for a moment as Fleming paced, muttering under his breath. She had to admit, if only to herself, that she was worried.

This was a crisis. Fleming's plan had utterly failed. Times like this were tests for a leader, Sarah knew. Would they rise to the occasion, learn from their mistakes, and use the experience for the betterment of their people? Or would they double down on leading their people to destruction?

It wasn't too late for Fleming to go in the first direction, but so far, he was leaning hard toward the second.

Maybe this was why Sarah was here. Why she'd gone through everything, from being shot to helping him take out the Council. Maybe it had all been leading to this moment.

She cleared her throat and leaned forward. "You need to sit down. Relax. Kurtz and his people are out there right now. They will find him. The whole city is after them. Three people can't hide in *New Haven* for long."

"Don't you think I know that?" Fleming snapped. "The new GMT will get them. Colonel Brickman got lucky. That's the only reason he's alive. Luck runs out, and usually much sooner than you expect. It's not him I'm worried about."

"Then what is it?"

Fleming let out a high-pitched laugh. The strange, unhinged tenor of the laugh set Sarah's teeth on edge.

"It's a hundred things. I'm responsible for this entire city. That's a job one man can't do alone. And so far, everyone I trust is letting me down."

Sarah tried to ignore the sting of those words. "What do you mean? Nearly the entire city's on your side."

"Sure, but what's it matter, if those closest to me are so ineffective? Take Firefly. Who the hell knows what happened at Fort Stearns, but it's clear he lost control of the situation. And then there's Kurtz, failing to take out Colonel Brickman at point-blank range."

"And what about me?" she asked hesitantly.

"Well, Brian McElroy is currently hiding somewhere on this ship. He was critical to Resettlement, and it looks like we've likely lost him forever. There's no way I could ever trust him again. That wasn't how things were supposed to go."

Sarah bit back the reply that almost sprang to her lips. She wanted to tell him to screw right off, but she knew he'd only take so much insubordination, and that would probably be crossing the line. She'd accepted that Fleming expected her to sleep with Brian for the greater good, but the fact that she'd failed in her mission to do so was almost too much to bear.

Attempting to seduce Brian McElroy had been like

trying to seduce a chair. She'd put out plenty of signals, many of them ridiculously overt, but he'd ignored every one of them.

The more worrying thing about Fleming's statement was that he was still talking about Resettlement in the present tense. Like it was still moving forward. He hadn't accepted that it had failed. At some point, he was going to have to realize that the entire Resettlement colony was likely dead. Hell, even most of the GMT squad they'd sent down to assess the situation had died. That was a pretty spectacular failure.

"I think that this could work for the best," she said. "CB is the perfect scapegoat for the Resettlement project. We can tell the people that it would have been a success, but CB sabotaged it. That's what caused the failure. You can get the city running on track again, and then we'll start over."

Fleming raised his voice almost to the point of shouting. "Resettlement is not a failure! We may have had a setback, but once we get a full assessment of the situation, we *will* move forward. We just need to step up the defenses." He took a deep breath and collapsed into the chair behind his desk. "CB *did* sabotage Resettlement, by the way. If he had believed in the project and truly dedicated himself and his team to its success, things would have gone very differently on the first night on the surface."

Sarah could see the desperation in Fleming's eyes and hear it in his voice. This speech was just an attempt to convince himself that it was true. She had seen the team members who survived the trip to the surface and heard their report. Fleming didn't have the ability to cope with failure. Sarah didn't know how to respond, but thankfully, she didn't have to.

There was a pounding on the door and a voice came from the other side. "Sir, we have a situation."

Fleming glanced at Sarah. He hopped from his chair and hurried across the room. He opened the door, a concerned look on his face. "What situation?"

"There's an intruder. Someone tripped the motion sensors on the fifth floor."

Fleming's eyes narrowed. "When and where?"

"An empty office on the west side. Happened less than five minutes ago."

Fleming hurried back to his desk and tapped at the monitor embedded there. A moment later, security footage appeared.

"We don't know how he entered the building without being detected," the guard said, stepping into the office. "We're on high alert here. Every entrance is covered."

Fleming ignored the man and squinted at the monitor, flipping from room to room on the fifth floor. When he found the footage of the intruder, he drew a sharp breath.

Sarah peered over his shoulder, and she too was startled by what she saw.

It was CB.

Colonel Brickman was standing in an empty office. He quickly moved into the hallway, and Fleming flipped the footage to the hallway camera. Then CB ducked around a corner and disappeared from view.

Fleming frantically flipped through footage, trying to find the missing colonel. With his other hand, he grabbed the radio off his desk. "Kurtz, this is Fleming. I need you to get everyone here, and do it quick! CB is in the building. I want you to make damn sure he doesn't leave alive."

Kurtz responded immediately. "I'm on my way. Stay in your office, with the guards inside. I'll have more posted outside the office soon. If CB is there, he is probably coming after you. He thinks taking you out is his only path to victory. Do not leave that room."

Sarah watched as Fleming slammed down the radio. A vein stood out on his forehead, and his face was growing redder by the moment. Fleming always controlled the situation. He made people do what he wanted and forced the outcomes to conform with his will. Now one man was refusing to play by his rules, and seemed to be a step ahead.

If Fleming didn't get himself under control quickly, things could get much worse for everyone.

CB, Jessica, and Brian waited silently, gathered around the radio CB had taken from the leader of Fleming's faceless GMT.

CB was beginning to wonder if they'd miscalculated, or if maybe Fleming had seen through their ruse, when a voice came through the radio.

"This is Colonel Kurtz. I need every badge that can hear my voice to converge on the Hub. Colonel Brickman is currently in the Council building, and ensuring that he does not leave is our top priority. Get your asses over there, post haste. Kurtz out."

CB looked at Brian and said, "My God, I can't believe you actually pulled that off. Well done! How exactly did you do that?"

Brian tilted his head a bit. "It was pretty easy. I set up the footage of you overlaid with some of the security footage from the cameras in the Hub. I just had to make sure that it was in an empty room, so that no one could verify if you were there or not. Once I had a nice new set of footage, I fed it back into the security system so that the camera itself interpreted the video I had made as live footage. I also made sure to trip the motion sensors for the area to get security to check the footage for that time. As far as they are concerned, you are sneaking around on the fifth floor of the Council building."

"Looks like Fleming bought it," Jessica said. "He is probably shitting himself, thinking you're going to burst into his office at any moment."

"Great work, guys. We should have a pretty easy time getting around, at least for a little while."

Jessica nodded. "We have our opportunity. Let's make the most of it."

CB smiled. "Then let's get to work on taking control of the flight deck."

11

———

JADEN LAY ON THE GROUND, momentarily stunned from the unexpected attack.

Just prior to the first shot, Jaden had sensed something. It was battle rage. Not the type that the Ferals experienced, the blind explosions of emotion. No, this was the strange combination of fear, excitement, and trepidation that only a more advanced mind could conjure. He'd experienced it many times, in fact, always just before attacking his opponent.

He silently cursed himself for not picking up on it sooner. Things were muddled with all of these Ferals nearby. Still, he should have caught it. He hadn't, and his team had paid the price.

Granted, if not for his warning, half the team would have fallen, but still. One loss was too many.

He looked to his left and saw Lesley on the pavement, clutching her stump of an arm. And suddenly—

It was 1919. Jaden had come to Chicago for a meeting of the vampires. He'd heard that Gustov had created a new prodigy, bringing their numbers back to one hundred. A young woman. He met the new vampire in a bar off of Water Street. She was danc-ing, but she seemed to sense him as soon as he entered. She saun-tered over, her skirt swaying with each step, every male eye in the place on her, and a few of the female eyes, too. When she reached Jaden, she didn't greet him. Instead, she reached up and touched his cheek with her hand—

—the recollection came in a flash, unbidden, a sensory memory of those soft fingers grazing his cheek. Fingers on a hand that was no longer attached to Lesley. She'd survive the injury, but unfortunately, any hit from a fifty-caliber weapon was a serious one. The force had spun her around and thrown her against the truck. Her torn-off lower arm lay ten feet away from the rest of her.

But she hadn't gotten the worst of it. She'd survive the injury. Tim and Adam had been in the cab of the flatbed truck, and they hadn't been so lucky. His memories of them—

It was 1708, a battlefield in northern France. Jaden had answered the call, coming to the aid of a vampire who was alone and being hunted. Jaden had been in the area on business involving a cannon and a general's daughter, but the panicked feeling from a fellow vampire had sent him racing into enemy territory in the dead of night. He found young Timothy huddled in a latrine—

—were many. He didn't have time to think about the tragedy now. The loss of potentially immortal beings he'd known since—

It was 1612. Jaden had been laying low in the new world for decades, but duty brought him back. In the shipyards, just after sunset, a cocky vampire had tried to sneak up on him. Jaden had easily caught him, grabbing him by the neck and saying, "If you want to last long, you'll need to be much faster than that. Or else, pick much slower targets."

—centuries ago. A loss that profound couldn't be grasped. Not now. Not if he wanted to avoid losing anyone else.

Only moments had passed since the attack, but Jaden realized affording himself even a moment of reflection was too much. Thankfully, the gunfire from the rooftops had stopped. It wasn't difficult to figure out why.

The Ferals that had gathered in the downtown area were already on edge, and the gunfire had been the fuse that blew the powder keg. Ferals were scurrying up buildings, clearly going after the sources of the gunshots. They were closing in on Jaden and his team, too, apparently deciding that all those who were not like them were a threat.

The team didn't need Jaden to tell them what to do. They went to work, clearing the area around their fallen teammates. Jaden quickly joined them.

He'd fought long odds many times in his lengthy life, but he might have been pushing his luck with this one. The Ferals around him pressed forward, closing in on the team.

The report of gunfire came from one the of buildings, and the Ferals froze for a moment, then turned toward it. This wasn't the sound of sniper rifles, like before. This was automatic fire. It must have been the unknown enemy, trying to fight off the Ferals.

Unfortunately for them, their gunfire was attracting even more Feral attention.

There were still plenty who kept their focus on Jaden and his team. The vampires worked quickly and surgically with their swords, tearing through their attackers. They moved fluidly as they fought, aware that there may still be snipers in those buildings and not wanting to give any of them a clear shot.

"Keep moving!" Jaden called to his team. "We need to get

some cover. Head inside there!" He gestured to the nearest building.

The Ferals seemed to be coming faster and faster now. Jaden would need to focus on taking out as many of these bastards as possible and trust his team to make it to the building.

He glanced down at the ancient swords in his hands. He wasn't generally the type to develop attachments to material possessions. He'd abandoned everything he owned—everything but these swords—more times than he could remember. But he'd forged these two blades himself, after a century of practice. And after more than six hundred years of using them as his primary weapons, he'd developed a certain bond with the blades. They were extensions of his arms, of his very soul. A single thought could translate to the death of an enemy with a flick of one of these blades. And it often had.

Turning to the Ferals, he resumed his dance of death.

After he'd dispatched the three closest Ferals, he glanced over his shoulder to check in with Lesley. What he saw brought a slight smile to his face in spite of the circumstances.

She was no longer huddling on the pavement. The bleeding from her elbow had almost stopped, and her eyes blazed red. In her remaining hand, she held a sword, and as he watched, she swung at the nearest Feral. The blade bit clean through, and the head fell to the ground.

Jaden almost pitied the sniper who had removed her arm. She was a vampire in search of true vengeance, and he knew she would not stop until she got her satisfaction.

It didn't take long for the team to make their way to the nearest building. According to the dilapidated sign, it had been a water-treatment facility.

"Lock's already been blown!" Robert shouted as he reached the door.

"Then let's get inside," Jaden answered. The team made their way into the three-story building. When everyone was inside, he said, "Stay away from the windows. We don't want to take any chances."

He sent two of his team members to do a quick sweep for Ferals who may have wandered inside.

Robert marched up to Jaden, his eyes wide. "What the hell just happened? Who was shooting at us?"

Lesley joined them, clutching her injured elbow. "I felt them. They were vampires. How is that possible?"

"It had to be Mark and Aaron," Jaden answered. As much as he hated to give that answer, he believed it had to be the truth. "Although, they weren't alone."

"Goddamn it, Jaden!" Lesley shouted. "I knew we should have killed those bastards. And yeah, there were more than two of them. I counted at least eighteen shots."

Jaden turned to the others and nodded. "Lesley's right. Almost. There were twenty. I'll forgive her missing two, as she was recovering from a sudden amputation at the time."

Lesley held up her stump at Jaden.

He chuckled. "Are you giving me the bird?"

"You're damn right."

"If we could get back to the task at hand," Robert said. "Err, no pun intended. I sensed a lot more than twenty."

Jaden nodded his agreement. "If they have twenty snipers, who knows how many soldiers they have, total?"

"How's this even possible?" Lesley asked.

Robert grimaced. "Those idiots from *New Haven* keep coming down to the surface. Maybe some of them got turned."

"We'll get the answers eventually," Jaden said. "For now,

we should help them realize that they have just attacked the most skilled and fearsome team of warriors to ever set foot on this Earth. It is time to let them know that we are the hunters and they are the prey."

"I like the sound of that," Lesley admitted.

"We'll leave two vampires here in the building. The rest of us will spread out through the storm drains. We can come out on the other side of their perimeter and attack them from behind. Who wants to stay here and draw their forces into this building?"

Lesley once again raised her stump. "I want to take them on in close quarters. I'm going to rip their arms off and then stab them through the heart with the bones."

"That seems highly inefficient," Jaden says, "but it's your call. Just don't let your emotions make you sloppy in battle."

"I'll stay with her," Akono said, after a moment.

"Good," Jaden replied. He looked over what remained of his team. "Let's show them what experienced vampires can do."

FIREFLY STARED at the Ferals gathered below in the street, surrounding the water-treatment building.

"I guess we know why Jaden has his people use swords," Shirley said, dryly.

Firefly turned, surprised to see her. Even with his vampiric senses, he hadn't known she was standing there. "Yes, it would appear the Ferals don't like noise much."

"Understatement of the year."

Firefly grunted his agreement. How many of his soldiers had he already lost? He didn't know, and he didn't know how to feel about those losses. On the one hand, he would never see those people again. On the other, they'd been freed from this hellish existence. "The good news is, the Ferals seem to lose interest quickly."

"Yeah. It didn't take long for them to chill out after we stopped fighting them."

It did present a conundrum, though. If they wanted to take out Jaden's team, they were going to need to use a lot more bullets. Which would bring the Ferals back down on their heads.

The good news was that Jaden's team had gathered in one building, effectively cornering themselves. Firefly's soldiers were moving into position now, surrounding the building. Any vampires who tried to exit would be gunned down before they made it ten steps.

Firefly's radio chirped to life, and Aaron's voice came through. "How we looking, Firefly?"

"Almost in position."

"Good." There was a long pause, and Firefly thought maybe his master was finished, but then Aaron continued. "One more thing. Don't attack the Ferals! We're not food, so if they don't see us as a threat, they'll leave us alone. Oh, and remember, Jaden must be taken alive. Do whatever it takes to make that happen. Take out the rest of his team, no matter the cost. Sacrifice yourself and every other soldier in the group, if need be."

Firefly gritted his teeth at this poor display of leadership, but all he could say in response was, "Yes, Aaron."

"That was two things," Shirley remarked after he'd signed off.

Firefly chuckled, but there was no humor in his laugh. The fact that Mark and Aaron would sacrifice their entire army to take out a dozen vampires told him everything he needed to know about their leadership. He would give anything for the chance to take those two out. He just prayed he would someday get the chance.

"I've got the two teams of twenty-five ready to go," Shirley said, getting back to business.

"Good. Who's leading?"

"Dominic and Rodney."

The two teams would enter from the doors on either side of the building and work their way to the middle. He'd given instructions for them to stay in tight formation and drive anything that moved toward the front doors. Then the teams waiting outside on the surrounding buildings would finish off anyone who fled the building.

It was a simple plan, but it was a solid one. All there was to do was to wait and see how it played out.

LESLEY AND AKONO waited inside the ductwork, silent and unmoving. The enemy was coming, they knew. It had been a long time since either of them had faced an intelligent vampire in true to-the-death combat, and they were both looking forward to the opportunity.

The sound of glass breaking came from the west. That would be the enemy breaking through the door on that side of the building, Lesley knew. She fought the urge to rush out to them, reminding herself of the oldest vampire rule: patience was the key to staying alive.

A sharp bolt of pain shot through her elbow, and her hand went to the injured limb. Akono glanced at her, concern on his face, but he said nothing. She was an old vampire, and she could handle pain. She'd been through worse. Already, a new layer of skin had grown over the bone, and she could feel the bone pressing on it as it began to grow. The next few days wouldn't be pleasant, but at the end of them, she'd be as good as new, with two working hands.

That didn't make her any less angry about the situation, and she was looking forward to expressing that anger to whoever had just broken into this building.

She watched through a vent, waiting for the enemy to pass by. She didn't have to wait long.

A group of twenty-five vampires filed past her location, every one of them carrying an automatic weapon. They moved slowly, carefully, checking every door as they went, but they appeared oblivious to her presence.

She shook her head in disgust. If they'd been more attuned to their vampire senses, there was no way she could have remained hidden while they passed so close. Sadly, the lesson she was about to teach them would be their last.

When the last two soldiers passed her vent walking side by side, she burst through, leaping into the air, sword drawn. She brought the sword around hard and sliced off two heads before her feet touched the ground. The moment her boots met concrete, she sprang forward, ducking into the office across the hallway.

Peeking through the crack in the door, she saw the other soldiers turn as the bodies of their two comrades hit the ground.

"Holy shit!" one of the soldiers cried out. He looked like he couldn't have been more than twenty, and based on his poor reflexes, he hadn't been a vampire long. Lesley almost felt sorry for him. Two of his friends had been killed and the attacker was nowhere in sight.

"Hey, look at this," another soldier said, gesturing toward the open vents.

"They're in the walls!" someone shouted. "Light 'em up!"

Lesley dropped to the ground as the soldiers began

shooting wildly, peppering the walls and ceiling with automatic fire. She silently cursed as she lay there, hoping she didn't catch a stray bullet. Her hopes of facing an intelligent vampire in combat were quickly slipping away. This was amateur hour. These soldiers might technically be vampires, but they didn't know enough to understand what that term fully meant. They were simply prey that was already bled dry.

When the soldiers finally stopped firing, there was a moment of silence. Then a lone howl came from the north. Another joined it. And still more, coming from every direction now.

Lesley grimaced as she gripped her sword. These idiots had just made things a lot more complicated.

FIREFLY BARELY DARED breathe as the howls of angry Ferals echoed off the surrounding buildings. From the sound of gunfire, it was clear the team that had entered through the west door had encountered the enemy. But the gunfire had stopped, so either that had been a surprisingly quick victory or...

He didn't want to think about the alternative. He brought his radio to his lips. "Dominic, I need a report, when it's safe to do so."

The reply came instantly through his earpiece. "We engaged with the enemy, sir. We've got two men down."

"Damn it. Did you take any of them out?"

There was a long pause. "I don't think so. We didn't actually see—"

Another burst of gunfire cut off the rest of Dominic's words.

It was quickly followed by a burst of gunfire from the eastern part of the building.

A noise came through his earpiece, something like a gurgle.

"Rodney?" Firefly asked. "Is that you?"

A female voice answered. "Rodney's dead, sir. He was standing by the wall and a sword just stabbed him through the chest like it had come from nowhere."

Firefly cursed as he heard the news. He'd been a fool to send these barely trained rookie vampires against experienced warriors. But it hadn't really been his choice, had it?

"Sir," the female voice continued, "I think they escaped, but I'm not sure."

"How many did you see?"

"None. Just the sword."

Firefly's mind raced. He realized he had no idea what to do here. Should he send in more troops or withdraw the ones already inside? He sorely missed the days when he'd been a member of the GMT and his job had been to blow up obstacles, rather than outthink them.

At the ground level, Ferals were surging toward the water-treatment building, drawn by the gunfire. There had to be a thousand of them down there. Some bashed their way through the doors, while others scaled the walls and smashed the windows to get inside.

"Everyone out of the water-treatment building!" he shouted into his radio. "You've got Ferals incoming. A lot of them. Don't fire on them, just get the hell out of there!"

The sound of gunfire once again filled the air, but this time it was coming from behind Firefly. He spun toward it, confused.

The Ferals on the street all turned toward the sound.

Then, after a moment, some headed toward the gunfire, while others turned back to the water-treatment building.

"We're under attack!" someone shouted through his radio. He knew that voice. It was Hector, who was stationed on a building nearby.

"The Ferals?" Firefly asked.

"No, I don't think so. Somehow, they got behind us. And they have swords."

A chill ran across Firefly's cold, lifeless skin.

Jaden's vampires were attacking.

12

JADEN and his team made their way through the storm drains and under the buildings. Four of the vampires had branched off to the north, and the other three, including Robert, stayed with Jaden.

As they walked, Robert sidled up next to Jaden. "So, what do you think? How'd Mark and Aaron get their army?"

Jaden had his suspicions, but he wanted to hear what the other vampire thought first. "Give me your best guess."

Robert thought a moment. "Well, unless they snuck a bunch of blood out of Agartha, which wouldn't have been possible, they couldn't have restored Ferals. I guess that means they turned humans."

"Yeah," Jaden agreed.

"So, I guess that means *New Haven*."

"Yeah," Jaden said again, glad his friend was working it through. "They're armed. Mark and Aaron left Agartha with nothing. So, unless *New Haven* crashed and Mark and Aaron just happened upon the crash site, there's only one plausible explanation. Fleming didn't listen to my warning."

"You think they set up a Resettlement colony already?"

Robert asked. "I thought Alex said they'd only been seriously talking about it for a few months. That would be insane."

"Sure. Insane, if you know the stakes as well as we do. But remember, humans are short-sighted and impatient. That's always been their downfall. I've been thinking of Resettlement in terms of centuries, but I've forgotten how abstract that concept would be to a human. It's so difficult for them to see beyond their own lifetimes. Something to remember in our future dealings with them."

Robert chuckled. "Jaden, you're the only creature I know who would take the time to discuss the limits of mortal imagination during a battle."

"What can I say? I enjoy multitasking."

Robert shook his head. "You know, it's not just humans who are impatient. Mark and Aaron have had their army, what, a couple days tops? Otherwise Alex would have known about it. And they're already attacking us."

"Perhaps. Could be they saw us being out as an opportunity too good to pass up." He saw the tunnel branch off ahead. "You and the other three go to the left. I'll go right."

Robert raised an eyebrow. "You sure you want to go alone?"

Jaden grinned, raising his swords. "I've got my two best buddies. I'll be fine."

He walked until he was three blocks from the water-treatment building, then exited through one of the drains onto the street. Looking around, he confirmed he was alone, then he scaled the nearest building.

When he reached the top, he looked around and grimaced at what he saw. Mark and Aaron's army was in position on most of the buildings surrounding the water-treatment plant. The army was much larger than he'd thought, at least a couple hundred strong. That wasn't counting the Ferals, who would likely lose control and attack once the fighting started again.

There had been nearly three million people living in the Denver metro area at the time of the third wave, and most them were now Ferals. If the fighting got too intense, it could bring every one of those Ferals crashing down on them. If that happened, his thousand years of existence could end today. Even he couldn't take on three million battle-raged Ferals.

He sensed vampires approaching, and a moment later he saw them walking through the alley below, totally unaware of his presence. He scanned the fire escapes and saw a few more soldiers, all with their guns trained in the direction of the water-treatment building.

As he moved into position, he heard gunfire. Clearly Lesley and Akono were engaging with the enemy. That meant the time was right to hit them from behind.

Just as he reached the alley and drew his swords, certain he'd caught these new vampires unaware, a Feral howled somewhere in the distance behind him. One of the soldiers turned and spotted Jaden. His eyes widened in surprise.

Jaden wasted no time worrying about this bit of bad luck. To him, being spotted was as good as a starting pistol at the beginning of a race. He leaped forward, his swords raised.

The soldier who'd spotted him moved impressively fast, raising his weapon and squeezing off a round before Jaden reached him. He miscalculated Jaden's speed and the shot went wide.

Jaden instantly rewarded his mistake by burying his sword in the soldier's left shoulder and driving it down and through his heart. He didn't wait for the soldier to fall, but turned to the vampire next to him, his sword already in motion.

Impossibly, the man brought his rifle up in time to deflect Jaden's blade a moment before it would have sunk into his neck. The soldier tried to lower his rifle, but before he could fire, Jaden swung his other sword. The man's head flew across the alley, landing near the feet of his fellow soldiers, who were all turning toward Jaden now and beginning to fire.

There were too many for Jaden to face head-on, especially with how well armed they were. He ducked behind a car as bullets tore through everything around him. He grabbed a headless body and threw it at the soldiers on the fire escape. The troops tracked the body and fired at it, perhaps thinking that it was Jaden.

While they were still distracted, he broke through a door on the left side of the alley and charged into the building.

INSIDE THE WATER-TREATMENT BUILDING, Lesley watched through a vent as the remaining soldiers met in the lobby. It was clear they were on the verge of panic. The sounds of Ferals crashing into the walls came from all around the building. Shattering glass, cracking wood, and howling. With every new sound, the soldiers pushed tighter together.

Lesley rubbed at her stump. It was starting to itch now, which was probably a good sign, but was annoying as all hell. She'd only killed two of the soldiers, and beyond that, all she'd accomplished was freaking them out. And now that forty-seven of them were gathered in one room like this, it would be suicide for her to attack. So, she just watched.

She saw a flash from across the room in another vent

and knew that it was Akono, signaling her. Good, at least she knew he'd made it through. If it did come to a fight, it would be two on forty-seven. Still not great odds, even against these new bloods.

Not that it would be a good idea to jump into the middle of a fight between the Ferals and these vampires. Best to let them kill each other and see what remained in the aftermath. Besides, Jaden and the rest of the team were taking care of the bulk of the soldiers outside.

As the first of the Ferals burst into the room, Lesley wondered how she and forty-six of her more seasoned vampires would have handled this situation. It would have been difficult, but they would have tried being passive. It may have been enough to calm the Ferals, or at least get them to ignore them and continue searching for the source of the noise. If that had failed, they would have attempted to push the Ferals back far enough to clear an exit and escape.

These green vampires were too panicked to attempt either technique. As the Ferals flooded the room, the soldiers unleashed a storm of automatic gunfire. They mowed through the Ferals, blanketing every entrance with a barrage of firepower.

For a few brief moments, it seemed as if the full-on assault was going to work. They pushed the initial wave back. Lesley was reminded that vampires—even green ones —were physical matches for the Ferals. Their speed, reflexes, and even their aim was much better than any human's. Most of their shots landed where they wanted them to, in the head or chest of a Feral.

But the success didn't last long. The Ferals screamed and howled as they fell, but still they kept moving forward, the horde behind them pushing ahead. The Ferals' bodies started to stack up in the three entryways leading to the lobby. Many of the Ferals were injured, but not killed, and they dragged themselves forward in an attempt to reach the soldiers by any means necessary.

Lesley tried to see through the doorway to get a feel for how many Ferals were out there, fighting to get inside. Her view was partially obstructed, but she could see far enough to know that there were hundreds and hundreds of the beasts trying to fight their way into this room.

She clutched her sword and waited. As much as she wanted to join this fight, she knew her best chance at survival was to remain hidden.

Some of the soldiers were reloading now, while others continued to fire into the ever-approaching throng. Try as they might, they couldn't seem to kill the Ferals fast enough.

A Feral broke through a wall leading to the lobby, while another came crashing through the ceiling. Still, the troops refused to give up. They fired in all directions now, even as the swarm of Ferals came faster and faster.

One of the Ferals charged through a pile of bodies, picking up one of its fallen comrades and hurling it into the ring of soldiers. The corpse slammed into one of the soldiers, knocking him back and creating a break in their formation.

Sensing weakness, the Ferals charged that spot. This time, the soldiers had no chance of killing the enemy before they reached them.

Lesley cringed as Ferals tore apart the soldiers, who stubbornly clung to their weapons, refusing to use their new vampiric skills to battle the Ferals hand-to-hand, even in the closest of situations. Soldiers were pulled down and ripped apart everywhere she looked.

Then, something near the center of the cluster of soldiers caught her eye. A man with a massive backpack. He slipped his arms out of the straps and set the pack on the ground. Opening the flap, he quickly began tinkering with whatever was inside.

Lesley squinted at the pack, trying to see through the opening as the chaos raged around her. She didn't know why she was so interested, but her instincts said it was important.

The vampire took a long look around the room, watching as his fellow soldiers fell. Then his expression hardened, and he turned to the pack on the floor.

Ferals were pouring into the lobby from everywhere now. It wouldn't be long before the soldiers were completely overrun. Still, the man's focus was on his pack, rather than the battle.

Lesley's eyes widened as she realized what the man had been carrying. She frantically tried to signal Akono, to tell him they needed to get out immediately. But in her heart, she knew it was too late.

The man reached into the pack and armed the charges. Then he reached for the switch.

———

FROM OUTSIDE OF THE BUILDING, Firefly watched, knowing the battle was lost. As soon as the soldiers started to kill the Ferals entering the building, the ones being attacked panicked, which sent a mental signal to those around them that there was a hostile presence. Other Ferals were drawn by the signal, until they, too, panicked, strengthening the unspoken message.

Even Firefly could feel it now, a strange, cascading wave of fear, excitement, and rage that seemed to grow stronger by the second. The feeling was so strong that it made him want to throw up.

And still more Ferals were drawn into the fight. They seemed to come from everywhere, swarming into the building.

Firefly thought about issuing an order to stop firing, but that would just mean that the soldiers would be ripped apart even more quickly by the frenzied creatures. He didn't know what to do, so he just watched in horror.

As things went from bad to so much worse, he stood with his finger on the button of his radio, wanting to give some heroic speech, or, barring that, at least a few words of comfort for his troops in their dying moments. Still, nothing came to mind, so he watched dumbly.

The exterior of the water-treatment building was so covered with Ferals that the walls seemed to be moving. Piles of fallen Ferals clogged the entryways, and the creatures had to fight each other to get into the narrow openings. Some pulled at the bodies, trying to clear the path, but most were too frenzied, and only wanted to get to their enemies as quickly as possible.

The most hellish part of watching was that time seemed to move slowly for Firefly, as his vampiric mind raced to process every detail of what was happening below. Even though the Ferals moved at incredible speed, he could perfectly follow their every movement. Every howl echoed through his head with perfect clarity. It almost felt like he could see things a moment before they happened.

But he was not expecting what came next.

For the briefest of moments, a brilliant light shot out of the doors and windows of the water-treatment building. The light was followed by an incredible wave of force.

The blast tore the entire building apart in an instant.

The Ferals around the doors were incinerated. Pieces of wood, concrete, and metal shot out in every direction. Shrapnel peppered the Ferals near the building.

Firefly was about two hundred yards away from the building, and the concussion wave hit him like a lead pipe to the chest. He was lifted off the ground and thrown back into the wall behind him.

He lay on the ground for a moment, not sure if he could move. If he were still human, he would never have regained his hearing, but his new body was already healing.

He struggled up to his knees and looked at the crater where the building had been a minute ago. There were hundreds of Ferals trying to get up around the large hole. Many of them were missing limbs or had large chunks of meatal or rock embedded in their twisted bodies.

Still, to Firefly's shock, they continued to push toward the source of the blast.

As Firefly's mind cleared, he realized something was very wrong. There was a vibration coming from inside of his chest. He thought he might be coming apart from the inside out. Then his hearing came back, and he realized the vibration was not coming from inside him; it was coming from all around him. The Ferals of Denver were howling in unison. The deep vibration shook the entire city. A million beasts were unleashing their battle cries.

Firefly searched the concrete until he found his radio. He brought it to his mouth with a shaky hand and gave one order. "Take cover. They are coming."

13

ALEX FOUND George standing on a balcony that overlooked a garden near the center of Agartha. She'd gotten a tip from one of the technicians that George often came there to be alone and think, especially when he was worried about something. Twenty minutes and four wrong turns later, she'd finally found the garden. Its only occupant was the director of engineering. He was so lost in thought that he didn't notice her until she spoke.

"Any radio contact from Jaden?" she asked.

He didn't look startled to find her by his side. She got the sense that maybe he was so used to being lost in his own thoughts that someone catching him unaware no longer bothered him.

"No, but I wouldn't worry. He frequently makes trips to Denver, and he usually doesn't check in. He's not exactly the 'checking in' sort."

"Yeah, I kinda got that," Alex said dryly.

George chuckled, his eyes still fixed on the greenery below, fed by artificial light. "It is a little odd, though. He's usually back by now."

Alex frowned. "What time did you expect him?"

George thought about that. "The trip to Denver should have taken about two hours. Say an hour to load up and another two hours' travel time back here. They should have been back about an hour ago."

"Huh." An hour late was no reason to panic. A thousand things could have set them back. An obstacle in the road. Trouble loading the ship. Any number of things. Still, dawn was closing in fast. "How often does Jaden spend the day in the city?"

George looked at her sharply. "The city? What do you mean?"

"I mean, if he doesn't make it back to Agartha before daybreak and has to hole up somewhere else. Does that happen often?"

He shook his head slowly. "I don't think it's ever happened. At least, not in my lifetime."

"Damn."

George's expression softened. "I wouldn't worry. They'll make it back. Jaden's very disciplined. So are his vampires. Once he gets the ship here, we can start work on it." He gave her a look. "Speaking of which, shouldn't you be sleeping?"

She sighed. "I'm surprised I got any sleep at all. With everything that's happening on *New Haven*..."

She paused, not sure how to continue. George had spent his life in Agartha. The citizens here were used to depending on the vampires to keep them alive. On *New Haven*, humans didn't have that luxury. They had to be more proactive. It would be difficult to get George to understand that mindset, but she was going to have to try.

"My team and I are going to prep for travel," she told him. "Just in case."

He blinked hard. "In case of what?"

"In case your vampires don't make it back by sunrise. I know you're not worried, but we have to play this safe."

George scratched his head. "You mean you're going to go to Denver? Shouldn't we just wait to hear from Jaden? I'm sure he has things under control."

She sighed. The subtle approach hadn't worked, so she was going to have to put this bluntly. "George, you don't know me well, but there's one thing you have to understand about the GMT. We don't wait around for others to do the hard work. We actually get our hands dirty ourselves."

"Honestly, Alex, that's a pretty condescending thing to say. Especially to the guy who risked his life to come rescue you and your team last night."

Shame washed over Alex. "God, George, I'm sorry. It's been a hell of a couple days. And stupid stuff comes out of my mouth all the time, even when I'm not stressed. I shouldn't have said that."

George looked back at the garden. "It's okay. Come on, I'll help you get some gear together and pick out a vehicle for your team to use. Just in case."

The two of them made their way through the city toward the garage, George leading the way. Alex hung back a bit, sometimes falling behind as she marveled at the city around her. It was nearly empty; the only beings they encountered were the occasional vampire. But what really astounded Alex was the darkness.

New Haven was always washed in daylight. The personal quarters didn't have windows, but nearly everywhere else, the exterior walls were transparent to allow for maximum light.

Agartha seemed to have been designed with the opposite approach. Passageways were dim and shadows were plentiful.

Seeing such a large area with only a few man-made lights illuminating it seemed odd, but she supposed it made sense. *New Haven* had been designed to keep vampires out, while Agartha had been built to allow vampires to stay in.

They soon reached the garage and Alex sent for Owl. They spent the rest of the time until sunrise selecting a vehicle and then preparing it for a potential journey. They needed it to cover ground quickly, but also, to be rugged enough to handle the obstacles that they knew lay between Agartha and the city.

Before long, the rest of the team had joined them and was helping to load the batteries and components onto the truck they'd be using. The hope was that they'd be able to use these parts to repair the away ship where it sat.

"One thing's for sure," Owl said with a grin. "It'll be better than driving the rover in a race against sundown."

Patrick put his hands on his hips. "That's not exactly a high bar to clear. If it can top twenty miles an hour, it'll beat the rover."

George walked up, a haggard look on his face.

"No luck?" Alex asked.

He shook his head. He'd been trying to contact Jaden's team on the radio for an hour, but there had been no response.

"How long until sunrise?" Chuck asked.

George glanced at his watch. "Twenty minutes."

"We want to be ready to leave at first light," Alex said.

George sighed. "I know Jaden wouldn't approve of this. He'd want us to stay in the city and let the vampires handle things."

"George, we can't just sit here and—"

He held up a hand, cutting her off. "Let me finish. I know Jaden wouldn't leave us stranded out there, and I don't intend to leave him, regardless of what he'd want. I'll lend you this vehicle and let you go, on one condition."

"What's that?"

"I want to come with you."

Alex looked at him for a long moment, surprised.

Owl shrugged. "It would be *really* helpful having his help with repairing the ship."

Alex nodded toward Wesley. "See if one of the vampires can help us find some gear for George. It looks like the GMT just got a new temporary member."

CB, Brian, and Jessica pressed onward through the tunnels.

"How much further?" Brian asked.

"There's not a direct route," Jessica answered. "Plus, we're going to have to wait for the shift change, if we want to have any chance of—"

"Hang on," CB interrupted. He didn't like the sound of his companions' voices. Raising his headlamp, he inspected them in the light, confirming his suspicions. "Listen, I want to apologize to you two."

"What? Why?" Brian sounded annoyed. "If you're going to say you're sorry for bringing us into this fight against Fleming, you can shut up right now. We've been over it, and we knew what we were getting into."

"It's not that. I've been pushing you like you're GMT members."

"So?" Jessica asked. "We need to push, if we want to carry out our plan."

"Yeah, but we also need rest. The truth is, you don't have GMT training. That's not a knock against you. I mean, each of you have skills no GMT member has. But pushing through the pain, carrying out a mission for days on end without sleep, and still being able to physically dominate an opponent when needed, those things take practice. It's no different than..." he waved at Brian vaguely, "programming a daylight to fry vampires."

"That analogy doesn't even make sense. You don't program a light."

"My point is, you two are wiped. I can see it in your faces. You need rest. And I wouldn't mind a little break myself." He thought a moment. "Jessica, we're near Sparrow's Ridge, right?"

She nodded slowly. "Damn near right under it."

"Good. I know a place. Just get us to Hanger's Point. You know it?"

Jessica raised an eyebrow. "Not exactly the best part of town."

"That's kinda the point."

Five minutes later, Jessica led them up from the maintenance tunnel onto a street in the worst part of Sparrow's Ridge.

Brian looked concerned. "This place makes Tankards look like a restaurant in the Hub."

"You ain't seen nothing yet," CB said with a grin. "Follow me."

He led them to a dilapidated building at the end of the street, then down a set of stairs to the basement. From there, he took them to a door at the end of the hall. He crouched down and picked the lock in a matter of moments.

Then he led them inside.

"Oh God, please tell me no one lives here," Jessica said.

They were in a filthy studio apartment. A small kitchenet sat at one end of the room next to a toilet with a sheet hanging around it. A small bed sat at the other end. There were no photos on the wall, and only a few items that marked the place as occupied.

Jessica bent down and picked something up off the floor. Holding it up to the light, they could see it was a small model of the GMT's away ship.

"Wait," Brian asked. "CB, is this your hookup pad? Do you bring girls here?"

Jessica raised an eyebrow. "I, too, would like to hear the answer to those questions."

CB felt his face flush. "No! This is Wesley's place."

The others stared at him blankly.

"Wesley?" Brian asked. "Are you sure you don't mean Patrick? Or Ed?"

"Yeah, Wesley seems like more of a Hub type of guy," Jessica agreed.

"What can I say? The man likes the simple life."

Jessica nudged the bed with her toe. "I guess so."

"The point is, it's a safe place to get some sleep."

"Tight space for three," Brian pointed out.

"We only need space for two. You both get some rest. I'm going to get us the help we need to pull this off."

It was a testament to how tired Brian and Jessica were that they barely argued.

As the other two settled in, CB took a moment to check his gunshot wound. He winced as he removed the bandage, not liking the looks of what he saw underneath. It looked like it might be infected. There was nothing to do about that now. If their plan worked, he could deal with it then. If not, it wouldn't much matter. A corpse didn't care about an arm infection.

Next, he dug through the dresser in the corner, looking for something to help disguise him. He tried on one of Wesley's hooded sweatshirts, but it didn't come close to fitting his much broader frame. Finally, he settled on a hat and sunglasses. He grabbed a bit of food from Wesley's refrigerator and headed out the door.

CB made his way through the streets of Sparrow's Ridge, sticking to the infrequent shadows when possible. He reached his destination and stepped inside.

Thankfully, Tankards wasn't too busy at that time of night. There were a dozen or so customers, but none of them seemed to notice CB. The bartender stared at him for a moment too long, but thankfully he just continued pouring drinks, careful not to look at CB once he'd identified him.

CB quickly made his way through the bar and into the back room.

The overweight, white-haired man behind the desk didn't look up when CB entered. "Employees only. Restroom's the next door over."

"I'm not here for the restroom. I'm here for a little help from an old friend."

The man looked up, his eyes widening. "Holy shit, CB. What are you doing here? Have you seen what Fleming's been saying about you?"

"It hasn't escaped my attention."

The man got up from his desk and shuffled to the door, making sure it was shut.

"Fleming had his lackey try to shoot me," CB continued, "and then he called *me* a traitor. How's that for irony? You've known me since we were kids, Billy. You ever seen me be disloyal?"

Billy grinned. "If anything, you're too loyal. Plenty of guys you probably should have stabbed in the back. Remember that Sylvester kid?"

CB chuckled. "Ugh, don't remind me."

Billy's expression grew serious. "I know what you've done for this city. You and your whole team. You guys are the ones that keep this bird in the sky. Hell, I remember when you lost your first team. You reformed the GMT out of sheer doggedness. Calling you a traitor is beyond low. Makes me want to punch that bastard in the face."

"I appreciate that."

Billy squinted at him. "You didn't come here to see what side I'm on, did you?"

CB couldn't help but grin. "Notice, I haven't asked."

"Good. I would have been insulted if you had. So why are you here? You said something about a favor?"

CB hesitated. "It's risky."

Billy let out a boisterous laugh. "I spend every day of my life serving booze to the roughest crowd in the city. I may not be running around the surface fighting vampires, but I've been knocked on my ass a few times. It'll take more than a politician to scare me out of helping an old friend. What is it going to take to get the city running on track again?"

"Thanks, man. Listen, I intend to either fix this city or die trying. Either way, it's going to be over soon."

"Sounds good so far. What's my part?"

"I'm involved in a bit of a cat-and-mouse game with Fleming. I need some help keeping him off balance. If you can get a bunch of people from the Ridge to call in reports of me being spotted all over the city, it should buy me some time."

Billy chuckled. "Shit, I'd do that for fun. Give me a real challenge."

CB looked his old friend in the eyes. "Fleming's not playing. If he figures out the reports are false, he's not going to be happy. If he starts pushing too hard, just let it go. I don't want anyone else to get hurt."

"You're from the Ridge," Billy replied. "We've got your back. We'll shovel some major confusion Fleming's way. But if you think this whole thing's going to end without anyone else getting hurt, I'm afraid you're as delusional as Fleming."

CB looked away, but he knew his old friend was right.

14

A FEW MINUTES AFTER SUNRISE, the doors to Agartha opened and a lightly armored truck rolled out. The vehicle had been designed to carry thirty passengers, but today it carried only seven. The supplies took up much of the space, but the truck was nowhere near capacity, and it sped along the tightly packed snow on the road at a good clip.

Owl glanced back over her shoulder at George. "Thanks for letting me drive."

"No problem. I saw how you handled that rover the night before last. If there's trouble, I want the best driver we have in control of the truck."

Alex grinned. "Besides, I told him you get cranky if you go too long without having your hands on the wheel of some vehicle or other."

Owl didn't bother denying it.

Alex was in the passenger seat, and George was seated right behind them. The rest of the team was a little further back, but sound carried in the vehicle and Alex could easily hear all their conversations. She turned to George and Owl.

"You two think you can get the ship up and running before sunset?"

"I certainly hope so," George said. "Hopefully, with plenty of time to spare. I need to get the truck back to Agartha tonight."

Owl nodded her agreement. "The batteries will be easy. As long as you're as good as we keep hearing, George, we'll be fine. I wouldn't think the repairs would take more than a few hours."

None of them mentioned the other task on their plates. Jaden and his vampires hadn't come home. That had to mean they'd run into trouble. Best-case scenario, they were holed up somewhere. But if they needed help, Alex didn't even know where to begin searching for them. Jaden had saved her and her team from Ferals twice, now. If she had the chance to help him and his team, she had to take it.

And what if it came to a choice? Board the away ship and save *New Haven,* or try to find Jaden? She didn't know the answer to that question. Probably because there was no good answer.

"Hey," Owl said. "You taking in this view?"

The truck was driving along a ridge that gave Alex a clear view of the landscape below the mountain. The sun glinted off the snow on the trees below. The ground was a field of glittering white, broken only by a smattering of giant rocks. The unexpected beauty took her breath away.

Owl spoke in a low voice that only Alex could hear. "I know there's a lot weighing on you. There has been for a while now. You take it all to heart, too. Always have, since your first day on the job. That's part of what makes you a good leader."

Alex frowned, startled by the truth of those words.

"We have a hard job," Owl continued. "A deadly job. I

mean, Simmons. Drew. Hope. We've lost some of the best friends I've ever had. It's easy to forget this job has its perks, too." She gestured out the windshield. "I mean, come on. How many people on *New Haven* have ever seen a view like that? Or how many in Agartha, for that matter?"

Alex stared at the snowy valley beyond the ridge and felt a sense of peace she hadn't known in a while. She tried to relish the moment, to just get out of her head and enjoy it.

Then another thought crept in. There were Ferals buried under that snow, just waiting for sundown. Every one of them had been a person once, and every one of them would thoughtlessly tear any human they got their hands on to shreds.

The thought almost made her laugh. Even on this beautiful vista she couldn't help but see the dangers and feel the closeness of death. But she appreciated what Owl was trying to do. "Thanks. You always know what to say to help me keep my head straight."

Alex glanced back at George. He was staring out the windshield too, but he didn't seem to be enjoying the view. His expression was drawn, and he was rapidly tapping his foot, sending a ratta-tat-tat echoing through the vehicle.

Ed tapped him on the shoulder. "You all right, big guy?"

George looked surprised at the question. "What? Yes, of course." After a brief pause, he resumed tapping his foot.

Ed touched his shoulder again. "No offense, man, but the foot thing is driving me nuts."

George's face reddened. "Oh, sorry. I didn't even realize I was doing it. I guess I'm a little edgy. I've never been this far from Agartha."

"No kidding?" Patrick asked. He called over his shoulder. "You hear that, everybody? Our boy George is popping his cherry on this mission."

George scowled, turning even redder. "Thanks for putting it so delicately."

Patrick nudged his arm. "Don't worry about it. You'll be fine. Just a couple things to keep in mind. One: don't let a Feral rip you to pieces."

George looked like he might be ill.

"Two," Ed said, jumping in. "Don't do anything that'll get *us* ripped to pieces."

Patrick nodded sagely. "Come to think of it, that's probably more important than the first rule. Number three: if you see Ed crying in the corner like a scared little bitch, slap him in the face and tell him to man up."

"Hey!" Ed shouted.

"That rule seems a bit sexist," Owl called back. "Who's to say a little bitch is more likely to cry in the face of danger than a man?"

Patrick shrugged. "I'm open to feedback." He turned back to George. "Final rule: have fun. Also, don't die. Rule four has two parts."

Wesley called up to George from a seat near the back. "Don't listen to him, George. Just concentrate on helping Owl fix our ship. We'll take care of the rest."

"Agreed," Chuck said. "It's dangerous out there, but so are we. Even those two idiots razzing you take care of business when it's mission time."

"Yep, we'll take good care of you," Ed agreed. "And you get bit by a Feral, we'll blow your head off before you turn."

"Wonderful," George said.

Alex reached back and slapped him on the knee. "Relax, you'll be fine. Remember, you volunteered for this mission. Whatever happens, you're going to have one hell of a story."

FLEMING SAT AT HIS DESK, staring intensely at his radio, trying to comprehend the report that Kurtz had just given. "I'm sorry, could you repeat that? Because I'm positive I didn't hear that right."

Kurtz cleared his throat and spoke again. "We got a report that Colonel Brickman was spotted near the water-processing facility."

Fleming gritted his teeth. "That's what I thought you said. But that would be impossible, as we have him cornered in this building. The only way that could be accurate is if he somehow slipped past your people. Since you have the entire GMT and nearly every badge in the city outside, tell me how that could happen."

There was a long pause, then Kurtz said, "I don't know, sir."

Fleming slammed his hand on the desk. "Then you'd better fucking find out!"

Sarah watched all this as she picked at her nails, a habit she had given up five years before. She got up and spoke into the radio. "Give us a couple minutes, Kurtz."

She clicked the radio off without waiting for a reply. She'd tried being the faithful employee, the trustworthy friend, and even the doting woman for Fleming. But she was beginning to realize that wasn't what he needed right now. He needed her to be the stern mother.

He stared at the radio in disbelief. "How dare you just—"

"Shut up. Another outburst isn't going to get you out of this situation."

He looked up at her, shocked. "Outburst? What else am I supposed to do? Have you seen the incompetence I'm dealing with? If we can't even control this ship, how the hell am I supposed to take back a planet?"

"Let me ask you a question," she said, keeping her voice as calm as possible. "Is Kurtz in charge of this city?"

"Of course not."

"That's right. Kurtz isn't in charge. You are. If Kurtz isn't cutting it, fire him and get someone who can do the job. But that's a problem for tomorrow." She slid around the desk, then leaned against it. "For today, the city needs you to do what you do best. We need you to be the man you were when you took control of this city. The one I took a bullet for. I need you to use your head, think it through, and problem-solve."

He squinted up at her, still angry, but at least coherent now. "What do you think I've been doing? There's a thousand problems coming at me every hour. How am I supposed to—"

"Then deal with them one at a time. Start with CB. Supposedly, he's in this building and at the water-treatment facility. At least one of those things isn't true. Think it through."

He glared up at her, and for a moment, she thought he was going to slap her. Then his radio chirped again, and Kurtz's voice came through. "Sorry to bother you again, sir. We've had another report. CB's been spotted in the agricultural sector."

Fleming looked confused. Then a slow smile spread across his face. "Thank you, Sarah. You're right. I let my emotions get the best of me. I need to concentrate on what I do best. And if Colonel Brickman thinks he's going to outthink me, he's going to be viciously disappointed."

Sarah nodded. "I can't wait to see you smash him."

Fleming picked up the radio. "Kurtz, ignore the CB sightings. They're false reports. He's trying to play us."

Kurtz's voice sounded hesitant when he answered. "Are you sure, sir?"

"Yes. And I'm not so sure he was in this building, either." He closed his eyes and was silent for a moment as he thought. "Here's what I want you to do. First, try to get the names of anyone who calls in a CB sighting. There'll be a price for those traitors to pay, when this is all over. Second, find someone we can trust in engineering and work with them to figure out how CB hacked into the security network. That may not be the last breach. I want every network room monitored. And if the door to any of them opens without authorization, I want you to bring the GMT down on the intruder's head before they make it two steps into the room. Understand?"

"Yes, sir," Kurtz immediately replied.

"Good. Make it happen." He clicked off the radio without waiting for a sign-off from the colonel.

Sarah smiled at Fleming, a true smile that made her eyes shine.

"What is it?" he asked her.

"It's good to have you back, sir."

Owl glanced over at Alex as the truck pulled into the old city of Denver. "This is going better than expected. Should I be worried?"

Alex shrugged. "Probably. But let's not complain. Enjoy the good luck while you can."

The road to Denver had been surprisingly clear. Jaden and his vampires must have pushed aside most of the obstacles, leaving the way open for the GMT's smaller, borrowed vehicle.

Owl slowed the truck as they approached the city center. Suburban homes and smaller commercial buildings gave way to larger structures as they approached the crash site.

"Sure is different driving in," Owl mused. "You get a better sense of the size of the city."

Alex nodded her agreement. The sprawl of the city was hard to ignore when you were driving through it. The only other time she'd driven through the city, she'd been so focused on getting to Agartha before sundown that she hadn't really taken it all in. She imagined what life would have been like before the infestation, maybe being a person who lived outside the city and drove in to work every day. This highway would have been crowded with cars. It must have been noisy, then. Though the noise would have been preferable to the oppressive, dead silence that hung over the city now.

A few minutes later, Owl pulled to a stop near the away ship's landing site. One glance out of the window revealed that much had changed since their last visit.

She glanced at Owl. "Stay in the truck with George for now. Until we know it's safe."

Owl nodded, her eyes fixed out the windshield. "*Safe* isn't the word that comes to mind when I see that."

Alex felt the same way. She turned to the team. "Everybody, stay frosty. We have no idea what we're walking into out there." With that, she stepped out of the vehicle and took a good look around.

The last time she'd been here, the area had had the same dilapidated, abandoned look of the dozens of cities she'd traveled to in her time with the GMT. Now, it looked different. There was fresh destruction. The place looked like a war zone.

Patrick cocked a thumb to his left. "Um, didn't there use to be a building there?"

Alex didn't answer. Instead, she headed toward the crater that now sat where the water-treatment building had stood.

"What could have done this?" Chuck asked.

"One hell of a lot of explosives," Wesley replied.

That was Alex's assessment, as well. She turned to the parking lot and saw the transport truck that Jaden's team had used. It lay on its side, a mangled wreck. Looking around the parking lot, she saw signs of a fight. Doors had been ripped from the surrounding buildings, and bullet holes peppered the rusted remains of ancient cars. Most of the windows were broken in the surrounding buildings, and the fire escapes were twisted and misshapen.

And then there were the bodies. Ferals' corpses lay strewn on the streets like trash, burning in the morning sun. The smell of them was almost overwhelming.

"Hey, Alex," Chuck called. "I found something."

"What is it?" she shouted back.

"Um, I think it's an arm."

Alex trotted over and found him in the shadows beneath an overhang, nudging a severed arm with his boot. It had been ripped off at the shoulder. The sleeve that still covered the arm looked all too familiar.

"I think it's human," Chuck said.

She bent down and rolled the arm over. Her heart sank at what she saw. A patch on the sleeve read "Fort Stearns, Resettlement Site 1".

"Holy shit," Chuck said. "How's that possible?"

Alex shook her head. "I have no idea."

Wesley walked over to see what they were looking at.

"Damn. Do you think they sent a team down to get the ship?"

Alex looked up at him. "This guy was killed in the street by a vampire. That happened at night."

The flatbed truck Jaden's team had driven to the city was sitting a bit further back from the crater and was still upright. The away ship was tied down on the bed of the truck.

Alex put her hands on her hips as she inspected the scene one more time. "Well, it appears to be safe now. Let's get Owl and George."

Owl was the first one to climb up onto the truck to get to the away ship. She wore a near-panicked expression.

"Is she going to be okay?" George asked.

"Probably," Alex answered. "She had a, um, special relationship with her ships."

"So I see."

Owl ran her hand along the side of the away ship, inspecting it for damage. When she reached the front of the ship, she glanced into the cab of the truck and grimaced. "We've got two dead vampires here."

Alex ran to check it out, followed closely by George. She opened the truck door and pulled herself up on the step and looked inside. A wave of nausea rolled through her. After everything she'd seen, she sometimes thought she was immune to being revolted to the point of physical illness. Then she saw something like this.

The vampire who'd been in the driver's seat was nearly gone from the waist up. His head had been torn from his neck, and there were three large holes in his chest. The other vampire still had his head, but he'd taken more hits in the torso, leaving his chest with a hollowed-out look.

She felt George climb up behind her before she thought

to stop him. He looked into the cab and gasped. "No." He stumbled back to the road. "They can't be dead. They're immortal. I've known Adam and Tim my whole life."

Owl hopped off the flatbed and ran over to Alex. "What the hell's going on here? These guys were killed with high-powered sniper fire."

"So, who was shooting at them?" Wesley asked.

Patrick turned to George. "Something you want to tell us? Maybe there's another city no one's bothered to mention?"

George shook his head, his eyes wide with horror. "No, of course not. We're the only city. I mean, I thought we were, until you showed up." His head spun toward Alex. "We know it wasn't anyone from Agartha who did this. That leaves *New Haven*. What have you done? You've killed our greatest protectors!"

"Okay, everyone take a beat and settle down," Alex said. "We don't know what happened here, and we don't know if the rest of the Agartha vampire team is dead. For all we know they're holed up in one of these buildings, just waiting for sunset." She thought a moment. "George, use the radio in the truck and see if you can contact Jaden. Owl, Wesley, Chuck, you three work on loading the batteries into the away ship."

"What about us?" Ed asked.

"You and Patrick are going to help me protect the perimeter while we figure out what happened here."

The team went to work, silently doing their jobs. The first hour seemed to go by quickly, and as the sun moved across the sky, the sunlight fell across new corpses, lighting them on fire and adding to the already putrid stench. Alex began to worry that the ever-increasing fires might set one of the nearby buildings ablaze. The buildings were mostly made from brick and stone, and the Feral bodies burned hot and fast, but smoldered out quickly. There didn't seem to be much danger of the fires spreading.

As Ed, Patrick, and Alex walked the perimeter, Ed asked, "So, what do you think?" *New Haven* Resettlers versus vampires. How does that even happen?"

"I still say they came down for the ship," Patrick replied. "Maybe sunset snuck up on them and a few soldiers got left behind."

"This is more than a few," Alex pointed out.

"Then maybe they all got stuck down here after dark." His eyes widened as an idea struck him. "Hey, if that's true, their ship is still down here. We could use that to get home."

Alex shook her head. "It doesn't make sense. There are too many dead Resettlers. You wouldn't need a team this big to recover a ship."

"I'm less interested in why they were here and more interested in whether they were human when they died," Ed interjected.

Patrick nodded slowly. "That sort of makes sense. Maybe they got stranded down here and then the Ferals turned them."

Alex wasn't satisfied with that explanation. Why would a bunch of newly turned vampires attack Jaden and his team?

"There's an easy way to answer the vampire question." Ed walked toward a severed leg laying in the shadows. He picked it up by the boot and ripped off the pants.

"You are super gross," Patrick said.

Ed ignored the comment and tossed the leg into the sunlight. It immediately burst into flames. "Yep, the Resettlers were turned."

Alex scratched her head. The situation made even less sense if the Resettlers were vampires. There had been a major battle here. "The way I figure it, the Resettlers and Jaden's vampires fought, which drew all the Ferals in the area. Then everything went to hell. The only question is why."

"Alex!" George stood next to the truck, waving his hands.

She smiled at the Barton brothers. "Maybe we're going to get a chance to ask Jaden what he saw firsthand." She trotted over to George. "You got something?"

"Something. But it's weak. Mostly static. Here." He raised the radio handset and tried again. "Jaden, do you copy?"

For a moment, there was only static. Then a broken voice came through. "...only...city...get...ground."

"That's Jaden," Alex said. "I never thought I'd be so happy to hear a vampire's voice."

George grinned. "I'm damn happy he's alive. Now we just have to figure out how to keep him that way."

Jaden's voice came through the radio again. "Ship... remember...underneath."

"It's been like this ever since I got him on the radio. I'm getting maybe every third word."

"We need to find a stronger signal. Tell you what, my team and I will take the radio and search the area. You help Owl with the ship. If we do find Jaden and his team, we may need to help them make a quick getaway."

15

"NOTHING LIKE A MORNING stroll to get the blood flowing," Chuck mused.

"We're in a city teeming with vampires," Wesley reminded him. "Can you not say 'get the blood flowing'?"

They were walking through the streets of Denver, working their way around the area in a circle to figure out where the radio signal was strongest. So far, they hadn't had much luck. George assured them that the signal would eventually strengthen, and all they had to do was head in that direction until they re-established contact with Jaden.

Alex walked in front of the group, her eyes flickering between upper-level windows and ground-level doorways. Based on what they'd seen near the crater, she knew there were vampire snipers lurking in the buildings. She was hesitant to walk in the middle of the street for fear of giving them an easy target. Yet, if she walked too close to the buildings, she would risk a Feral potentially lunging at her from the shadows. There was no safe option, so she'd chosen a middle ground, walking close enough to the buildings so that they weren't completely in the open, yet far enough away that a Feral would have to risk a serious sunburn to attack them.

The key was keeping the team alert. It was a lot easier to stay on your toes when you were, say, under tons of sand in an ancient Las Vegas casino, rather than walking through a city on a sunny day. Alex knew this situation could turn just as bad as that one had, though.

She'd given Patrick the radio in the hopes that it would keep him from getting impatient and doing something stupid. So far, it was working, though Ed was practically steaming with jealousy that his brother had been given a special duty.

"You know what I can't get used to about the surface?" Chuck asked. "The way the ground feels so dead."

It was a strange way to put it, but Alex understood what he meant. On *New Haven*, there was always a slight vibration. It traveled from the deck up into your feet; it was a comforting sensation to those who had grown up on the ship. And not feeling it was odd, almost like your feet weren't touching down at all.

"It is pretty weird," Ed agreed. "But I think the opportunity to kill vampires kinda makes up for it."

"Agreed," Chuck said with a smile.

Patrick raised the radio to his mouth. "Jaden, do you read? We are trying to save your undead ass. Do you read?"

A broken voice came through, but Alex was only able to catch a few words.

Patrick looked at Alex. "No improvement."

"Then we keep moving."

They'd walked for twenty more minutes in a variety of directions before they noticed the signal strengthening. They then continued northeast ten more minutes before finding a spot where they could clearly hear Jaden.

"Pass me the radio," Alex said.

Patrick's eyes narrowed and his mouth fell open. He looked genuinely offended. "Wait, you're saying I did all that work, and now I don't get to keep the radio for the payoff?"

She held out her hand, a stern look on her face.

"Fine." He slapped the radio into her waiting hand.

"Jaden, you there?" she said into the radio.

His voice was still a bit staticky, but she could understand his voice. "Alex, you need to be careful. There are enemy soldiers in the city."

"Yeah, we kinda figured that out from the giant crater. Where are you?"

"We're underground. In the storm drains."

"Okay, give me a location. We'll come to you."

"Probably a good idea, if you don't want me to burst into flames," Jaden said. Through the static, she could hear the annoyance in his voice. Daysickness. Of course, he was going to be cranky. "Okay, there's a building a few blocks north of the crater. It has three tall windows on the front. There's a metal sign on the top that says 'Union Station'."

"Yeah, we can find that." She'd seen the building in the distance.

"Good. If you're walking straight at the building, there's a manhole cover about a half block away."

"Manhole?" That was a strange combination of words she hadn't heard before.

"Damn you sheltered humans," Jaden muttered. "It's a metal lid covering a hole in the street. I'll open it a little for you so you can come down."

"On our way." Alex put the radio on her belt and turned to her team. "Looks like we're headed underground."

"Of course, we are," Wesley said with a grin. "Wouldn't

be a GMT mission if we didn't go somewhere dark and scary."

They found the spot without difficulty, and the manhole cover was open a crack, just as Jaden had told them. Alex called down, "We're going to open the cover the rest of the way. Sunlight incoming!"

Patrick pulled the cover aside and they all dropped down into the storm drains.

Alex was the first to go down. After she landed, she stepped out of the sunlight and let her eyes adjust to the darkness. Before long, she could see large figures in the shadows. Jaden and six other vampires.

"Alex," Jaden said, "why am I unsurprised that you didn't stay in Agartha?"

ALEX and her team stood in silence as they listened to Jaden recount what had happened the previous night. The unexpected sniper ambush. The Ferals going on a rampage. The explosion at the water-treatment facility.

When he'd finished, there was a long silence.

Finally, Alex spoke. "I don't understand. If the vampire soldiers are the Resettlers from *New Haven*, why would they attack you? Were they going after the ship? Did they want to get home?"

Jaden sighed. "I'm afraid it's not that simple. There are two vampires named Mark and Aaron. They were Ferals until recently, when they returned to their intelligent form. I took them in at Agartha for a while, but I threw them out after they tried to take advantage of my hospitality. I believe they're here to take their revenge on me. With a new army under their control."

Wesley scratched at his chin. "So, how the hell did they get all the Resettlers under their control?"

"They must have found the Resettlement site and personally turned all the Resettlers."

Alex held up a finger. "Hang on, I'm still stuck on another part of the story. Two Ferals returned to intelligent form. The only way to do that is by drinking blood, right?"

"Correct."

Alex spoke slowly, afraid she knew where this was going. "And when did this happen?"

Jaden met her gaze with a cold, unwavering stare. "Mark and Aaron showed up shortly after you left Agartha the first time."

"I was afraid you were going to say that." She felt a chill run through her. "I only know of one human who was killed by a vampire near Agartha around that time."

Wesley's eyes widened as he started to understand. "These are the vamps that killed Drew?"

Alex nodded slowly. She expected to feel anger, but instead she just felt cold. "These bastards killed our friend, and then Jaden took them in, knowing what they'd done."

"They were Ferals, in the grip of mindless hunger," Jaden explained.

"Did you even consider that they'd just killed Drew?" She asked, her voice even. "Whose side are you on, Jaden? The vampires or the humans?"

Jaden took a step forward, and there was a slight snarl in his voice when he spoke. "I'm on the same side I've always been on. The one fighting for the continued existence of life on this planet. I saved Mark and Aaron from starvation, yes. And I saved you and your friends when you were dumb enough to stay out on your little rover after dark."

Alex took a small step back. She'd never seen Jaden like

this. His emotions seemed so close to the surface, like they were threatening to boil over.

He took a deep breath. "I'm sorry. It's the daysickness. It makes me act... different." He squeezed his eyes shut for a moment. "Look, I made mistakes, and my friends have paid dearly for them. I won't apologize for taking Mark and Aaron in. They were confused and suffering when they showed up on our door. But I will apologize for letting them go once they revealed their true natures. I should have ended their miserable lives, then and there."

"But you didn't," Alex pointed out. "And now everything has gone to shit."

"This is not the ideal scenario," Jaden admitted.

Alex cocked her head, unable to believe what she'd just heard. "Not the ideal scenario? Is that what you'd call it?"

"Alex," Wesley said, putting a hand on her shoulder, but she brushed it away.

"These two monsters killed three hundred people. People who wanted nothing more than to make a better life. Now these two vampires you let go have my fellow *New Haven* citizens as their undead slaves. That's more than just not ideal. It's fucking horrific."

A strange sound that was almost a growl escaped Jaden's throat. "It could be much worse. If the settlement had been wiped out by Ferals, rather than by Mark and Aaron, we'd have hundreds of Ferals returned to their intelligent, human state. They'd be running around, out of control, each with their own agenda. We'd have hundreds of Marks and Aarons. At least now, it's contained."

"So, what, we just let them run free in Denver?"

"No!" His voice was a full snarl now. "We kill Mark and Aaron. That'll set the others free."

Ed patted his rifle. "Finally, a plan I can get behind. Let's do it."

Alex ignored him, keeping her gaze fixed on Jaden. "And what then? We have three hundred vampires. We can't take them back to *New Haven*. Are they going to live in Agartha?"

"I don't... I don't know. I haven't thought that far ahead." Jaden put his hand over his eyes and lowered his head.

For the first time, Alex noticed that the other members of Jaden's team were struggling. None of them had spoken a word since Alex and her team arrived. Two of them were leaning against the wall; their half-opened eyes looked drugged. The rest were slumped on the floor in various states of consciousness.

She turned back to Jaden. "You still with me, big guy?"

For a moment, he didn't respond. Then he let out a deep sigh and rubbed his eyes. "You have no idea how difficult it is to function during the day. We're all strong enough to pull it off, but just barely. Any of the newly turned vampires who are awake really hate life now." He paused a moment, then looked at her. "I'm curious if you're really as capable as you seem to think you are."

Patrick took a step forward. "I'll bet Captain Goddard's capable enough to kick your tired ass."

Alex flashed him a look, then turned back to the vampire. "Jaden, if you have an idea, spit it out."

He took so long to answer that she was beginning to think he hadn't heard the question, but then he spoke.

"As much as I hate to say it, now may be our best chance to kill Mark and Aaron. They're trapped by the daylight, just like us. If we can find them and get to them..."

Chuck frowned. "Assuming we can make it through the million or so Ferals down here and get past any vampire soldiers they left as guards."

"Yes," Jaden said with a weak smile. "There is that. There are six of my vampires left. I believe two more may still be alive in another location. They were attempting to lead the Ferals away and got separated from the group."

"Those are long odds, Captain," Chuck said. "He's daysick. Not thinking clearly."

Jaden didn't bother arguing.

"Listen, Jaden," Alex said, "you helped my team. Saved us from certain death twice. That doesn't mean I'm not pissed about all this, but it does mean I owe you our help. We owe it to the Resettlers, too. There's no way we're going to leave anyone from *New Haven* as a vampire slave."

"Oh, thank God," Patrick muttered. "I thought Chuck was going to talk you out of it for a second."

"You want someone to hunt down vampires, you've come to the right place. That's what the GMT is all about."

Jaden looked at Alex and smiled. "We'll give you all the support we can."

"Thoughts on where we should start?"

Jaden nodded. "If you can help me get my other two team members, we can even the odds a little."

"Sounds like a plan."

Ed shook his head in wonder. "Heh, the GMT teaming up with vampires for a mission. Who would have expected that?"

16

"THE FLIGHT DECK is the most heavily protected part of the ship, from an electronic security standpoint," Jessica said.

"Makes sense," CB replied. "One thing you don't want on a ship is the wrong person getting their hands on the controls."

They were back in the tunnels in the belly of *New Haven,* making their way toward the flight deck. A few hours of sleep had made a world of difference for Jessica and Brian, and even CB had managed forty minutes of shuteye before his sense of caution and his instincts told him it was time to move on from Wesley's apartment.

He'd put it off long enough. It was time to make their big move. He only hoped the false leads from the residents of Sparrow's Ridge would keep the faceless GMT off their tails long enough for them to pull it off.

"Our only hope," Brian said, "is to get into the server room. Then I might be able to hack the system."

"Will we be able to control the ship remotely from there?" CB asked.

Jessica shot him a look. "Afraid not. You really don't know how this ship works, do you?"

CB chuckled. "I guess I was too busy risking my life on the surface, getting you parts, to learn about the flight mechanics."

"Yeah, well, while you were playing hero, some of us were getting our hands dirty up here."

"Oh, my hands got plenty dirty down there," CB objected with a smile. "Blood's hard to wash out from under your fingernails."

Brian shook his head. "You two have a truly strange way of flirting."

CB flushed. "We weren't... It was just a friendly conversation."

Jessica raised an eyebrow. "We weren't flirting? Too bad." She quickly changed the subject, before he could respond. "Look, the flight controls are a physical system. It was built that way so no one could hack in and take control of the ship."

Brian nodded his agreement. "Don't get it wrong, there are plenty of systems on this ship we can control by hacking in. We could have some serious fun. But controlling the actual flight of the ship? No, sorry."

Jessica stopped walking and pointed up. "This is it. Here's how we get into the control tower."

They stood silently, each contemplating the severity of what they were about to do. Taking control of the ship, what they would have been called a mutiny back in the pre-infestation days. Everything they'd been working for had been leading to this.

"All right," CB said. "Up we go."

Brian tilted his head. "Hang on. 'Up we go'? That's your motivational speech? I've heard you in dozens of briefings, and you always get the team psyched for the mission. You can do better than 'up we go.'"

CB chuckled. "I guess it's not the most eloquent speech I've given. But honestly, what else is there to say? We've already been through hell together, and we know what's coming next is going to be even more difficult. And that's not even considering what happens after. If we lose, we'll be killed. If we win, we get to work our asses off putting this city back together and convincing the people we aren't traitors. Either way, it's not going to be easy."

Jessica looked at Brian. "I thought you said he was good at motivational speeches."

"The positive part's coming," Brian replied. "At least, I hope so."

"I'm afraid it's not," CB replied. "There's nothing I could say that would make this easier. But I will say this. As much as I love Alex and the GMT, there are no two people I'd rather have by my side on this mission."

"There it is," Brian said with a grin.

Jessica's eyes shone as she stared at CB. "That was... It was really touching."

"I meant it," the colonel replied. "Now, come on. Like I said before, up we go."

CB laced his fingers and gave Brian a boost up into the ductwork. Then he gestured for Jessica to step into his hand.

Instead, she grabbed him by the shirt and pulled him close. For a moment, CB pulled back in surprise, but then he leaned toward her. Their lips touched, softly at first, but soon the passion overtook them both.

Finally, Jessica pulled away and smiled. "I figured a little extra motivation couldn't hurt. Get us through this and we can see where that goes. Now, how about that boost?"

As he lifted her into the duct, CB promised himself he

would live through this. He wanted to experience a thousand more kisses like that one. And he was eager to see where those kisses would lead.

Jessica and Brian each lowered a hand. CB jumped, catching them both, and they pulled him up.

"Um don't worry, I wasn't watching," Brian said, once CB was in the duct. "And if I had been, I wouldn't want to say another word about it, because it would already be super awkward. Hypothetically."

CB was suddenly grateful for the darkness in the ducts, so Jessica couldn't see him blush.

They came out of the ducts in a hallway on the bottom level of the control tower. CB stuck his head through first, and when he saw it was empty, he breathed a sigh of relief. Other parts of the mission would depend on good fortune, but this hallway was the only place where their success or failure would depend solely on dumb luck.

They moved through the hallway quickly and quietly, making their way to the door to the server room. When they reached it, CB stood watch while Jessica removed a panel and Brian went to work hacking the locking mechanism.

The lock opened with a soft beep, and Brian grinned. "Easy as that. I thought you said this was going to difficult, CB."

"Why do I wish you hadn't said that?" Jessica asked.

They stepped inside, and CB saw an organized maze of wires plugged into rows of servers. He stood by the door while Brian got to work. None of them spoke as the low hum of the electrical equipment filled the air. CB stayed close to the door, listening for any approaching workers in the hallway. Brian was too in the zone to notice anything outside his tablet screen, and Jessica paced back and forth, one moment, listening at the door with CB, and the next moment, looking over Brian's shoulder.

After about ten minutes, CB asked, "How's it going, Brian?"

For a moment, CB thought Brian hadn't heard him, but he finally responded. "Great. I'm getting control of quite a few systems. My only concern is that even if I override the locking mechanisms to get us onto the flight deck, Fleming's people will also have control of the systems on their end."

"Which means his faceless GMT will be able to waltz right on to the flight deck," Jessica said.

"Exactly," Brian confirmed.

CB grunted in annoyance. "There has to be a way for us to lock down the flight deck. If not, there's no point to us even getting in there. It's going to take time for us to change the course of the ship, and we need those fake GMT goons locked outside."

Brian said nothing to that.

CB and Jessica exchanged a glance.

"Any thoughts?" Jessica asked.

"Just a moment," Brian answered. "I've got us into the security system. Jessica, jack your tablet in. I'll route the feed to you, so you can make sure our route is clear."

Jessica did as he asked, and less than a minute later, she was watching a live feed from security cameras on her tablet.

Their entire level was surprisingly empty, but a few moments later Jessica gasped.

"Shit. Look at this, CB, we've got company."

CB peered over her shoulder and let out a curse at what he saw. Six of the faceless GMT members were marching down the hallway, their weapons drawn.

Jessica glanced back at CB. "I don't suppose this is a routine security check."

"Unless a lot has changed in the last forty-eight hours, GMT isn't in charge of ship security. And even if they were, they sure as hell wouldn't need that kind of firepower while simply walking their rounds."

Jessica sighed. "I figured as much." She glared at Brian. "This is your fault for saying this was going to be easy."

Brian didn't seem to notice the comment. "I'm almost done. Give me twenty seconds."

"We may not have twenty seconds." CB scowled at the security footage on the screen. "Is there another way out of here?"

"We're in a data room." Jessica gestured to the floor. "The cables run under our feet. They built these rooms with a raised floor to accommodate all that. Pop out one of the floor tiles and we should be able to squeeze down through there. But first, let's see what I can do to keep them from getting through this door too quickly."

She marched to the door and pulled off the panel with the controls. Then she quickly shorted them out so the door wouldn't be able to be unlocked with a security card.

"Got it!" Brian's eyes were beaming with triumph.

CB clapped him on the arm. "Good work. Let's get the hell out of here."

Brian grabbed a hook off of the wall. Then he stuck it into a slot in one of the floor tiles and pulled it up. He squatted and shone his headlamp into the crawlspace below.

"There's only about a two-foot gap between the raised floor and the steel deck," he said with a frown. "Looks like I'm going to have to suck in my gut."

CB squatted next to him and peered into the crawlspace. "We'll make it work. Let's get moving."

Brian squeezed beneath the raised floor first, quickly followed by Jessica. CB was the last down, and just as he ducked his head under the raised floor, someone began pounding on the door to the data room.

"Colonel Brickman!" yelled a voice from the other side of the door. "Lay down your weapon and open this door. We are placing you under arrest. If you do not comply, things are going to get very uncomfortable for you."

CB's muscular frame was almost too large to fit in the crawlspace, and he had to army crawl, his back and chest scraping against the top and bottom of the space. From behind him, he heard a distinctive hissing whine.

He touched Jessica's foot and whispered, "As soon as we're under the next room, we need to get out of here. They're cutting through the door. It'll only take them a minute or two to get through."

Jessica passed the message up to Brian, and a few moments later he pushed up a tile and climbed through into the next room. Jessica and Brian quickly followed.

CB looked around quickly as he emerged, trying to get a handle on their situation. They were in some type of office. Two maintenance workers stared with wide eyes at the three people who had just emerged from the floor tile.

Jessica touched CB's arm. "There is an entrance to a large duct system at the end of the next hallway. If we can get past the GMT, we can make it there."

CB nodded quickly, ignoring the sting at hearing those fakers being called the GMT. "Let's do it."

They listened, waiting until the GMT made it through the door and loudly charged into the next room. Then Jessica led the way, taking them out of the office and down the hallway. At the end of the corridor, they reached a door. Jessica tried the knob and cursed.

"I take it the duct work is behind this door?" CB asked.

"Sorry, I didn't think it would be locked." She went to work prying the panel off the door controls and plugging in her tablet.

The distinctive sound of boots slapped against the deck echoed through the hallway, and a black-clad face appeared around the corner at the end of the hall.

The faceless GMT member froze as he saw them. Then he shouted, "They're over here."

CB glanced at Jessica. "Work fast." Then he drew his pistol and fired a warning shot above the man's head.

It was a risky move, as it could attract other guards to their location, and it would help justify the fake GMT's use of deadly force. But it would be worth it if it bought them enough time to get through the door.

Just as he'd hoped, the man disappeared back around the corner.

There was a loud click behind CB, and Jessica said, "Got it!"

CB backed through the door without turning, never taking his eyes off the end of the hallway until he was through and the door shut.

He turned to see the room. "Uh, so we're trapped again?"

A few feet in front of him stood a chain-link fence with an old-fashioned lock on the gate. Beyond the fence was a huge eight-foot-by-eight-foot duct.

"What is this place?" Brian asked.

"It's our way into the main ventilation system." She gestured toward the huge duct in front of them. "This vents to the outside. It lets out stagnant air."

"Huh," Brian said. "And you want us to get in there?"

She shrugged. "I don't see a lot of other options." She pointed at the lock on the gate. "I can't hack this one, but I'm hoping you can, CB."

CB grinned. He raised his pistol and shot the lock. Then he gave the gate a small nudge and it swung open with a squeak.

They went through the gate and climbed into the massive duct system. It was like walking down a metal hallway. Every footstep clanged and every word they spoke echoed.

They hadn't been walking long when they heard the sound of heavy boots hitting sheet metal echoing from behind them.

"Damn, we better move faster," CB said.

Suddenly Jessica stopped. "Shit. I just thought of something. What time is it?"

Brian glanced at his watch. "About two."

"I need the exact time."

He looked again. "One fifty-seven. Why's that important right now?"

"Because in three minutes, those fans are going to turn on and suck out the old air. It turns on for five minutes at the top of every hour. That's how we regulate the air we breathe on *New Haven*."

Brian nodded slowly. "So, what you're saying is it's about to get really breezy in this hallway."

Jessica nodded. "If we don't secure ourselves in the next three minutes, we'll probably die."

CB grinned. "How much you want to bet that the faceless GMT doesn't know that?"

Brian looked around, his gaze nervously darting from floor to ceiling. "I notice there isn't a whole lot to hang on to down here."

CB pulled his knife from his belt. "Guess we'll have to make our own."

He stabbed his knife through the sheet metal wall of the duct, working it to create a two-inch hole. Then he pulled his belt from his pants and wrapped it around the knife.

Brian's voice was urgent when he spoke. "We've got less than a minute."

"Plenty of time," CB muttered. He put the knife back into the hole in the sheet metal, pushing it all the way in this time until the handle cleared the hole. Then he twisted it sideways so it lay lengthwise against the wall. He tugged on his belt, and the knife clanged against the other side of the sheet metal, holding fast.

"Instant handhold," he said. "Jessica, come here."

She complied, and he wrapped the belt around her arm once.

"This isn't going to be comfortable, is it?" she asked, grabbing the belt above her arm.

"Probably not." There were only about six inches of belt remaining past Jessica's arm. CB grabbed hold of it and turned to Brian. "You're going to have to hold on to my waist, buddy."

Brian hesitated.

In the distance, there was a loud click and they heard hydraulics.

"That's the outer vents opening!" Jessica shouted. "Grab on, Brian!"

Brian stepped forward and threw his arms around CB's waist. "Like I said earlier, not awkward at all."

The sounds of boots against sheet metal were getting louder now, but it was quickly dwarfed by the sounds of the powerful motors bringing the fans to life. In the distance, the black-clad members of the GMT ran toward them.

"Hang on tight!" Jessica shouted.

The blast of air hit CB like a baton to the chest, knocking him off his feet. He'd expected the wind to be strong, but he hadn't considered it would be anywhere near this powerful. He held tight to the belt, squeezing as hard as he could with both hands. Brian clutched his waist, hanging on to keep from being sucked down the corridor that had transformed into a wind tunnel.

CB glanced at the hole in the duct, thinking of how he'd wrapped the belt around the knife and hoping it would hold.

The five faceless GMT members struggled to remain on their feet in the powerful wind, a battle they quickly lost. If CB hadn't been holding on for dear life, it almost might have been funny. They slid down the hallway, frantically trying to find a grip on the sheer metal of the duct walls and floors.

As the power of the fans increased, so did the speed of the GMT members whooshing toward CB and his friends. One by one, they slipped past CB, Brian, and Jessica. As the fifth and last member slid past, he desperately grabbed at them, and CB felt a sudden jolt. Looking back, he saw the black-clad soldier had grabbed Brian's leg and was hanging on for dear life.

CB clutched the belt with all his strength. The added weight of the extra man made a huge difference. CB was having trouble holding on, and he knew if he was struggling, Brian had to be too. He felt the hands around his waist slip.

Brian lost his grip, and he slid free of CB and toward the vent at the end of the duct and the thirty-thousand-foot drop outside the vent.

CB spun, his reflexes responding before his mind could,

and threw out an arm, desperately grabbing for Brian. His fingers closed around Brian's outstretched wrist.

The sudden jolt was almost enough to make CB lose his one-handed grip on the belt, but he managed to hold fast.

The fans had to be blowing full-blast now. CB, Jessica, and Brian were all parallel to the floor.

CB held on with all his strength, all his willpower. But still he knew he couldn't last long like this. He shouted to Brian, straining to be heard over the rushing wind. "Kick him off! I can't hold you both!"

Brian peered down at the masked man still clutching his leg. Then he drew back his other foot and brought it down hard. The foot connected with the man's face, and the soldier lost his grip and careened down the corridor, carried like a loose piece of paper in a strong breeze.

The jolt of Brian's kick almost caused CB to lose his grip again, but he dug his fingers into each other as he gripped the belt, and he managed to hold on. Veins stood out on his forehead as he used every ounce of strength to keep him and Brian from flying out of the vent after the GMT members.

Then he felt a hand on his arm, taking off a bit of the pressure and making it possible to maintain his grip. It was Jessica. Her face was contorted in pain, and he saw the arm the belt was wrapped around was white. CB silently cursed his own stupidity. In trying to save her, he'd wrapped her arm in a tourniquet, and now the blood flow to her lower arm and hand was cut off. The belt dug deep enough into her flesh to break the skin, and drops of blood flecked into the wind from the contusions above the belt. Despite her pain, she held on to CB's arm.

With a grunt of effort, Brian reached up and grasped CB with his other hand.

Still, CB knew they wouldn't be able to keep this up for long. He'd been an overconfident fool to think they'd be able to survive this torrent of wind with a single knife wedged into the wall.

He felt Brian beginning to slip again, and he didn't know if he had the strength to save him again.

Then he heard the most beautiful sound in the world: the hydraulics moving. The vents were closing.

A moment later, the fans slowed, and Brian, Jessica, and CB collapsed to the floor, gasping in exhaustion, pain, and relief.

17

FIREFLY WOKE WITH A START, his body already beginning to stand. It was as if he was being physically pulled to his feet. There was only one thing that could do that, he knew. An order from his masters. Somehow, even from a distance, they were calling him, and his body was responding even before his mind was fully awake.

He felt like utter shit.

The world looked strange, blurry. It seemed to swim before his eyes each time he blinked. And that was far from the worst of it. A feeling akin to nausea threatened to overwhelm him. But this nausea wasn't only in his stomach; it was a sickness that sang from every cell of his body. He could even feel it in his teeth.

He'd had his share of rough mornings after a night of drinking at Tankards, but this felt like every hangover he'd ever had all rolled into one. His body throbbed with pain.

The worst part was that he knew there was a very simple cure to the sickness: sleep.

For the first time in his life as a vampire, he was experiencing daysickness. All his body wanted was to rest until the sun went down. If he lay down in this storm drain and closed his eyes, he'd be asleep in an instant and the pain would be gone. But his masters compelled him to come, so that was what he must do.

It was no wonder all the vampires he'd encountered during the day in his time with the GMT had been so pissed off. The way he was currently feeling, he'd probably rip out the throat of anyone who came into his immediate vicinity.

He ran through the maze of storm drains, instinctively knowing which way to turn at each junction. Once, he made a wrong turn, but he only made it a few steps before his instincts recognized the mistake and forced him to turn around.

The tunnels were crowded with sleeping Ferals, a fact that made Firefly nervous when he thought about it too hard. But they didn't rouse when he ran by, or even when he leaped over them. He understood why. He was a vampire. It wasn't worth the daysickness to go after someone who couldn't even feed their hunger. If he still smelled human, the experience of running through this tunnel would have been far different, he knew.

His leg brushed against a Feral as he ran by, and he shuddered. The world had turned upside down. He would give anything to go back just a few days, to refuse to lead the Resettlers to their first night on the surface. If he could somehow get up to *New Haven*, he'd pay Fleming a visit. He'd slice the councilman from throat to balls and he'd pull out the man's insides. Then he'd sink his teeth into Fleming's soft neck and drink deep. He could almost feel the hot blood flowing across his teeth and down his throat—

He shook his head, pushing away the fantasy and the hunger it had stoked. Truth was, if he were on *New Haven* right now, he'd be on fire, scorched by the sunlight that filled the ship at all hours.

Not that a fire sounded too terrible right now. Compared with the daysickness, fiery death would almost be a relief.

He found Mark and Aaron waiting in a large, open area where several tunnels came together. About twenty Resettlers stood around them, all looking about as good as Firefly felt.

Mark nodded toward Firefly when he saw them. "There he is. Our brilliant field commander."

Firefly wanted nothing more than to rip the vampire's face off, but he just came to a stop and stood silently before his two masters. Where had these two been during the battle last night? They'd given Firefly a couple of orders and then disappeared.

Some leaders.

Aaron crossed his arms and scowled at Firefly. "It seems we underestimated our opponents last night. And that we overestimated you."

"It wasn't a great outcome," Firefly started, "but if we—"

"Shut up," Mark ordered.

Firefly's jaw snapped shut.

"We were overconfident in our numbers," Mark continued. "We lost fifty in that damn explosion alone." He turned to the gathered vampires, watching their faces contort in the discomfort of their daysickness. "I know you all feel like shit right now. That's to be expected. And, to be honest, you deserve to feel like shit after last night. Now, we're going to stand here in silence, until the rest of your pathetic brothers and sisters get here."

The wait couldn't have been more than five minutes, but it was the longest five minutes Firefly had ever experienced. There were two warring needs inside him, both equally powerful. His vampire body was designed to sleep during the day, and every nerve was screaming out to do so. But the need to obey his masters was even stronger. And waiting in silence with nothing to distract his mind made it even worse.

Finally, mercifully, after nearly two hundred vampires had gathered, Aaron spoke. "All right, this looks like everybody that's left. First, I want to apologize for last night."

Firefly tilted his head in surprise. Apologies didn't seem like Aaron's MO.

"I want to apologize for trusting you idiots so much. Let me assure you that will not happen again."

Mark nodded along with his partner's words. "That said, we have a rare opportunity here, and we're not going to let it sail by without taking a swing. Jaden and his disciples are hiding in the shadows, just like us. And I'd bet my ass they're not sleeping. They'll be hunting us. That's why your primary order is to protect Mark and I at all costs."

Firefly swallowed hard, understanding the implications of that order. He knew he'd jump in front of a bullet or murder his best friend to protect his masters now. There was nothing he'd be able to do to stop himself.

Mark continued, "Most of you will stay here with us, in case those Agartha vampires do show up. Firefly, you're going to take a team of twenty and go looking for Jaden's crew. If you find them before they find us, you give a shout and hold tight. We'll send our army, and once they get there, it's on. Nothing fancy, this time. Just a good old-fashioned fight, where we outnumber the enemy, twenty to one."

Firefly nodded, then turned to gather twenty of the soldiers.

But Aaron spoke again. "One more thing, before you go. You think you're in pain now. We understand. We feel it, too.

But this is nothing. Wait and see how it feels when we order you not to sleep for a week. Then, you'll know real pain. And if you mess this up again, that's exactly what's going to happen." A tiny smile touched the corner of his lips. "Move out."

Firefly wished he could punch Aaron in the face. Just one solid hit would make him feel so much better. Instead, he gathered his twenty scouts, including Shirley and Hector.

He led them out of the area where the vampire army was gathered and down one of the tunnels.

When he was far enough away to be out of vampires' earshot, he stopped walking. "Everybody, hold up for a second."

They stopped and turned to him, their eyes simmering with pain and fury. But as they looked at him, Firefly thought maybe he saw a tiny bit of hope there, too.

"Look, this is bad," he began.

"You think?" Hector asked. "Thanks for letting us know. I thought Resettlement was going pretty well, until you said something."

Shirley looked up at him, her eyes wide. "What are we going to do, Captain?"

He desperately wished he could tell her he had a plan, some way to get them out of this hellish situation, but he wasn't going to lie. He owed them more than that. "I don't know. But I promise you this: I will work like hell to find a way out."

"A way out?" Hector said, skepticism clear in his voice. "What's the best-case scenario? We get free of Mark and Aaron, we'll still be freaking vampires, right? And with no blood to drink, we'll eventually turn into those Feral creatures. That's what happens to vampires who don't feed, right?"

Firefly grimaced. "One step at a time. We have to figure out a way to get free of Mark and Aaron, then we'll worry about the rest. But for now..." He trailed off, not sure how to continue.

"For now, we obey our masters," Shirley said, her voice hollow.

"Yeah," Firefly confirmed. "Let's split up and spread out. It's time to find Jaden and his vampires."

ED LIFTED the manhole cover and climbed out onto the street. The others quickly followed, scurrying out of the hole and into the safety of the sunlight.

Wesley stretched, an easy smiled on his face as he stood up on the road. "Ah. I never thought I'd be so relieved to be on a city street on the surface."

Alex got to her feet, her eyes scanning the windows of the surrounding buildings. "Don't get too relaxed. They've still got the vampire snipers."

"Heh, I'm not worried," Ed said. "If these vamps are Resettlers, that means they're probably former badges. Those guys can't shoot for shit."

Patrick nodded. "You should know. You were the worst of them."

"Maybe until I got to the GMT and Alex gave me a few lessons."

"Yeah, now you're just the worst shooter on this squad. You could probably even beat a few of the worst badges these days."

No one laughed at the joke, and a heavy silence hung in the air. Though none of them said it, they all knew what was causing their melancholy. Ed had just pointed out that the vamps were former badges. Which meant every member of the GMT knew just about every one of them. There were friends and former coworkers among the enemy now.

Chuck turned to Alex. "Do you think there's any chance of saving them?"

Patrick scowled. "You mean the assholes who tried to help Fleming settle his dumb city? They're vampires now. There's no coming back from that."

"It's not that simple," Alex said. "They're citizens of *New Haven*. Also, remember that Fleming staffed Resettlement with the people who opposed him. Hell, if you hadn't made it onto the GMT, you'd likely be among them."

Ed's face darkened at that, but he couldn't deny the truth of it.

"Honestly, I don't know if there's anything we can do to save them," Alex continued. "If there's any chance, we'll try our damnedest." She looked around at her team, meeting each one of their eyes. "That said, every one of them is a vampire and we have to consider them our enemies if we're going to live through this. That means no hesitation when the time comes. Things could get ugly fast, and I want every one of you ready to take out any vamp who moves against us, even if they look exactly like somebody you used to know. Like Jaden told us, they're not in control of their own bodies right now."

Wesley frowned. "Do you really think they'd kill us? They haven't been vampires long. Maybe there's enough humanity left in them that they'd—"

"Stop," Alex ordered. "We can't afford that kind of thinking, Wesley."

"She's right," Chuck said. "I've done a lot of reading on the infestation. People who'd been turned attacked their friends, their communities, and even their families. If there was a way for humanity to override the control of a vampire master, I'm pretty sure the world wouldn't be the way it is today."

Patrick stifled a yawn. "Good point. I'm convinced. Let's kill every vampire that's not firmly on the good-guy team. Now, can we stop talking about it and start doing it?"

Alex nodded. "I'm going to check in on Owl, and then we'll get to work."

She contacted Owl on the radio, and the pilot sounded in good spirits.

"How are the repairs going?" Alex asked her.

"We're cranking through them," Owl answered. "George is one hell of a worker. Can I keep him?"

"I think Jaden might have something to say about that," Alex said with a laugh. "Listen, we're trying to contact two of Jaden's vampires on the radio, but we're not sure our signal's reaching them."

"Get somewhere high," Owl said. "The signal will carry better."

"Roger that. We'll be in touch."

"Good, because we'll have this ship ready to go in a couple hours, and I'm really itching to go punch Fleming in the face."

"That's a relatable sentiment. Talk to you soon." She lowered the radio and thought for a moment. "We're going to need a way to transport the two vampires to Jaden. Patrick and Ed, you two get the truck we drove from Agartha."

"On it, Captain," Ed said. "I'm driving, though."

"Like hell you are!" Patrick replied.

"Work it out." Alex turned to Chuck and Wesley. "You two, follow me."

She climbed the nearest fire escape, carefully avoiding

getting too close to any windows on the way up. Chuck and Wesley followed, serving as her backup as she climbed.

When she reached the rooftop, she turned her radio to the channel Jaden had given her and tried to hail the vampires.

It wasn't long before a male voice answered. "Who is this?"

"It's Alex Goddard, from the GMT."

There was a long pause. "Alex? This is Igor. What the hell are you doing in Denver?"

"Long story, but I just spoke with your boy, Jaden, and he'd very much like to see you."

Igor chuckled. "The feeling's mutual. Natalie and I are stuck in this damn building and feeling a little isolated, at the moment."

"Well, give me your location and find something to cover up with. We're coming to get you."

18

JADEN CLEARED his mind and concentrated on his breathing. The tunnel around him seemed to fade as he went deeper into his meditative state. He'd found that meditation was the most effective treatment against daysickness, other than actually sleeping. It didn't make the symptoms go away, but it did make him less aware of them.

Then Robert spoke, bringing him back to reality. "What's the plan for taking out Aaron and Mark?"

Jaden took a few more breaths before answering. "Removing their heads should do the trick."

"I'm not in the mood for jokes, Jaden. We need to find them, get past a small army, and take them out. That's going to require a plan, which is sort of your department."

"I'm aware." Jaden still hadn't opened his eyes. He hoped that if he kept them closed, a bit of the peace he'd felt while meditating would remain, pushing out the anger and aggression that always threatened to spill out when he was awake during the day.

"I'm not trying to push, but we suffered greater losses last night than we have in over a century. I can't bear to think about it now. I just want to get the rest of us home safely."

Jaden thought a moment before answering. When his mind was clouded with daysickness, it always took a bit longer to see the obvious. "We need to take one of their soldiers captive. Once we do that, we can use them to locate Aaron and Mark."

A sound like a small growl escaped Robert's throat, revealing his disagreement. "They won't betray their masters. Even if they want to, they won't be able to."

"We don't need them to betray their masters. In fact, we'll use that forced loyalty against them. If we take them through the tunnels, they should feel more discomfort as we near Mark and Aaron, since they'll feel some sense that they are betraying them. We can use their pain as a homing beacon. Then we break through their defenses and kill them."

Robert grunted his approval. "We can send the humans in first. They will be a good distraction, and they'll buy us a few moments to get to Mark and Aaron."

Jaden thought about that for a moment before answering. "I think in this case, we should try to keep these humans alive. They have a role to play in the future of our cities and the human race. I have a feeling Alex will be the bridge between our worlds."

"You're a soothsayer, now? I thought you were too old to believe that bullshit."

"Not a soothsayer. Just a creature whose instincts have had a long time to tune themselves." He paused a moment. "I enjoy having her around. Her passionate recklessness... It reminds me of a part of myself that died a long time ago. Watching her makes me feel alive."

"I didn't think you were the sentimental type anymore."

Jaden opened his eyes for the first time and looked at his old friend. "Neither did I."

Robert frowned. "At some point, we have to talk about what happened. Vampires died. Our friends died."

Jaden looked down at the tunnel floor. Over the centuries, he'd gotten used to humans dying. Their short lifespan meant that saying goodbye to humans he cared about was a regular occurrence. But losing a vampire? One he'd been close to for centuries? And not just one, but multiple? It was too heavy a concept to think about right now. He was afraid it would crush him. "We will. But first, we have to live through today."

"GET us as close as you can to that loading door," Alex said.

Ed threw the truck into reverse and reached out of the window, adjusting the sideview mirror. "Patrick, hop out and back me up."

Patrick scoffed. "Really? I thought you were this big, awesome driver. You need someone to wave you into a door?"

Alex sighed. "This really isn't the time, guys. Chuck, you mind?"

"Not at all." Chuck hopped out of the truck and ran to the back to wave Ed in. Alex joined him.

They were in the transport vehicle outside of the building where Igor and Natalie were holed up. The two vampires had said they would be waiting somewhere near the loading dock door.

Alex crept toward the shadows covering most of the dock, her pistol in hand. She stopped at the edge of the shadows.

A moment later, two figures filled the doorway. As they stepped through the door, Alex vaguely recognized them as two of the vampires who had helped Jaden save the GMT on the road to Agartha. They wore the same pained, haggard expressions as Jaden and Robert had. Daysickness was no joke, apparently.

"Hey, Igor and Natalie. Glad to see you two are all right. Let's get you back to Jaden."

Igor smiled weakly. "You're going to need to back that truck up farther, unless you brought a fire extinguisher."

"Sorry!" Patrick called from the cab of the truck. "My brother can't drive for shit."

Alex nodded toward the building. "Any Ferals awake in there?"

This time Natalie answered. "Not currently, but if we hang around long, the human stink will waft in there, and they'll wake up fast."

Chuck raised an eyebrow. "Human stink?"

"Oh, it's not a bad stink," she added quickly. "Sort of a combination of blood, musk, and citrus."

"It's quite pungent," Igor agreed.

The truck rolled to a stop less than an inch from the edge of the shadow.

"That's as close as I can get it, Captain!" Ed shouted.

Alex looked at the vampires. "That work?"

"I guess it'll have to," Natalie muttered.

"Okay, then, follow me." Alex leaped into the covered back of the transport.

Igor and Natalie quickly followed. The sunlight touched their skin for just a moment as they passed through the sliver of exposure. When they landed, thin tendrils of smoke rose from their skin.

"You all right?" Wesley asked.

"We'll live," Igor replied. "Where are we meeting Jaden?"

"They're in the storm drains," Alex answered. "We can access them through a manhole in an alley. It's completely shadowed. Will that work?"

Natalie nodded. "Indirect sunlight stings a little, but it doesn't burn us."

Igor looked at her. "It'll be good to see the others again. I wasn't sure everyone would make it through."

Alex felt a sinking in her stomach. These two hadn't talked to Jaden or anyone else since last night. They didn't know. She exchanged a glance with Wesley and saw from the sickened look on his face that he was feeling the same way.

"I'm sorry to tell you this, but not everyone made it," she said softly. "Between the explosion and the rampaging Ferals, six of your vampires died."

Igor's eyes widened in shock.

"No," Natalie whispered. Then her voice grew louder. "It can't be!" Her fist lashed out, slamming into the seat in front of her, and the blow rang through the truck. The metal bench was left dented as she drew her first back.

The truck skidded to a stop and Chuck, Ed, and Patrick ran back, weapons in hand.

"It's okay!" Alex shouted to them. "We're fine! She's just... taking in some bad news."

Igor put a hand on Natalie's shoulder and turned to Alex. "You're in no danger from us. Emotions run higher during the day, and this... It's a lot to take in. We haven't lost that many vampires in a long time."

Alex turned to Ed, Patrick, and Chuck, who were still staring dumbly at the vampires. "Get us moving. We don't have time to waste."

When the truck started rolling again, Natalie turned to Alex. "You said six died, but you didn't say which six."

Alex shook her head. "I'm sorry, I only know that Jaden and Robert are alive. I haven't had a chance to learn the names of the others."

"They died trying to retrieve your ship," Natalie said. "Perhaps you should learn their names. Learn them and honor their sacrifice."

Alex couldn't meet the vampire's eyes. She knew Natalie was right.

BRIAN STOOD in front of the control panel, his tablet once again plugged into the system. "You sure we should be taking the time to do this, CB? Hacking in is going to take time. The security on the weapons systems is tricky. I'm talking heavy firewalls."

"It has to be done," CB growled. "If the GMT makes it back here, we don't want Fleming's goons shooting them out of the sky."

Brian nodded. "I'll do my best."

Jessica glanced down the corridor behind them. They hadn't seen any faceless GMT members since the team that got sucked out the ventilation system, but CB understood Jessica's trepidation.

"It's going to be okay," he told her.

Jessica smiled. "Now, I know you can't promise me that. Don't start lying to me, Colonel." She paused. "Shutting down the ship's defensive weapons seems a little risky, doesn't it?"

CB shrugged. "We've gone a hundred and fifty years without an aerial assault. I think we can risk it."

Brian nodded. "Agreed. I just wish one of us had access. They stripped all three of our permissions an hour after we went rogue."

"Here's a thought," CB said. "Try Alex's credentials."

Jessica nodded slowly. "Of course. They think she's dead. Why would they bother removing her permissions? That's brilliant."

"Let's not get ahead of ourselves," Brian said. "Do we even have her password?"

CB chuckled. "She wasn't big on cybersecurity. Her password is VAMPKILLERS2GO. All caps."

Brian chuckled as he keyed in the password. Then his eyes widened. "Holy hell, it worked. I'm in!" He tapped at the tablet another moment. "All right... External turret defense systems are off...now. Normally, this would be setting off all sorts of alarms, but I suppressed them. Honestly, they gave Alex way too high a level of access. Totally unnecessary for her job."

"You complaining?" Jessica asked.

"Not today." He sighed as he unplugged his tablet.

CB gave him an appraising look. The poor guy looked even paler than usual. It was clear he'd pushed himself to the limit, and was now attempting to go even further. And he was too proud to ask for a break.

"Hey, you two mind if we rest for a couple minutes?" CB asked. "I need to change my bandage."

Jessica and Brian exchanged a glance that was mostly relief, but also contained more than a little surprise.

"You sure it's safe?" Jessica asked.

CB looked around. "This is as good a spot as any. No one can sneak up on us here." With that, he sank to the floor and began unbuttoning his shirt. "You said you grabbed some food from Wesley's, Jessica?"

She nodded. "Just some bread."

"Well pass it around. Let's refuel, as long as we're stopped."

They ate in silence for a few minutes. The bread was stale, but CB thought it was just about the tastiest thing he'd eaten in months. An empty stomach could teach a tongue to love even mediocre food, he figured.

When Jessica had finished, she moved to CB's side and reached for his shirt buttons.

"Um, should I leave?" Brian asked.

"I'm just helping him change his bandage. Relax."

When she'd pulled the old bandage off, she let out a soft gasp, which she failed to stifle.

"That bad, huh?" CB asked. He'd known the wound was infected since checking it at Wesley's place, but he'd been trying not to think about it.

"It's not great," Jessica replied. "You need to get that taken care of sooner rather than later."

CB chuckled. "Sure. Maybe I can just ask Fleming for a time out, so I can get some medical attention."

"I'm serious, CB. And so is this infection. As soon as this is over, you need to get it looked at. If you let it go, it'll kill you."

Brian let out a laugh. "The great and fearsome CB survives hundreds of vampires, assassination attempts, and working with Alex Goddard, but dies from a microscopic bacteria. That's irony for you."

CB glanced at the wound and grimaced at what he saw. Jessica was right.

He started to wrap it back up, but Jessica took the bandage from him.

"Here. Let me."

CB looked at Brian. "Don't worry, I don't plan on dying

anytime soon, from a bacteria or anything else. I've got a city to save and a team to find before I kick the bucket."

"You really think the GMT's alive?" Brian asked. "Fleming seemed pretty sure they didn't make it."

"Yeah, well, Fleming's been underestimating Alex from the day he met her. That girl's too stubborn to die."

"Good point. I don't know what I was thinking." A soft smile crossed Brian's lips. "For a long time, I dreamed that I might end up with Alex. I know that it's a silly thought. She's miles out of my league."

Jessica gave him a look. "Brian, you are a major catch for any woman. You are almost certainly the smartest person alive. Like, in the whole world. Plus, you're a good guy. What's not to like?"

Brian's face reddened. "That sounds like something my mom would say."

"Maybe your mom's smarter than you think she is."

"Yep, socially awkward nerds like me get all the girls." He chuckled again. "I appreciate the kind words, and I don't mean to sound negative. It's just... In a situation like this, where the odds of us getting out alive are so low, it kinda makes you think about the things you never got around to doing, you know. I wish I had at least asked Alex out." He paused again. "I hate to say it, but I kinda wish that I had slept with Sarah. I mean, I hate her, and everything, but it would have been nice to get laid one last time. Plus, it really would have pissed her off when I didn't come over to Fleming's side and she realized that she slept with me for nothing."

"This took a weird turn," Jessica said. "Now. I'm the one who wants to leave the room."

CB looked Brian in the eye. "You are going to make it to the other side of this."

"Oh, yeah?" Brian asked, the skepticism clear in his voice. "How do you figure?"

"Because I'm Colonel Arnold Brickman, and I say we're going to live."

Brian raised an eyebrow. "Please, tell me you have more than that."

CB leaned forward and smiled. "I do. I have a plan."

Jessica put a hand on his arm. "I think you've kept us in the dark long enough. What's the plan?"

"Want to know one of the biggest secrets on *New Haven*?" CB glanced back and forth between his two companions. "There is a vampire on board."

They both stared at him blankly.

CB frowned. "I was kinda hoping for a bigger reaction, there."

Jessica shook her head. "I don't believe it. How could a vampire have even gotten on the ship?"

CB smiled. "He's been here since the ship took off one hundred fifty years ago. He was one of the original crew."

"Holy hell," Brian said, his face growing even paler. "You're serious."

"His name is Frank, and apparently he volunteered to be turned. We kept him in a sun-proof cage, and over time, he became a Feral. We were waiting for him to die, but he never did."

Jessica leaned forward and squinted at him. "If you're pulling our legs—"

"I'm not," he quickly interjected. "After we realized that Ferals could turn back to human form, we gave Frank some blood. Our goal was to convince Fleming that Resettlement was more dangerous than he believed. Needless to say, it didn't change his mind. But I've been visiting Frank daily, ever since. I bring him blood, and we talk."

"You couldn't have mentioned sooner that you have a vampire friend?" Brian asked.

"I guess he is sort of a friend. I respect the hell out of him. He's a true hero. He sacrificed himself to help humans live."

"That's where you slipped off to earlier," Jessica said, as the realization dawned on her. "The ultimate weapon you were talking about. It's Frank."

CB nodded. "I needed to steal some blood for him." He raised a finger. "We don't have an army, like Fleming. And we don't have the GMT. But we have Frank. He'll be our army."

Jessica beamed, clearly warming up to the plan. "Fleming's always said vampires aren't as dangerous as we say. Let's prove him wrong by letting him face one, up close and personal."

"Exactly!" CB replied. "And we can do it without endangering too many lives. Frank can move fast enough to make it to Fleming without killing the rest of the guards around him. We'll limit the deaths and only take out the people we absolutely have to."

"That's a bold plan," Jessica said. "What if Frank decides he wants control? Couldn't he just go around the ship and kill us all?"

CB was quiet a moment. "This may sound strange, but I believe Frank will do anything to protect this ship and the people on it. He's already sacrificed more than any of us have, and he's not going to see his sacrifice go to waste."

Jessica smiled. "I love the way you see the best in people. Not many have that kind of faith. This plan is insane, but I think it's the best one that we've got, and I'm behind you."

Brian looked back and forth between the two of them. "I'm sorry, am I missing something?"

"Possibly," CB answered. "Wouldn't be the first time."

"The whole point of *New Haven* is that it's vampire proof. If we let Frank out of his cage, he'll burn up in three steps. Unless you have a way to protect him from the sun, he's basically worthless to us."

"That's true," CB allowed. "And even if we could keep him from burning up, he is still much weaker during the day. Fleming's people might be able to take him down."

"So why are you still smiling?"

"Because we're not letting Frank out during the day. That's the whole reason we need to get control of the ship."

Brian's eyes widened. "Are you saying what I think you're saying?"

CB nodded. "For the first time in its one hundred fifty-year history, this ship is going to fly into darkness. *New Haven* is about to experience its first night."

19

ED PULLED the truck into the alley above where they'd agreed to meet Jaden and his vampires, and Patrick hopped out and pushed the manhole cover aside.

Natalie and Igor still looked pretty shaken from the news of their friends' deaths, and they were clearly eager to get back to Jaden. The truck's tailgate was just in front of the manhole so the vampires would be able to slide off the back of the truck and directly down the hole.

As Natalie was about to hop off the tailgate, she turned to Alex. "Thank you. All of you. We would have been stuck in that building until nightfall, if not for you and your team."

"Well, we would have been eaten by Ferals, if not for you and yours. Twice, actually. So I think you are still one up on us." Alex glanced back into the truck and saw her team gathering their gear. She turned back to the vampires. "Why don't you two go ahead? We'll be down in a couple minutes."

Igor and Natalie looked at her strangely, but then nodded. Natalie stepped off the back of the truck and plummeted straight down the manhole. Igor quickly followed.

"Guys, come here a second," Alex said.

All five of them gathered in the back of the truck, their equipment slung over their shoulders and their faces hardened for battle. Alex knew that they would follow her into that manhole without question, even knowing that their deaths very possibly waited for them down there. That was why she felt that it was important to ask the question she was about to voice.

"You signed up to be members of the GMT," she said. "That meant going to the surface during the daytime and gathering supplies for the continued survival of *New Haven*. It was a dangerous job, but you knew what you were getting into."

"Best job in the world," Patrick said with a grin.

"Maybe so," Alex allowed, "but in the past few months, I've asked you to do far more than what you signed up for. And now, I'm asking you again. I'm asking you to team up with vampires to help kill some other vampires. Doing so will free the Resettlers, but it won't make them human again. This is pretty far outside your job scope. That's why I'm asking, rather than telling. Every one of you has a choice."

"Not the way I see it," Ed replied.

"Let me finish. We have a duty to *New Haven*, and we could be putting that at risk by joining Jaden's mission. Anyone who isn't one hundred percent behind what we're doing, I want you to go back and help Owl and George with the ship. You'll still help us take back *New Haven* when the ship is ready, and I won't think any less of you. Once we're down in that hole, I'll start giving orders again, but for now, it's up to you."

Chuck, Wesley, Ed, and Patrick looked at each other for a moment. Then Chuck walked to the edge of the truck without a word, hopped off, and climbed down into the manhole. Wesley followed close behind.

Patrick squinted at Alex. "You didn't really think we'd puss out, did you, Captain?"

Ed nudged him. "I'm pretty sure that whole speech was meant for Wesley. She wanted to give him an out in case he was scared of getting an owie on his leg again."

With that, the Barton brothers went down the manhole. Alex followed, a proud smile on her face.

———

JADEN and his eight vampires stood waiting in the shadows below the street. From their dour expressions, it was clear that they had just been discussing their losses with Igor and Natalie. Alex was glad she'd given them a minute alone before sending her team down.

"So, what's the plan, Jaden?" she asked.

"First, we need to find one of their soldiers. We can use him or her to lead us to Mark and Aaron."

Patrick frowned. "I thought you vampires could sense each other. Can't you just, you know, feel them out?"

"I wish," Robert answered. "We have a sense of other vampires, but it's weak. Think of it like hearing an echo in the mountains. You know you heard the sound, but it's tough to tell exactly where it came from. Besides, all these Ferals down here are putting out so many raw feelings that it's tough to sense anything else. The stronger the emotions, the easier it is to sense. And these damn Ferals have a lot of pure emotions, even when they're sleeping."

Jaden nodded his agreement. "The closer we are to the source, the easier it will be to pinpoint. Though it still won't be perfect."

"Okay, so step one is to capture a vamp," Alex said. "Seems like a good start. GMT, this will be the only time I tell you not to aim for the head and heart. Make sure to unload on the non-vital areas, though."

The two teams moved out, heading slowly through the twelve-foot-wide tunnels. Each side of the tunnel had a narrow walkway with a rusted railing. The center was meant for drainage, though it was nearly dry now, with just the occasional puddle.

The group crowded close together as they moved down the walkway. Every footstep echoed in the otherwise silent tunnel.

Something felt odd to Alex as she walked, and it took her a while to figure out what it was. She heard breathing coming from her teammates, but not from the vampires. She was struck by the fact that she was surrounded by the undead. She had to stifle a shudder at the thought. It had never occurred to her that she'd one day be walking into battle with vampires by her side.

Up ahead, the light from Alex's headlamp fell across a slumped form on the other walkway. A Feral, she realized. She raised her pistol. "Heads up, team."

Jaden glanced at the sleeping Feral. "I got it."

Before Alex could respond, Jaden leaped into the air, vaulting to the other walkway. In a single motion, he drew his sword and sliced off the Feral's head. His hand snaked out, catching the falling head before it hit the ground. Then he set it gently on the walkway.

A moment later, he landed soundlessly back on their side of the tunnel.

"Damn," Wesley whispered. "I like having a vampire on our side, for once."

They'd only gone another fifty yards before Jaden held up a hand, motioning for them to stop.

After a moment, Alex whispered, "What is it?"

"A vampire close by," he answered. "It's awake."

Alex turned her head, shining her headlamp around the tunnel. A row of four-foot-tall pipes blocked the corner where the tunnel turned, a hundred feet ahead. If someone was planning an ambush, this would be an ideal location.

She motioned for her team to shut off their headlamps. They'd have to trust the vampires' eyes in this darkness. When the last headlamp was switched off, they were enveloped in a darkness so complete, it almost felt like a physical weight on Alex's shoulders.

They waited in silence for a full minute, no one moving, and the GMT trying their damnedest not to breathe too loudly.

Then, a soft shuffling sound came from up ahead. It was followed closely by a whisper. It was too faint for Alex to make out the words, but it was definitely someone speaking.

A sliver of light appeared ahead. With her eyes adjusted to the darkness, the faint light allowed Alex to make out the vague shapes of her team around her. The voices were just loud enough for her to understand their words now.

"I think I feel it," the distant voice whispered. "It's like a tickle at the base of my spine. Whatever it is, it's coming from someone strong."

Another voice answered, "I feel it, too. They must be close. We have to call it in."

Alex's breath stopped at the sound of the second voice. Even as a whisper in the dark, she knew it. She'd heard that same voice coming through her headset on many missions.

A hand touched her arm, and she knew it was Wesley. He recognized the voice, too.

She felt her pulse pounding in her ears as the adrenaline surged inside her. She wondered if the vampires could hear her heart beating.

The footsteps stopped ahead, and she heard a click. A radio being switched on, maybe?

"This is Firefly. I think we have them. We feel them close by."

The voice that answered was cut by a bit of static as it came through the radio. "Understood. Don't engage them until backup arrives. We're sending them now."

Jaden and his team crept forward, moving in near silence. Even from a few feet away, Alex could just barely detect the sound of their clothing brushing against itself and the tiny noise of their footsteps.

"What was that?" one of the distant voices asked.

Alex tilted her head is surprise. Apparently, vampire hearing was no joke.

"I don't know," Firefly replied, "I thought I heard something, but it might have been my imagination."

In the distance, Alex heard the click of the hammer of a gun being thumbed back.

"I'm sure it was nothing," Firefly said. "Our army's on the way. We need to just hang back and relax."

Something in Firefly's voice sounded odd to Alex, like maybe he was trying to put on a show for whoever was listening.

Jaden and his team stopped before they reached the turn. Both groups were aware of each other's presence. Just around the corner, death waited for the first person to show themselves.

Alex slowly crept ahead, motioning for her team to follow. She thought about how Jaden had described daysickness to her. He'd said it was like the worst hangover you'd ever had. And Alex knew a thing or two about hangovers.

As she walked, she slipped her arms out of her jacket. Then she turned and found Patrick in the darkness. She grabbed his shotgun and gave it a soft tug. He held on for a moment, but then let her have it.

She motioned for her team to cover their ears. Hoping they got the message, she hung her jacket on the barrel of the shotgun and approached the turn, moving past Jaden's team and staying close to the inside wall.

She stopped when she reached the corner, pressing her back against the wall and watching for movement. Seeing none, she slowly eased the barrel of the shotgun into the light.

Immediately two guns fired, and bullets tore through the coat. Alex pushed the shotgun forward, angling it as far toward the shooters as she could without exposing herself, and fired. The blast echoed through the confined space of the tunnel. Someone around the corner cried out in pain at the noise.

The GMT sprang into motion, sliding past Alex and into the tunnel. Ed was the first around, and he immediately fired his automatic weapon. Alex ducked around the corner and saw that he had hit a female vampire in the leg with multiple rounds. She somehow kept her feet and raised her rifle.

Before she could get a shot off, Chuck fired his weapon. His bullet struck her in the shoulder, knocking her back into Firefly.

Firefly's mouth opened in shock and surprise at seeing his old teammates standing in front of him. He stared for only a split second, then he grabbed the injured vampire, threw her over his shoulder, and ran back the way that he'd come.

But Jaden and his team were in motion now. They rounded the corner with blinding speed and charged after Firefly. He was moving fast, but the woman he was carrying him made him slower than the other vampires.

Ed squeezed off another burst of fire, and the vampire Firefly was carrying cried out in pain as a round struck her in the back.

Robert was the first to reach Firefly. He grabbed the injured vampire by the leg and lashed out with his foot, kicking Firefly in the back. Firefly stumbled, losing his grip on the female soldier and falling to the tunnel floor.

Robert threw her face down on the ground and put a knee against her neck. He pulled her arms behind her back and held her there.

Alex knew Robert had one vamp down and Firefly had fallen, but she couldn't see if there were others with Firefly and the female. She reached up and turned on her headlamp.

When she looked past Firefly, she gasped.

At least a dozen Ferals were racing down the tunnels toward them.

"The gunshots woke them!" Jaden shouted. "There'll be a lot more coming. Get ready!"

Firefly rolled to his feet and raised his pistol, but the Ferals were already on him. He managed one shot before a Feral slammed into his arm, knocking the weapon from his hand. Three other Ferals hit him in quick succession, sending him onto his back, hard.

One of the Ferals sank its teeth into his lower arm, and he cried out in pain.

Alex dashed forward, holding her pistol in a two-handed

grip. At least five Ferals had already sped past Firefly, going for other members of the team. She knew she should help them. But they weren't about to be devoured by four Ferals, and Firefly was.

He'd been a GMT member. And once a GMT, always a GMT. The Ferals would dismember him in the next few seconds if she didn't act quickly.

She squeezed off four quick shots. Each round went through the head of one of the Ferals holding Firefly.

But she didn't have time to consider whether she'd made the right decision. As the four Ferals fell, she heard an animalist scream. She spun toward it and saw a group of Ferals piling onto Robert, who was still holding down the female vampire.

He leaped to his feet, drawing his sword as he stood. The vampire underneath him tried to stand too, but her injured leg slowed her progress. A Feral grabbed her, sinking its claws into her arms, and another one grabbed her head and pulled. A third Feral sank its teeth into her neck and began devouring flesh, tendon, and bone alike. A moment later, her head tore free of her body. The Feral holding her head let out a victorious howl and smashed the head against the wall of the tunnel.

Robert made short work of the Ferals attacking him. If he was less deadly than Jaden, it wasn't by much. His motions were less fluid than Jaden's, but his strikes seemed even more brutal. As he finished off the last Feral attacking him, he turned his attention to those attempting to get by him to reach the humans.

Now that Robert was up and moving, the narrow walkway and his frenetic speed prevented Alex from taking a shot at the Ferals rushing toward them. That was all right, though; the last four Ferals didn't stand a chance against Robert.

After quickly dispatching three of them, Robert turned, catching the last Feral in the neck as it tried to speed past him. The sword cut through cleanly and the head fell from the creature's shoulders. Before it hit the ground, a shot rang out.

Robert spun around, his mouth hanging open in surprise. The right half of his skull was missing, leaving a C-shaped hole where the rest of his head should have been. He paused for a moment, then collapsed, tumbling over the rail and landing in a small puddle in the center of the tunnel.

"No," Alex whispered.

Firefly stood, rifle raised, taking aim at another one of the vampires.

This time, Alex didn't hesitate. She unloaded her weapon into Firefly's arms until the rifle slipped from his hands.

A cry that was somehow even more animalistic than the Ferals' howls came from behind her, and then Jaden charged past. His eyes glowed a furious red, illuminating the tunnel around him. Alex had never seen him move like that.

Firefly raised his injured arms and threw a punch as Jaden reached him, but the older vampire batted the hand away like it was nothing. He grabbed Firefly and slammed him into the rail hard enough to bend the metal.

Jaden let out a gut-wrenching snarl and grabbed one of the metal posts holding the railing, ripping it from the concrete and smashing Firefly in the face with it before the younger vampire could even raise his hands to defend himself.

Firefly tried to throw one more punch, and Jaden

dodged, letting the blow graze harmlessly past his head.

Then Jaden drove the metal post through the side of Firefly's left thigh and then through his right one. With the metal impaling both legs, Jaden squeezed the ends together until they touched, immobilizing the former GMT member's legs. Then he ripped another post from the ground.

Firefly was wriggling in pain now as Jaden grabbed both his arms and held them behind his back. Jaden drove the other post through Firefly's biceps, once again twisting the ends to pin his arms behind him. Then he shoved him face-down onto the ground.

Jaden's eyes blazed red as he stood over the whimpering Firefly. He reached down and wrapped his fingers around the other vampire's skull.

Alex realized with a start that Jaden was about to rip Firefly's head off, just like the Ferals had done to the female vampire. She quickly pushed her way toward him, shuddering as she glanced at Robert's unmoving body in the water.

"Jaden, no!" she shouted.

The old vampire turned and glared at her, his lips curled in a nasty snarl.

"We need him to find his masters!" she said. "They're the real enemies. You said it yourself, this vampire is just their slave."

Jaden turned back to Firefly and stared at him for a long moment, his fingers still squeezing his skull. Firefly's wide eyes darted around madly as if searching for someone to save him from this animal.

Finally, Jaden stood, raising himself to his full height and pulling Firefly up with him. Then he let go, and Firefly dropped to the concrete.

20

ALEX WAS RELIEVED to see Jaden's eyes return to normal as he turned to face the other vampires, but his voice sounded dead when he spoke.

"Someone, get Robert's body. We need to regroup." With that, he picked up Firefly with one hand and began walking back the way they'd come.

Natalie jumped down and grabbed Robert's body, then quickly rejoined them.

Jaden told them they'd be returning to the place where they'd convened underneath the alley. It was an out-of-the-way spot, an offshoot of the main tunnels, so it seemed unlikely that any vampires would stumble across them.

As they walked, Alex wondered why they weren't encountering any Ferals. Even the one who'd been sleeping last time they'd passed through here were gone. She wondered if perhaps it was Jaden's inhuman cry that had sent them scurrying. Maybe they'd realized he wasn't someone they wanted to tangle with today. Or maybe there was some honor among vampires. Maybe they'd heard the pain in that cry and were leaving him alone, for now.

Whatever the reason, the GMT and the Agartha vampires seemed to have the tunnels to themselves for now.

Wesley sidled up to Alex and leaned close. He spoke in a whisper. "Holy shit, Alex. That was insane. Why did Firefly—"

"I don't know," she answered tersely, cutting him off.

"Okay, but is he even still Firefly? I mean, does his consciousness—"

"I don't know."

"Yeah, I get that. I'm just saying, do you think he's going to—"

She turned toward him. "Wesley. I do not know. We are in uncharted territory here. It's going to take time to sort it out. So, could you please just give me a few minutes?"

He blinked hard, taken aback by her harsh response. "Yeah. Sorry, Captain."

She bit back the apology that almost came out. She felt bad speaking to him sharply at a time like this, but she needed to focus if she was going to keep them alive. She was all too aware of the questions, and she didn't have any useful answers.

When they reached the area under the alley, Jaden set Firefly face down on the tunnel floor and went to work setting up a perimeter.

Alex walked over and knelt beside Firefly. The metal bars through his arms and legs had been twisted together, effectively hogtying him, but she was still careful to not get too close to his face.

"Are you in there, Firefly?" she asked, softly.

He slowly turned his face to her. The despair was clear in his eyes. "I'm here, Alex. I'm damn glad you and the team are alive. Is Owl okay?"

She almost told him Owl was at the ship, but she

stopped herself. Maybe giving him information about the team wasn't the best idea. She had no idea how much he could communicate back to his masters. "She's fine."

"Good," Firefly said with a weak smile. "I didn't know... I wasn't sure you would make it after Fleming had Sarah sabotage the away ship." The smile left his face and the despair returned. "I'm so sorry, Alex. I should have stopped Fleming. I'm sorry for everything."

As sincere as the apology sounded, she wasn't about to start handing out forgiveness just yet. "If that's really you in there, why the hell did you shoot Robert?"

"You don't understand the control that my masters have over me. I want to help you kill Mark and Aaron, I swear to God, but if you freed me, I would kill Jaden's entire team and drag Jaden back to my masters the first chance I got. Those are my orders."

Alex felt the anger rising in her chest. It made her sick to hear him give up like that. "You have to fight, Firefly. You're strong. You need to resist them."

He shook his head weakly. "It doesn't work like that. My body has no choice but to obey. Their will overrides my own. I don't know why you saved me, but it would be best for all of us if you just finished me off right now."

Alex glanced down at the Resettlement patch he still wore on his jacket. She thought of the dinner she'd had with him at the fancy restaurant in the Hub. The way he'd been so smug and refused to see the truth. Three hundred people had paid the price for his arrogance, and plenty more still might before this was over.

Fleming was an asshole, but at least he was a naive asshole. Firefly had been to the surface and seen the Ferals up close. He should have known better, yet he'd still gone ahead with Resettlement.

And yet, there were plenty of times Firefly had come through for her. He'd saved her ass half a dozen times on missions. She'd fought back-to-back with him in the NSA facility only a couple months ago, both trusting each other completely, nothing but their faith in each other keeping them alive.

She reached down and put a hand on his shoulder. "I'm not giving up on you yet, Firefly. You have a lot to make up for, and I want to make sure you have the chance to do it. We just need to find your masters and take them out. Jaden says that should free you from their control. Can you tell me where they are?"

Firefly opened his mouth, but no words came out. He squeezed his eyes shut in frustration. "No, I can't tell you that. I just tried, and my body would not let me say the words."

"You always make it hard for me to be on your side. I was hoping for a little help. Is there anything you can tell us?"

He thought a moment. "I think so. I can give you details that don't directly put my masters in danger."

She nodded slowly. "I'll take what I can get."

"Okay." He drew a deep breath, even though he didn't need it. Force of habit, Alex supposed. "There were three hundred people turned at Fort Stearns. Aaron and Mark had burrowed under the main building days before, waiting for us to come back. Fleming sent us all down the day you went to Denver."

"What a coward," Alex muttered. "Had to get us out of the way before he made his move."

"Yeah," Firefly agreed. "Look, you were right about everything. Fleming is a fool. I am a fool. We retreated to the main building to protect ourselves from the Ferals, but we just ended up cornering ourselves. Mark and Aaron turned us all in a matter of minutes."

Alex grimaced. She was glad she hadn't been there to see that bloodbath. "How many of you are left?"

"About two hundred, I think. They were still gathering when I went out looking for Jaden."

Alex patted him on the shoulder again. "Thanks, Firefly. That does help. I am going to find a way to take those bastards out and free you."

Firefly didn't look any less forlorn to hear that. "What then? Do we wander the earth until we turn Feral? I would rather die." He looked up at her, his eyes pleading. "I deserve to die. I betrayed you, I betrayed the Council, I failed our people. And now Shirley..."

She thought back to the female vampire whose head had been ripped off. Alex had thought she'd looked familiar, but she hadn't been able to place her. Now she got it. It had been Shirley, Firefly's second-in-command on the Resettlement project.

"I'm sorry, Firefly."

"I'm going to ask one more time, Alex. Kill me. Please. It's the only way to make sure I don't hurt anyone else."

Alex forced a tiny smile. "Those metal bars through your arms and legs are doing a pretty good job of that. I'm not going to kill you. You've screwed up a lot of lives. You're not wrong about that. But you're a damn vampire now, so you're going to outlive me. You'll have plenty of time to make up for the things you've done. Besides, I happen to think you're worth saving. You gave us the radio that helped us make it to Agartha. You wanted humans to take back the Earth. You just went about it in an idiotic way."

"You'll get no argument from me, there."

"I'm sort of the poster child for being an idiot," she said.

"Remember when I stole the daylights for Fleming? If I don't forgive you, how's that going to look?" She paused, her face growing more serious. "As far as what happens after we free you, I don't know. There are a lot of smart people on our side. We'll think of something."

Firefly looked up at Alex. "You know, when you first joined the team, I thought you were an egotistical asshole. I told Drew you wouldn't last three missions. But you proved me wrong. You'd never leave a man behind, would you? Even when it's the sensible thing to do." A single tear slid down his cheek.

Alex swallowed hard, pushing down a lump in her throat. There was no time for sentimentality. Not today. "Pull yourself together, soldier. You just got recruited back into the GMT, and we have a hell of a lot of work to do."

With that, she stood up and walked away. There was another conversation that she needed to have, and this one would be just as difficult.

She approached Jaden slowly, not sure how to begin. What did you say to an immortal vampire who just lost his best friend? She didn't know, and she had an idea saying the wrong thing might earn her a broken bone or two. It was partly her fault that Robert was dead. If she had let Firefly die and concentrated on helping Robert, this tragedy wouldn't have happened.

If there was anything she knew about Jaden, it was that he was pragmatic. She hoped he'd be able to move past this and continue with the mission. Still, she couldn't help resting a hand on the hilt of her sword as she approached him.

Jaden stood over Robert's body, and he kept his eyes fixed on his dead friend's face as he spoke. "I'm not going to hurt you. You can let go of your sword."

"Oh, I didn't—"

"It's all right," he said. "I understand. You think I blame you for Robert's death. If you would have helped him instead of Firefly, my friend would be alive."

"The thought had crossed my mind," she admitted.

"Battle is battle. There are hundreds, maybe thousands of moments I would change if I could fight them over again. You didn't fire the bullet that killed Robert, and I don't blame you for his death."

Alex relaxed slightly. "I'm sorry, Jaden, I know that he meant a lot to you."

"You have no idea what he meant to me." His voice was cold. "Robert and I have been like brothers for seven centuries. We have seen civilizations rise and fall. He's been by my side for so long that I'm finding it hard to imagine what a world without him in it even looks like. It is like losing the mountains or the ocean. It's impossible to think of them suddenly being gone."

Alex stared down at Robert's body. Her gaze kept drifting to his ruined head, and then she'd quickly look away.

Jaden was right. There was no way she could understand the bond he had with Robert. She'd only been teammates with Chuck, Ed, and Patrick for a couple months now, and they already felt like family. Still, she needed to find a way to get Jaden's head back in the game. The clock was ticking, and nightfall was getting closer every minute.

She suddenly realized Jaden was looking at her.

"It is understandable that you can't find the words," he said. "How do you ask me to put my loss aside, so we can get back to work? After all, there are things to do and time matters." He chuckled, but the laugh was joyless. "I know everyone around me hates the extreme patience I present when dealing with problems. And maybe it is a fault. This is a reminder that time does matter. Robert was not immortal. Nothing truly is."

Alex figured that was about as good an opening as she was likely to get. "What do you say we get started, then? I have an idea how we can pull this off."

She dug around in her backpack as she explained her plan. When she found the small item she was looking for, she handed it to Jaden.

When she'd finished speaking, he stared down at the small object resting on his palm for a long moment. Then he closed his hand around it. "Follow me."

Jaden stalked over to Firefly, who recoiled when he saw who was approaching.

Jaden crouched down beside him. "Don't worry, I'm not going to hurt you. Well, no more than I have to."

First, he twisted the metal behind Firefly's back, tightening the way the younger vampire's limbs were bound. Then he reached inside Firefly's jacket and yanked off the shirt underneath.

"At the same time," he continued, "I can't have you ruining our element of surprise when we get close to your masters, which is exactly what your body would force you to do. Open up."

Firefly looked up at him, confused.

"Open your mouth, dummy," Alex explained.

Firefly did so, and Jaden jammed the shirt into his mouth. Then Jaden stood up and brushed off his hands. "There. The prisoner is gagged and ready. Shall we get started?"

FLEMING GAZED out the window in his office, frozen and staring exactly as he'd been doing for the last ten minutes. Outside, a crowd was gathering.

Sarah stole a quick glance out the window, hoping that Fleming wouldn't notice. She winced at what she saw. Every time that she thought the crowd of malcontents was at its peak, more showed up. The crowd was slipping out of the small square in the front of the Council building where they'd initially gathered and into the street. There simply wasn't room for all of them in the square.

These were the people loyal to Colonel Brickman and the GMT, she knew. Their signs made their loyalty clear. "CB was framed!" read one. "The Council was an inside job!" said another. And then there was Sarah's least favorite, the one that made her stomach turn. The one that felt like a time bomb waiting to go off. "Where are the Resettlers?"

Fleming hadn't publicly said anything about Resettlement, which in and of itself was a pretty clear indication to those people paying attention that there was a major problem. How long would it be before the truth was revealed, and even those loyal to Fleming turned on him?

But that wasn't the sign that bothered Fleming most. The one he was fixating on read: "Fleming lies!" A vein stood out on his head as he stared at that one.

"Can you believe that?" Fleming asked them for the third time. By this point, Sarah and Colonel Kurtz knew better than to answer. "Have I stretched the truth from time to time? Of course. Lying is part of politics. Why is this news that needs to be scrawled on a sign and paraded through the Hub?"

Kurtz cleared his throat. "Sir, maybe you should step back from the window. Just in case."

Fleming didn't seem to hear. "What these ungrateful

bastards don't understand is that every time I lied, every single time, it was to make their lives easier. The truth is a heavy burden, and the average person shouldn't have to bear it. That's what they elect us for."

Sarah had spent the last few minutes considering why that sign bothered him so much, and she thought she finally understood the answer. Politicians often lied, it was true. But when the people refused to believe the lies, that was the beginning of the end for any politician. That was when they lost their power. And power was the one thing Fleming most cherished.

"Sir," Kurtz said again. "The window. Would you please step back?"

This time, Fleming turned toward him and blinked hard as he took in the man's words. "I'm sorry, are you implying that my people, the people I have given so much to serve, would take a shot at me, Colonel?"

"It's just a precaution, sir."

Fleming turned back to the window. "We are in a crisis, and this type of protest isn't acceptable at a time like this. I want you and the badges to go down there and tell those people to go home, Colonel Kurtz. Anyone who disobeys is to be considered a traitor and must be shot."

Kurtz and Sarah exchanged a glance. Sarah saw the same panic she felt reflected in Kurtz's eyes. Fleming was really losing it, and they both knew it. Killing citizens for protesting would be his last move. If that happened, the city would revolt. It would be civil war.

"They still love you," Sarah said quickly. "They've just forgotten it. If you use too much stick right now, you could lose them forever. You need to remind them you are their best hope for the future."

Fleming turned toward her, and she saw that his eyes

were bloodshot. He hadn't slept since the attempt on CB's life two days ago, she realized. He wasn't taking care of himself. Maybe that was why he was losing control.

"When was the last time that you ate, sir?" she asked.

Fleming tilted his head in surprise. He hadn't expected that question. "Why does that matter?"

"I know that every moment counts right now, but if you aren't at the top of your game, everything could fall apart. I'm going to get you some food and Kurtz and his badges will get rid of the crowd. Peacefully. You need to get some sleep, or you will start making mistakes."

Fleming stepped close and glared at her. But she couldn't back down now.

"Sir, you are a great man, but you are still a man. Your body has needs. Don't push yourself over the edge."

Fleming said nothing for a long moment. Then he turned back to the window.

Sarah gritted her teeth. She'd tried, but she'd failed. If she couldn't get through to Fleming, no one could. As much as she hated to think about it, she needed to start planning an exit strategy that would allow her to survive when the people took Fleming down, once and for all.

Then Fleming spoke. "Fine. I'll eat. Kurtz, I don't care about this crowd. Let them wear themselves out shouting and protesting. They're just another distraction from the real goal. We need to keep our focus on getting rid of CB."

Kurtz nodded briskly, and the relief was clear in his voice when he answered, "Of course, sir. I think that's a good call."

"I'm going to eat and then rest, like Sarah suggested. I'll sleep for an hour, and when I wake up, I expect to you to tell me that CB is dead."

Sarah hurried out of the room to get Fleming his food.

She felt a twinge of guilt that the thought of turning on Fleming had even entered her mind, but she was relieved that he had come to his senses. Things were back on track. Soon, CB would be dead, and they could start deciding what to do about Resettlement.

BRIAN STARED down at his echolocation device.

"How we looking?" CB asking impatiently.

"Hard to say."

CB frowned. "You have a device that can see around corners and down every passageway on this level, and it's still hard to say?"

"Yep."

Ever since their rest, the three of them had been making much better time. After turning off the defense turrets and hacking the necessary systems in the control tower, they were making their way to the GMT hangar. It was a desperate move, since Fleming's men would almost certainly be looking for them there, but they needed a few more people on their side to pull this off. CB figured that if anyone remained loyal to him, it had to be the support staff he'd worked hand-in-hand with for twenty years.

Besides, the road to Frank the vampire started at the GMT hangar.

Brian was still struggling to keep up, but he made up for his lack of speed with the fact that his invention had saved their asses multiple times already.

CB didn't know what was going on in the rest of the city, but whatever it was must have had Fleming spooked. The tunnels were crawling with badges and faceless GMT soldiers. They'd had some close calls, but so far, they'd managed to stay out of any more entanglements.

Brian made an adjustment on his device. "There we go. I got it now. The tunnel's clear ahead. Let's move."

The three hurried down an empty passageway. CB knew that going to the GMT hangar was potentially dangerous. If Fleming didn't have troops stationed there, he surely had someone watching the place. If they were spotted, they could end up cornered in the hangar. CB just hoped there were enough staff people loyal to him that they could fight their way out, if need be. Besides, no one knew the GMT headquarters better than him, and he knew of a few passages that weren't common knowledge. They just need to get there.

A clanging noise coming from behind them caused CB to turn. An access hatch in the ceiling hung open above the spot they'd just passed.

"Oh, shit," CB muttered.

A pair of legs dropped through the access panel, and a moment later the rest of the man became visible and he dropped to the ground.

"Run!" CB shouted. He turned and took off, hoping his two companions would be able to keep up. If he set a fast pace, they'd have no choice but to do their best to match him.

He heard the loud thumps of three more bodies dropping from the access hatch to the ground, but he didn't bother looking back. It would only slow him down.

How had the badges found them? The only explanation CB could think of was that they'd been waiting up there watching for anyone to pass below. That must have been why the echolocation device hadn't spotted them.

Was Fleming really so desperate that he was stationing

groups of badges to peek through random access panels in the off chance the fugitives might wander by? Sadly, CB believed that the answer to that question was yes.

From behind him, he heard the crackle of a radio, and one of the badges said, "We got them! Sector Twelve!"

That meant that reinforcements would be on the way. Not good.

CB risked a glance back and saw that Jessica was only a few steps behind him. Miraculously, Brian was keeping up as well, though his face was beet red, and it didn't look like he'd be able to keep it up much longer. Even though he hated to do it, CB slowed his pace half a step to make sure that Brian stayed with the group.

A shot rang out, echoing through the tunnel. CB looked back again, making sure his friends hadn't been hit. They were both uninjured, but Jessica wore an expression of absolute fury. For a moment, CB thought that look must be because someone was shooting at them, but he quickly realized he was wrong. He knew her well enough to realize that she was pissed that they were discharging a firearm in these tunnels, where a stray round could easily damage a vital system.

Even a rookie badge knew not to fire a weapon anywhere near a vital system. They were on a nuclear-powered airship, after all. A very unlucky shot could potentially bring the whole city down. But these badges didn't seem to care. It looked like all bets were off when it came to killing the three fugitives.

CB rounded a corner and slowed to a walk. He grabbed Brian as he passed and pulled the echolocation device out of his pack, shoving it into his hands. "We need a way out of here."

They walked fast as Brian frantically tapped at the

screen. "No clear exits, and more badges are closing in fast." He tilted the screen so CB could see the groups of people heading down every hallway.

He turned to Jessica. "Where's the nearest hatch to get us back up top?"

Jessica thought for a moment. "If we go left at the next turn, there should be a ladder that leads up into the sanitation building in Sparrow's Ridge."

"Good enough."

Brian pointed to the screen, which showed a team moving toward them fast from that direction. "That's going to be a problem."

CB looked at the locator. He thought that if he timed this just right, he may be able to power through. "Hang tight until I say otherwise," he said in a low voice.

He watched the soldiers on the screen rushing towards them. Just as they were about to round the corner, he sprinted at them.

The first badge appeared, and CB hit him full force, his shoulder lowered as he plowed into him. The badge careened back into the man behind him and both tumbled to the floor.

CB kept charging forward. He hit the biggest man in the group square in the chest, smashing him against the wall. The man's head ricocheted off the concrete behind him and he slumped to the ground, unconscious.

One down. But the two he'd plowed over were already trying to get up.

The fourth and final badge raised his weapon, but CB was already entangled with the other two, making it impossible for the man to get a clear shot without hitting his fellow badges. He tried to track CB with his gun, but the fight was too chaotic.

He was so focused on CB that he didn't see Jessica creeping up to him, a baton taken from one of the fallen badges clutched in her hand. She swung it hard, connecting with the back of his head and taking him out of the fight.

Brian was trying his best to help, too. After CB scored a monster blow on one of the badges' knee, Brian kicked him as he fell. His foot only delivered a glancing blow to the man's side, but CB appreciated the effort.

The badge managed to struggle to a standing position, and he threw a hard punch, hitting Brian in the stomach. Brian doubled over and fell to his knees, gasping for air. The guard snatched the baton off his belt and raised it, ready to bring it down on the back of Brian's head.

CB made a move toward the badge, but Jessica struck before he could get there, bringing her baton down on the badge's wrist. There was a loud crack, and his arm bent at an odd angle. His baton clattered to the ground.

Jessica struck again, hitting him in the side of the head, and he went down.

Brian stared up at her in wide-eyed surprise, still struggling to regain the wind that had been knocked out of him.

"Come on, we have to go." She grabbed Brian's hand and assisted him as he got to his feet.

CB quickly followed them as they raced down the passageway toward the access hatch.

Brian checked the echolocation device as he ran. "They're not... far... behind us," he choked out between gasps.

A moment later, his point was proven as the badges who'd first spotted them through the access panel rounded the corner behind them.

One of them had a radio to his mouth. "Looks like they took out Phil's team. They're right under Sparrow's Ridge."

CB, Brian, and Jessica kept running, focusing on the ladder that would take them up to street level and trying to ignore the men chasing them. They didn't have much farther to go. They just had to push a little longer.

CB reached the ladder that led up to the hatch first. "Get up there. I'll be right behind you."

The other two didn't bother arguing. It would have been a waste of the precious time they couldn't afford. Brian went up the ladder, and Jessica quickly followed.

The badges approached at a dead run, and one of them fired. The shot was wild, as CB would have expected a shot fired by a running man to be. CB raised his own weapon, leveling it at them. He aimed at the oldest man in the group, thinking he'd likely be the team leader.

He fired, and his aim was true. The shot hit the badge in the knee, and the man dropped to the ground, screaming.

The other badges ducked back behind the corner, trying to avoid taking a bullet in the leg, or worse.

CB knew he wouldn't have long until they recovered their courage. He quickly climbed the ladder and came up through the hatch. Brian and Jessica were waiting for him.

"We heard the shots," Jessica said. "You all right?"

CB nodded. "I was one of the people doing the shooting, this time." He paused for a moment, then quickly added, "Don't worry, I was careful."

"You'd better have been," Jessica muttered.

CB looked around, taking in their surroundings. They were on the first level of the sanitation building in a large, open room. They were near the wall, and thankfully the room appeared to be empty.

His eyes settled on a locker full of gear, and he ran to it. Then he dragged it back and placed it over the hatch. "There. That'll make it difficult for the badges to follow us."

"We should keep moving," Brian said. "They've probably already radioed in our location."

CB couldn't argue with that.

They ran to the nearest door.

"This way," Jessica said, pointing to a door to their right. "If I remember correctly, we can get to an exit through here."

CB was the first to reach the door. "Hopefully, we can blend in on the streets of the Ridge without attracting too much attention. If we're lucky, we might be able to make it all the way to the hangar without the wrong people spotting us."

He pulled open the door and froze.

Standing on the other side of it, a raised gun in his hand, was Colonel Kurtz.

21

CB AND KURTZ froze in surprise as they stared at each other.

Jessica didn't. She wrapped her arms around CB's midsection and pushed her shoulder into him, shoving him out of the path of Kurtz's weapon. Kurtz gritted his teeth and fired.

The round echoed like thunder off the walls around them, and CB waited, expecting to feel the impact of the bullet. But the pain never came. Instead, Jessica cried out, and a different kind of pain filled CB.

The bullet hole in Jessica's forearm seeped dark blood. She stumbled backwards, clutching her arm.

The rage erupted from CB in a wordless shout. He grabbed Kurtz's wrist, twisting it up and away. The gun went off, but the shot was wide, and it ricocheted off the wall behind them.

Kurtz tried to pull his arm out of CB's grip, but CB was simply too powerful. He twisted the wrist again, much harder this time, until there was a pop.

Kurtz yelped in pain and his hand went slack, letting the

gun fall to the ground. CB drew his left arm back and slammed his elbow into Kurtz's face, breaking his jaw.

Kurtz staggered backward, blinking hard in a futile attempt to clear the tears from his eyes. To Kurtz's credit, he didn't go down easily, which made CB happy. He wasn't done with Kurtz yet.

As CB stalked toward him, Kurtz pulled his baton from his belt with his uninjured hand and shifted to a defensive stance. CB glanced at the baton. It was the same type the faceless GMT used.

Kurtz swung the baton, but CB surged forward, catching the other colonel's wrist and bringing the arm down hard even as he swung his knee upward. He slammed the wrist into his knee and heard it snap.

With two broken wrists, Kurtz collapsed to his knees, clutching both arms to his chest. CB threw a hard right hook that connected with his temple, knocking him unconscious.

With the colonel down, CB frantically turned back to Jessica. He was relieved to see Brian was already tending to her.

"The bullet went straight through," Brian said. "If we can stop the bleeding, she'll be okay. Hand me some of those shop towels." He gestured to a folded stack of towels on a counter just inside the door.

CB quickly grabbed a few and dashed back to Brian.

"I'm fine," Jessica said. She looked pale and her voice sounded weak. "We need to keep moving."

"Not until we get this arm wrapped," Brian said firmly.

CB stood silently watching, feeling helpless as a sick sense of worry crept up inside him. He'd seen plenty of injuries in his time with the GMT, and more death than he cared to remember, but this felt different, somehow. Jessica wasn't a soldier, who'd volunteered for a mission to the surface to fight vampires. She was an engineer, who was just trying to do the right thing by her city. The fact that Fleming had brought so much pain and destruction to *New Haven* made CB furious. And the mere thought of Jessica paying the ultimate price in the fight to stop him made him sick with dread.

He'd carried a torch for Jessica a long time, but over recent weeks it had grown into something deeper. He truly cared about her, and the thought of her dying scared him in a way that he'd never quite felt before.

Brian finished bandaging the arm as best as he could with the towel. "All right, I think that will do for now."

"Good," Jessica said. "If you two are done fussing over me, let's get moving."

CB helped her to her feet. As they moved through the door into the work area, she put her good arm around his shoulders, leaning on him as they walked. Six workers dressed in identical orange jumpsuits and hard hats turned toward them.

"Guess we forgot to use the echolocator to make sure the path was clear," CB grumbled.

"Uh, yeah, my fault," Brian said softly. "Sorry about that."

The workers stared at them, no one speaking.

Screw it, CB thought. They'd been spotted. Nothing to do now but put his faith in the people of Sparrow's Ridge.

"My name's Arnold Brickman," he said. "You can call me CB. As you may have heard, I've had some trouble with the authorities recently. My friends and I are trying to bring Fleming down, but we find ourselves in a bit of a tight spot. The badges are turning the city upside down looking for us, and we need a little help."

For a long moment, no one spoke.

Then one of the workers, a woman who looked to be in her late fifties, turned to the others. "What are you waiting for? CB needs our help."

Five minutes later, CB, Jessica, and Brian walked out of the sanitation building, dressed in orange jumpsuits and wearing hardhats, and stepped onto the crowded streets of Sparrow's Ridge.

Five beams of light cut through the darkness in the storm tunnel under Denver. They shifted and bobbed as the GMT members moved, the light from their headlamps the only illumination.

Igor led the way, Firefly dangling from one hand. So far, Jaden's plan had worked beautifully. Firefly's physical discomfort at his perceived betrayal grew as they got closer and closer to his masters. They knew which turns to take by his squirms.

The group mostly walked in silence, the vampires still in shock at the loss of Robert, and the humans conflicted at the current state of their former teammate.

The silence was suddenly broken as a voice crackled in Alex's ear. In the quiet of the tunnel, even the other humans could hear Owl's staticky voice coming through the earpiece.

"Alex, we got it."

"You fixed the ship?" Alex asked.

"Yep. It was a bit trickier than I'd expected. The person who sabotaged this thing wasn't messing around. We had to jury-rig a couple components, but we're up and running."

"That's fantastic." She spoke softly, not wanting to give away their location to any enemies who might be lurking nearby. "Get everything ready for takeoff. We might not have the luxury of being able to give you much notice before we head your way. We have a job to finish, and then we will be right up."

"Copy that. Stay safe out there."

After she signed off, Jaden slowed his pace a bit, falling in beside her. There was just enough room for two to walk side by side on the walkway. It didn't take a keen understanding of vampire physiology to know he'd heard every word of her conversation with Owl.

"Alex, we don't have a lot of time before dark," he said. "I think you and your team should head up and get back to your ship."

She raised an eyebrow in surprise. "What, and miss out on the fun? I thought you needed our help."

"We did. And you helped plenty. You got Natalie and Igor back to us."

"Okay, but the job's not over yet." She was acutely aware that everyone on both the Agartha team and the GMT were listening closely to this conversation.

"Indeed. But honestly, this job is better suited for vampires. I know it's not what you want to hear, but it's true. With all the Ferals down here, we stand a better chance without you. Not to mention Mark and Aaron. They'll be able to smell your human scent when we get close." He stopped and turned toward her. "You and your team have held your own so far, but we both know things will be different after sundown. Facing a vampire, Feral or intelligent, at night is an impossible task for any human. Go to your ship. We'll meet you in Agartha when we've finished here."

Alex opened her mouth to respond, but Jaden spoke before she could.

"I respect your desire to see the mission through, but I am going to take the choice out of your hands. If you and your team don't climb up the nearest ladder and get into the safety of the daylight, I am going to wake every Feral in these tunnels. I would rather not do that, but I need your team gone."

"Jaden, don't be an idiot. We can help."

He turned to Natalie. "Do you have Firefly's gun?"

"Right here, boss." She held up the weapon, aiming the barrel at the ceiling of the tunnel. "Want me to fire a couple rounds?"

"That's up to Alex."

Alex stared at him for a long moment before answering. "Goddamn it, Jaden. Fine. You want us gone? We're out of here. GMT, let's head topside."

In the beam of her headlamp, she saw a ladder not far ahead. From what Alex could see of her teammates' faces, they didn't look too pleased about this turn of events.

Chuck was the first one up the ladder. When he reached the top, he called down, "You undead types might want to watch yourselves. Sunlight incoming."

The vampires jumped back as he lifted the manhole cover and light streamed into the tunnel.

Wesley scurried up after Chuck, then Patrick moved to the foot of the ladder. He paused and said, "Man, I was really looking forward to fighting a nest of intelligent vampires under the city. That's the kind of mission every little boy dreams about."

His brother patted him on the back. "Don't worry, buddy. You'll get your chance."

Alex rolled her eyes and nodded toward the manhole. "Get moving, you two."

As she climbed out onto the street, Alex checked her watch. They still had over an hour before sunset.

She saw the transport truck less than a block away. She gave a wave, and it began rolling forward. When it reached them, Owl leaned out from the driver's seat, a grin on her face. "Need a ride?"

Alex climbed into the passenger seat while everyone else piled into the back. As she slid into her seat, she asked, "Is the tracker working?"

"Obviously," Owl replied. "You think I happened to be right above you?"

She tapped on the tablet on the seat between them, and an image of a map appeared with a red dot in the center. As they watched, the red dot began to move.

"Think Firefly suspects anything?" Owl asked.

"I don't think so. I'm sure he doesn't know about the tracker."

Jaden had shoved the tracker into Firefly's leg while adjusting the metal bars just after Alex had told him the plan. Firefly had been in too much pain to notice the tiny device. Or, so Alex hoped. She'd clued in the rest of the team through whispered messages, and she'd even managed a quick radio chat with Owl before they started down the tunnel with Firefly.

"Jaden did a good job making it sound like he wanted us to leave," Chuck called from the back.

"Yeah, and how about that acting performance by me?" Patrick added. "I wonder if *New Haven*'s theater company is holding auditions anytime soon. I'll bet I'd kill it on stage."

Ed looked offended. "If anyone's killing it on stage, it's me. I have the voice of an angel. Mom always told me so."

"Can we focus, please?" Alex asked. "We need to stay on top of that signal and pray the next part of the plan works."

Owl drove slowly, tracking along with the red dot on the screen. Alex watched in silence, wondering what was happening twenty-five feet below the truck's wheels.

JADEN CREPT through the tunnel at the rear of his team. He liked to be in a position where he could see the whole team and any threats that might pose a danger to them.

This was a test of his mental discipline, he knew. Between the daysickness and Robert's death, his mind was already on the verge of giving over control to his animalistic rage. To keep his mind right, he needed to keep his focus one hundred percent on the task at hand.

And then there was this crazy plan of Alex's. As soon as she'd explained it, he'd immediately disliked it. There were too many variables, too many ways it could go wrong. Two things had convinced him to agree to the plan.

Firstly, he knew that Mark and Aaron were selfish bastards, who cared about their own safety above all else. Those two would send wave after wave of their soldiers after Jaden and his team, never daring to risk their own physical safety, until the fight was truly over. Unless Jaden wanted to fight his way through the remaining two hundred Resettlers, he needed to find Mark and Aaron's location. This seemed like the best option to do so.

Secondly, and even more importantly, Jaden didn't totally trust his own judgement in his current condition. Daysickness messed with a vampire's mind, as well as his emotions. Small things could seem more important than they really were, while crucial details were easily overlooked.

Since he couldn't trust himself, he had to select someone

else to trust. He'd chosen Alex. Though he didn't know her well, he had seen evidence of her rash, sometimes immature actions. But he knew that was a byproduct of her passion. She was battle-hardened, and a capable warrior with experience in planning and executing missions.

So, even though he didn't love the plan, he'd decided to follow it. The most difficult part was still to come: trusting Alex and the GMT in battle.

Igor led the way, Firefly dangling from his hand. As they reached a cross section, Igor slowly began walking to his left, just as he'd done at every other cross section. Even from the back of the group, Jaden could see Firefly relax just a bit.

Wrong way. Igor turned back and started down the right-hand path. Firefly immediately began wriggling, desperately trying to get free. It was the strongest reaction he'd had, thus far. They were close to Firefly's masters.

Igor paused, glancing back at Jaden. The older vampire nodded, and Igor headed into the tunnel to his right.

He'd only made it a few steps before a rifle's crack split the air. At the sound of the gunshot, Igor dropped Firefly and jumped back, ducking to safety around the corner.

The rifle fired again, and Firefly let out a muffled shout.

"Wait!" one of the vampires called. "I think that's the captain!"

The sound of ten pairs of boots slapping against the tunnel floor filled the air, and Jaden grimaced. These new vampires were like a pack of wild dogs. A vampire should be able to move almost soundlessly, but these new bloods had no idea how to use their abilities. And clearly, Mark and Aaron didn't consider teaching their progeny a priority.

The thought of it stoked the fire of anger already raging in Jaden's chest. Turning a human and teaching it the ways of the vampire was a sacred duty, and it should not be taken lightly. In his long life, Jaden had only turned three humans, and each time, he'd dedicated the following hundred years to their education. That was why he now had an army of skilled warriors, instead of this rabble of armed dullards that were barely better than Ferals.

Jaden felt sorry for the Resettlers. They hadn't asked for this. He hoped he wouldn't have to kill too many more of them, but he wouldn't hesitate if the situation required his application of the deadly arts.

"Don't let them get the prisoner!" Igor shouted.

The Resettlers moved fast, grabbing Firefly and pulling him deeper into the tunnel.

Natalie sprayed a few rounds in their general direction to sell their pursuit. She even chased them a little way down the tunnel.

Igor called after them, "Don't let them get away!"

Jaden put a hand on his shoulder. "I think that's enough." Then he raised the radio to his mouth. "Alex, they took the bait. Just make sure they don't wiggle off the hook."

"We got this, Jaden," she answered. "We'll let you know when they stop."

"We'll be ready."

Natalie trotted back toward them. When she reached them, she turned to Jaden. "What do we do now?"

"We do the thing we've become so good at over the past few centuries," he answered. "We wait."

22

Alex and Owl watched as the red dot on their display stopped directly below them.

"Think this is it?" Owl asked.

"Let's hope so," Alex replied. "The sun isn't going to be up much longer, and we need to finish this before night falls and things get way more complicated. Facing a vampire army during the day is bad enough. When night arrives, these guys are going to be unstoppable."

They watched for another thirty seconds, making sure the dot wouldn't start moving again, then Alex radioed down to Jaden.

"They stopped," she said. "I think we got them."

He answered immediately, "Roger that. Give me a moment to move in and confirm."

As they waited, Alex looked around the area. They were parked in the middle of a large intersection where two wide roads crossed. Glancing around, she saw four manhole covers, one near each corner. Good. Multiple ways down meant multiple points of attack.

Still, she didn't love the thought of descending in a spot

where Mark and Aaron could see them coming. They needed something that could serve as a distraction.

"What's the plan, Captain?" Ed called from the back. "Are we going down to kill some vampires, or what?"

"Hang tight. It shouldn't be long now." She thought a moment. "Owl, remember that palace in Las Vegas?"

"The one where we almost died under three tons of sand? Yeah, I have a vague recollection. Why?"

"I'm wondering if we could use the same approach here."

Owl stared blankly for a moment. Then she got it. "Alex, we don't know exactly how large that room is down there. It would be guesswork. Assuming we could do it at all."

"Well, you are smarter than I am. Give me your best guess."

Owl looked around. "I think that the tunnels meet up here. Theoretically, I think it's doable."

Alex was about to respond when her radio crackled to life.

"Alex, the army is gathered in a large room. I'm going to see what I can do about clearing out the army so you can take out Mark and Aaron. You up for the task?"

"Get the Resettlers out, and we'll take care of those two bastards." She paused for a moment. "Think you could give us ten minutes before you make your move? I have a really dumb idea."

"Ten minutes, no more. We're losing daylight, and you don't want to face Mark and Aaron at night."

Alex couldn't disagree. She remembered Firefly's story about how those two had taken out three hundred Resettlers in a matter of minutes. "Roger that. And make sure your vampires are out of the room before you send the signal. We'd hate to accidentally kill your people."

"I would also hate that. Wait for the signal and then attack. Good luck, Alex."

"Same to you, Jaden." She turned to her team, wishing she'd thought of this plan sooner. They'd have to move quickly now. "Owl, drive the transport about a block away. Chuck and Wesley, use your cutters to get down a foot or two into the street and fill it with enough explosives to collapse a tunnel. Everyone else with me."

The team got to work, moving quickly, aware that the signal from Jaden could come at any moment. Alex didn't know if the explosion would allow enough sunlight down into the tunnel to make a difference, but it would be one hell of a distraction, and it might give them an alternative route from which to attack.

She just prayed Jaden could come through on his end of the plan to draw the Resettlers away. The whole point of this was to save the Resettlers, and it would sort of defeat the purpose if the lot of them died in a hail of gunfire.

When Wesley and Chuck finished cutting their hole in the pavement, they loaded it with explosives from Wesley's pack.

"This might be overkill," Wesley said.

"This is the rare case when I say, better too many explosives than too few," Alex replied.

"Then I guess we're ready," Wesley said.

Patrick and Chuck waited by one of the manhole covers, and Alex and Ed waited by another. Wesley and Owl stood by a third manhole cover, ready to climb down as soon as the explosives were detonated.

They were in position and ready. All they needed was the go signal from Jaden.

FIREFLY GROANED, unable to get any words out around the gag in his mouth, though his body desperately wanted to shout. He had information that could possibly help his masters, and everything, from the metal rods through his limbs to the shoulder wound he'd sustained when his soldiers accidentally shot him, took a backseat to that.

His orders had been to get information on Jaden and his team's whereabouts. Now he had that information, and his body needed to obey.

But all that came out were muffled grunts.

Jaden had done a thorough job of stuffing Firefly's T-shirt down his throat. If Firefly had still needed to breathe, he'd have been in serious trouble. As it was, the lack of air bothered him far less than his inability to speak.

Two of the Resettlers carried him, one supporting his legs and the other lifting him by the shoulders. As vampires, they were each certainly capable of carrying him alone, but both probably wanted credit from their masters for bringing him back.

They entered the wide area where Mark and Aaron waited, surrounded by over one hundred of their soldiers. The rest of the army must have been searching the tunnels, Firefly figured.

The large, circular room had a raised walkway around the perimeter. The rest of the room was an open area, presumably where rainwater gathered, fed by the three smaller tunnels before flowing out of the larger fourth. Two sets of stairs led up from the main area to the walkway.

The two masters stood on the raised walkway, their backs to the wall, observing the room in front of them. From their perch, they could clearly see the entrance to every tunnel.

As the vampires carrying Firefly entered, the Resettlers all raised their weapons.

"Don't shoot!" the vampire carrying Firefly's legs shouted. "It's us. And we have Firefly."

Mark and Aaron squinted down at Firefly's sorry condition.

"What the hell happened to you?" Aaron asked.

Firefly tried his best to answer but he was still unable to speak with the gag shoved down his throat.

Mark said, "Get that crap out of his mouth and get the metal bars out of him."

The soldiers did as they were commanded.

Firefly groaned in pain as they pulled the metal rods from his arms and legs. As soon as they were out, he tried to stand, but he quickly fell back down. The gunshot wound in his shoulder was already nearly healed, but his legs and arms would take longer to recover.

One of the soldiers, a man Firefly recognized as Dustin, pulled him to a standing position and helped him maintain it.

Mark frowned down at him. "Give us a report, Captain."

Firefly told them how he had located Jaden and his team, along with the GMT from *New Haven*.

At the mention of the GMT, a murmur ran through the room. Every one of the Resettlers respected the GMT, and most were just realizing that they might have to fight them. Jaden and his vampires were an unknown quantity to the majority who hadn't faced them the previous night, but all of them knew the GMT. And they were clearly afraid.

After Firefly explained who the GMT were to Mark and Aaron, the two vampires scoffed.

"Vampire hunters, huh?" Mark asked. "Please. They're

human. We have nothing to fear from them. Tell us what happened next."

He told them how he had killed Robert, which brought a smile to their faces, and how he'd been captured, which removed those smiles. He explained that the GMT had left the tunnels and was headed back to Agartha.

When he finished, Mark turned to the soldiers who'd brought Firefly back. "How did you manage to rescue the captain?"

One of the soldiers responded, "We heard them coming down one of the tunnels. As soon as they rounded the corner, we opened fire, and they dropped him."

"Nice work. At least someone around here can do something right." Mark glared at Firefly.

Aaron thought for a moment. He looked at the soldiers who had brought Firefly back. They must have been around twenty years old, and they didn't have the look of battle-hardened warriors. "Doesn't it seem a little strange that these children got the drop on Jaden and his vamps? And that he'd abandon his prize so easily? Something's not right, here."

As Aaron finished speaking, an object whizzed through the air and landed with a metallic clink in the middle of the room.

Every eye turned toward it, spotting the grenade a split second before it exploded.

———

As soon as the grenade exploded, Jaden surged forward, rushing through the tunnel and into the room where Mark and Aaron's vampire army was gathered. He quickly scanned the area and saw that the effect of the grenade he'd thrown was even more devastating than he'd expected.

Alex had given Jaden the grenade, as well as the tracker. As much as Jaden enjoyed keeping things simple with his sword and his fists, he had to admit that a little technology was nice to have, occasionally. After the infestation and the complete failure of technology to save the humans, Jaden had soured on it, but perhaps it was time to give human tech another chance.

He'd instructed his vampires to avoid killing the Resettlers whenever possible, but it looked like the explosion had taken out at least one of them. Eight others were on the ground, with various injuries. Apparently, *New Haven's* brand of grenades was quite a bit more powerful than the ones Jaden had used back in the pre-infestation days. They must have an excellent weapons department turning out all these little gadgets.

The rest of the vampires inside the room reeled, momentarily stunned by pain the thunderous explosion caused in already daysick heads. It didn't feel so great to Jaden either, but at least he'd been prepared.

Two guards stood between him and the main part of the room, and they'd been far enough from the explosion that they still had their wits about them. They raised their weapons as Jaden charged.

Even though the purpose of this mission was to save the Resettlers, Jaden knew he wasn't going to be able to get out of this without hurting a few of them. He held a sword in one hand and his other one was empty. He swung at the guard on the left, and his blade cut cleanly through the vampire's wrist. The hand fell, and Jaden snaked out his own hand and snatched the vampire's gun before it hit the ground.

The other guard trained the barrel of his weapon on him, and Jaden had no choice but to defend himself. He quickly removed the vampire's head.

His way cleared, he spun toward Mark and Aaron. He'd only get one chance at this. Though it was Alex and the GMT's job to take care of Mark and Aaron, Jaden wasn't about to let this opportunity slip by. He rushed forward, bringing the pistol he'd stolen up as he ran. He took aim at Mark and fired.

A vampire leaped into the air, throwing herself into the path of the bullet. The round struck her in the chest, and she tumbled to the ground. Jaden fired three more rounds in quick succession, but two vampires dove in front of Mark, protecting their master.

Jaden cursed silently. That was it. He was out of time. If he messed around in here much longer, the vampires would swarm him. As it was, he was already going to have a difficult time making it safely back into the tunnel. Thankfully, every eye in the room was on him now. Attacking one of their masters had been an excellent way to get their attention.

He turned and booked it toward the tunnel from which he'd emerged. Every vampire had been focused on staying between Jaden and the masters, so his path was clear. He quickly reached the tunnel and ducked into it.

"Get him!" Mark screamed. "Take him down!"

The rumble of nearly two hundred pairs of boots hitting the ground in unison shook the concrete.

"Time to move," Jaden said as he reached his waiting friends.

His vampires fell in step behind him, racing down the tunnel. Only Natalie held back for a moment, peppering the approaching vampires with gunfire to keep their interest and sell the retreat.

As he ran, Jaden heard Aaron calling in the distance.

"Wait!" the vampire master yelled. "This could be a trick. You twelve, stay here and protect us in case Jaden doubles back."

Damn, that wasn't good. Alex and the GMT's job had just gotten a whole lot harder.

Though trusting humans to come through in a pinch hadn't always paid off for Jaden in the past, he didn't see how he had much choice this time. He raised his radio to his mouth. "Alex, we got most of them out, but twelve are hanging back with Mark and Aaron."

"We're on it," Alex immediately replied. "You just keep moving. See you when this is done."

Jaden clipped the radio to his belt and hoped the GMT was as good as they thought they were. They were about to face fourteen vampires.

In the distance, Jaden heard a howl. Dozens of more howls responded to the call.

Those sounds could only mean one thing. The Ferals were joining the fight.

"Blow the lid off, Wesley," Alex ordered.

Wesley hesitated just a moment, scanning his teammates to make sure they were in position. "Fire in the hole."

He hit the detonator.

A massive explosion rocked the street, sending asphalt and concrete shooting in all directions. It rained down around the GMT like hail. They all huddled behind cover and waited for the debris to stop falling.

Alex ducked her head out and saw that Wesley's explosives had succeeded in opening a massive crater in the road. As the last rocks clattered to the ground around them, she called to the team. "Let's move!"

She didn't have to ask twice. They'd grown antsy listening to the explosion and gunfire below the street as Jaden drew the soldiers away, and now they were primed for battle. At Alex's orders, they sprang into action.

Patrick pulled aside the manhole cover and disappeared downward, Chuck right behind him. Wesley and Owl ran down theirs as well.

Alex was about to start down her manhole when she glanced at the hole in the pavement. Part of the street had collapsed, forming a ramp down into the storm drain. "Ed, follow me."

She ran to the top of the ramp and started downward. The scene below was chaos. Vampires darted around, confused, dodging the thin beams of sunlight that made their way down from the street. Others were struggling to free themselves from the rubble under which they were pinned.

All of that was to be expected, but there was one thing that Alex hadn't expected, and it took her a moment to process what was happening. Dark figures were pouring into the room from the tunnels, attacking the vampires.

Ferals, she realized. The Ferals were attacking.

She saw two figures standing on the raised walkway, dressed differently from everyone else. Rather than the Resettlement outfits, they wore clothing Alex had seen on the vampires working in Agartha.

These had to be Mark and Aaron.

The vampires who'd turned Firefly and so many others. The vampires who'd caused all this trouble, who'd forced

Firefly to kill Robert. The same vampires who'd killed Drew outside Agartha on that evening that felt so long ago now.

She jumped from the ramp onto the walkway. Then she raised her pistol in a two-handed grip, took aim at the taller of the two vampires, and fired, putting a bullet into the vampire master's chest.

23

As the world exploded around him, Firefly struggled to his feet. It was incredible how fast his limbs were healing after his being impaled mere hours before. He might have taken time to marvel at this occurrence if the ceiling weren't caving in.

They were under assault from all sides, it seemed. First Jaden had lobbed a grenade into the middle of the room, hacked at a couple vampires, and run back out again. Then Mark and Aaron had ordered him and eleven others to stay and protect them. Another huge explosion had rocked his already throbbing head. Then Ferals had poured in from all sides, and—most shockingly of all—the GMT had dropped in from above.

Firefly leaped into action, his body moving without thought, his injuries forgotten. His masters were in danger, and he would tear his own body to shreds if it meant obeying his orders to protect them.

Instinctively, he grabbed the weapon off the vampire who'd been killed by Jaden's grenade and raised it, preparing to fire at the nearest threat. It was Patrick, that obnoxious shotgun-toting GMT member, scurrying through one of the manholes and down the ladder. Firefly gritted his teeth as he took aim, knowing he had no choice but to fire on the man.

But then something strange happened. Out of his periphery, he saw a Feral rushing in the general direction of Mark and Aaron. The urge to destroy this Feral was just as strong as the urge to destroy Patrick. Both posed a serious threat to his masters, and each needed to be eliminated.

The order he'd been given had been to protect his masters, he realized. Mark and Aaron hadn't instructed him to focus on any target in particular. And in the gray area of that order, he found something he'd never expected: he found free will.

He spun toward the Feral and fired, putting a round through the creature's head. No sooner had the first Feral fallen than he saw five more charging down the tunnel behind it.

To his right, he saw Owl and Wesley climbing down another ladder, and he felt the urgent tug of his body's wanting to destroy them. But he quickly realized that if he kept his focus on the Ferals and imagined how much damage they could do to Mark and Aaron if they reached them, he could overcome the urge to go after the GMT members.

He truly believed that the Ferals posed just as great a threat to his masters as the GMT, and that made all the difference.

As he took down two other Ferals, he saw some of his soldiers going after the GMT members. He had to find a way to stop them without disobeying orders.

"Resettlers, listen up!" he shouted. "We've been ordered

to protect our masters, and our masters are in danger from the Ferals. Protect Mark and Aaron! Kill the Ferals!"

The soldiers looked at Firefly, some of them seemingly surprised by the order. A few of them nodded, understanding what he was trying to do. But all of them turned their attention on the Ferals and fought back the wave pouring through every tunnel.

ALEX STEADIED her pistol and fired again, sending a second slug into the tall vampire master's chest. He staggered backward, struggling to maintain his balance, but after a moment he toppled onto his ass.

As he fell, she risked a look around. Firefly and the remaining Resettlers were focused on the Ferals pouring into the room. That was the good news. The bad news was that most of her team was, as well. They were all fighting to keep the seemingly endless tide of Ferals from making it into the room and destroying them all.

"Mark!" she heard the other vampire master cry out.

It was always good to know who you were killing. Alex turned back to Mark. He was still on the ground, which was a good sign, but there was no way in hell that she was going to assume that he was dead until she'd removed his head from his shoulders.

As she raced toward him, she saw something in her periphery: a Feral leaping at her.

She spun, raising her pistol and putting a quick two rounds into the creature's head. Her shots were effective, killing the Feral, but that didn't stop its forward momentum.

The Feral's corpse slammed into her chest. She tumbled backward, going over the railing and tumbling off the raised platform where the vampire masters stood. She hit the ground below hard, the heavy, rancid creature landing on top of her.

There was one rule that applied to fights of every scale, from sparring matches in the GMT training facility to massive battles with undead hordes in the storm drains under the ancient city of Denver: you never wanted to find yourself lying on your back.

She struggled to get out from under the dead Feral. To her right, she saw an especially large Feral loping toward her, its teeth bared.

A gun nearby fired three times, and the running Feral went down. Owl lowered her pistol and held out a hand to Alex.

"Guess I'm good for more than just flying the ship, after all," the pilot said with a smile.

"I never doubted it for a minute," Alex replied, taking her friend's hand. Owl pulled, and Alex managed to wriggle out from under the dead Feral.

When she got to her feet, she looked around and took in the chaotic scene. Firefly's vampires were still focused on fighting the Ferals, but more and more of the mindless creatures were making it into the room, now.

She looked to her right and saw the last vampire guarding the tunnel go down, overwhelmed by five Ferals piling on top of him. The eight Ferals behind them pushed past, their eyes fixed on Alex and Owl.

"Heads up, Owl." Alex raised her pistol with one hand and drew her sword with the other. She knew that eight Ferals would be too much for the two of them, but there was no way that she was going down without taking as many of those bastards with her as possible.

The sound of automatic fire came from her left, and

three of the Ferals went down in a hail of bullets. Then a shotgun blast took out another.

Alex turned and saw Patrick, Ed, Wesley, and Chuck all converging on the spot where they stood.

"Circle up!" Chuck shouted. "I want every quadrant covered!"

The four of them stood back-to-back, unleashing death on any Ferals who approached from any direction.

A wave of pride ran through Alex, but she pushed it aside. There was no time. If they survived this, she would let them know how amazing they were. But there was a lot that needed to be done before that could happen.

She glanced up at the platform where the masters stood. She couldn't see either of them from her location. "Cover me, Owl."

"You got it."

She dashed up the steps, and as she reached the top, she saw Mark lying where he'd fallen after she shot him. Aaron, however, was nowhere to be seen.

She heard a snarl from behind her.

"Alex, look out!" Owl shouted.

Alex turned just in time to see Aaron flying at her.

She raised her pistol and squeezed off two shots. The vampire moved with uncanny speed, dodging the first shot completely and moving out of the way of the second far enough that it just barely grazed his arm.

And still, Aaron came.

From below, a Feral leaped up at her, but it fell before Alex had even fully registered it, thanks to a bullet hole in its head. She'd have to remember to thank Owl for that one later.

Alex trained her pistol on Aaron again, but before she could fire, he reached her. He lashed out, knocking the gun from her hand. She let it go, shifting her sword to a two-handed grip.

Aaron let out an animalistic snarl and drew back his hand.

If he'd thrown a simple punch, his quickness probably would have allowed him to land the blow, but drawing back his hand telegraphed the motion to Alex. He struck hard, clearly trying to quite literally knock her head off, but Alex was ready.

She sidestepped and the strike went wide, missing her completely. He was momentarily off-balance, and Alex was not going to let an advantage like that slip by.

She brought her sword up, swinging at his neck.

Even off balance, he could dodge. But not far enough. The sword clipped his neck, slicing a half inch into the skin.

The vampire's eyes widened, and his hand went to the wound, a look of shock on his face. The shock quickly dissolved, replaced by an expression of pure fury.

"Kill this woman!" Aaron bellowed.

At the sound of the order, every vampire in the room turned toward Alex.

FIREFLY WAS ENGAGED in a vicious fight with a Feral when the order came. Thankfully, he was pulling the trigger and firing a bullet into the Feral's brain when Aaron's words hit his ears. Otherwise, he surely would have turned to Alex, the danger from the Feral forgotten, and attempted to shoot her even as the creature right in front of him tore him to shreds.

"Kill this woman!"

Firefly raised his weapon as the Feral he'd been fighting

fell, and he raced across the room, every fiber of his being suddenly dedicated to getting a clear shot at his friend, Alex Goddard.

But Alex was no dummy. It was clear that she instantly understood what Aaron's order meant. By the time Firefly turned toward her, she was already in motion, putting Aaron between herself and the ten remaining vampire soldiers who had a biological imperative to kill her.

"Protect Alex!" Chuck shouted.

The GMT shifted their focus from the Ferals still rushing into the room to the vampires targeting their captain. Not that it mattered. Firefly knew the GMT members could pepper the soldiers with bullets all they wanted, but unless they struck a killing shot, the vampires would ignore their injuries and follow their orders.

Up on the platform, Alex was avoiding the vampires' attacks. Between their master and the Ferals flooding the room, the Resettlers couldn't get off a decent shot.

From his place down below, Firefly saw a look of fiery resolve on Alex's face, and something deep inside him smiled. She wasn't giving up. In fact, quite the opposite. Aaron had succeeded in severely pissing her off. She'd try to end this quickly, he knew.

She drew back her sword and thrust it forward. Aaron raised a hand to protect himself, and the blade sank straight through his palm.

Firefly saw the struggle on both their faces. Aaron attempted to grip the blade with his other hand even as Alex pushed, driving the tip closer to his chest. She pressed hard, gaining ground centimeter by centimeter.

Then Aaron lashed out with his foot, kicking her square in the chest. She managed to keep her grip on her sword as she flew backward, and the blade sliced Aaron's hand in half. He cried out, staring at the wide slit that had appeared in his hand.

Alex flew backward ten feet and hit the concrete wall, then slid to the ground.

Firefly immediately took aim. He finally had a clear shot at her.

She struggled to her knees, fighting for every breath.

He told himself he would not fire. He forbade himself from shooting. He put everything he had into stopping himself from pulling that trigger. The world around him seemed to fade. All that was left was him and his weapon. He fought the urge to fire like a man riding a rocket. He felt thick blood trickle from his ears and his nose, but he pushed that aside, too. All that mattered was that he didn't shoot Alex.

For a wonderful moment, he thought he might win. But then he realized he was already pulling the trigger.

"No!" someone shouted.

As he fired, he saw movement out of the corner of his eye.

Chuck dove in front of Alex. Firefly's bullet slammed into him, and he collapsed to the ground.

AS THE BULLET HIT CHUCK, Aaron charged at Alex, his teeth bared. He looked almost feral.

She gasped, struggling for breath, her friend and teammate fallen by her side. This would be over in a moment, she knew. The vampire charging at her was damn fast, even during the day.

Time seemed to stop for Alex, and she pushed aside both her grief for her friend and the way her lungs were screaming for oxygen. She thought of Simmons and the tender way he used to hold her at night, his body pressed against hers. She thought of Drew, his boyish enthusiasm, and the way he'd turn even the direst situation into a game. She thought of Hope and the potential within her to be a great GMT member. She thought of CB and the way he'd fought his way back after losing his entire team to Ferals in a single night, only to inspire and lead an entire generation of GMT hopefuls.

But most of all, she thought of the people of *New Haven*. That was what she was fighting for. The very future of humanity. If Mark and Aaron won today, they'd probably target Agartha first. Once they'd brought that city down, they'd turn their attention to *New Haven*. And when they had those two cities, they'd have every human on Earth in their grasp.

All of this flashed through her mind in an instant.

She set her jaw with grim determination and sprung to her feet, bringing up her sword as she stood. Then she swung, aiming not for where Aaron was, but where he'd be in a moment.

Her blade sang as it flashed through the air, and it struck its target, slicing cleanly through Aaron's neck. The vampire master's head separated from his body and flew through the air, hitting the wall behind Alex with a thud, that terrifying snarl still frozen on his face.

As the vampire master's body fell, Alex went down on one knee, still gasping for breath.

She looked around, and she saw the expressions of the faces of the vampires in the room change, much of the tension leaving them. Firefly wiped at the inky black blood leaking from his nose with the back of his hand.

"Resettlers!" Firefly shouted. "Take out the Ferals!"

"Firefly," Wesley called. "West tunnel!" He nodded toward a tunnel that had been left unprotected when the vampires turned their focus on Alex; it seemed to be the main spot through which the Ferals were getting in.

Patrick and Ed moved up to the platform, trying to position themselves to better protect Alex. Wesley and Owl stayed on the steps leading up to the platform, laying down heavy fire from above, while Firefly and his team attacked the west tunnel.

They fought together, vampire and GMT, all focused on the same goal.

Alex struggled back to her feet and drew a painful breath. She stumbled over to Chuck.

He was still breathing, but he was bleeding badly from a massive wound on the inside of his left shoulder. The bullet had gone all the way though. He was still conscious, but he looked pale and not entirely alert.

The blood seemed to be driving the Ferals into an even greater frenzy. Alex knew that any Feral in the area who wasn't already headed their way soon would be.

Ed reached the platform, scooped Chuck off the ground and threw him over his shoulder. "Alex, can you make it on your own?"

She drew in a painful breath and took a step toward him. "You think I'm going to puss out on you, Ed?" They had to get out of here fast. The daylight wouldn't last much longer, and they needed to be gone before it was. "GMT! Let's move out!"

As she was turning toward the ramp leading to street level, a figure stepped into her path.

Mark.

There were two holes in his shirt where she'd shot him, but the flesh underneath was almost healed. From the looks of things, her bullets had missed his heart by mere inches.

He smiled joylessly as he stared at Alex. Then he opened his mouth and bellowed a command. "Everyone! Listen to me!"

That was as far as he got before the upper half of his head disappeared, and a splatter of brain matter and bone hit the wall next to him.

Patrick chambered another round as smoke trailed out of his shotgun barrel. "Nah. I only listen to Alex."

All around the room, the Resettlers staggered, as if they'd just been released from heavy weights attached to their arms and legs.

"We're free," Firefly said, his voice filled with wonder. "We're really free." He shook his head, clearing it, then grabbed the radio off his belt. "Resettlers! Quit chasing Jaden and get back here! The GMT needs our help."

Alex started up the ramp leading to the street, then hesitated, looking back at Firefly. Their eyes met and neither said anything for a long moment. They'd been through so much together. They'd been teammates, friends, rivals, enemies, and allies. And in the end, they'd saved each other.

Finally, Firefly spoke. "Alex, go! We got this!"

Alex nodded quickly, turned, and charged up the ramp into the dying evening light.

The GMT raced to the transport truck, half a block away. When they reached it, Alex hopped into the passenger seat and turned to Owl. "Get us to the away ship, fast."

"On it," Owl said as she threw the truck into gear and started moving.

Alex spoke into her radio. "George, you there?"

It took a moment before he responded. "Alex? I'm beyond happy to hear your voice."

"Get the ship ready to fly. We'll be there in two minutes."

"Good timing," he replied. "I was just about to leave without you, but then I remembered I have no idea how to fly this damn thing." His voice grew more serious. "Alex, you have to hurry. We don't have much daylight left. We're going to be cutting this razor-close."

"Don't worry," Alex answered. "We do this all the time."

As the transport roared toward the away ship, Alex could hear howls erupting all around them. The Ferals were now very aware of the humans in the city. Between the noise of the battle and the powerful emotions that had to be surging through the Ferals they'd fought in the tunnel, Alex was willing to bet that there were thousands of the creatures waiting to attack. That wasn't even considering the smell of the blood splattered all over them from Chuck's gunshot wound.

In the back, Patrick was tending to Chuck, wrapping his shoulder to stop the bleeding, but the Ferals in the buildings on either side of the street went wild as the transport drove past.

Alex looked out of her window and toward the western sky. The sun was setting and Ferals were emerging, standing in the shadows next to the buildings.

Her radio chirped to life, and George's panicked voice came through. "Alex, we're out of time! The shadows are almost to the ship, and the Ferals will be able to attack in just a minute."

Alex gritted her teeth as her heart clenched in her chest. Could it really end like this? Just blocks away from their working ship? Would they arrive just in time to see Ferals tearing the ship apart and hauling George from the wreckage?

Then the radio chirped again, but this time it was

another voice that spoke. "George, you didn't think that I would let a bunch of Ferals kill my favorite human, did you?"

"Jaden, is that you?" George asked.

"Of course. Is there another vampire who'd call you his favorite? Alex, are you listening?"

"I'm here, Jaden," she answered.

"I need you to get George airborne as quickly as possible. I'd prefer if you and your team lived, as well. I'll buy you as much time as I can, but it may not be a lot."

Alex stared out the window at the teeming masses of Ferals waiting in the shadows. "Jaden, I don't think even you and your team can hold off this many Ferals."

"Maybe not, but we're not alone. I just got a new army of nearly two hundred vampires, thanks to you, and they're itching for a fight."

The transport turned the corner, bringing the away ship into view. Hundreds of Ferals stood in the shadow of the nearest building, huddled shoulder-to-shoulder, some as close as thirty feet from the ship.

The Feral horde stood directly between the transport truck and the away ship.

"Can we go around them?" Alex asked.

Owl shook her head. "By the time we circle around, it'll be full dark. And we can't plow through without them piling onto the truck and tearing us to shreds. We need another way."

Just then, manhole covers all around the street popped up, many flying as high as five feet into the air. Jaden and his team sprang up, followed by the remaining Resettlers.

Jaden held a sword in each hand as he dashed into the horde of Ferals who were blocking the GMT's path. The other Agartha vampires followed close behind him, and together they cut a wide swath through the crowd.

Firefly and his team fanned out, firing on the Ferals at the edge of the shadows, driving them back, further from the away ship.

The Ferals were so disoriented by the smells of blood and humans that they were slow to respond to the attack. The vampires managed to take out half of the group in less than a minute. Jaden continued to slice his way through the Ferals, and soon there was a path large enough for the transport.

Owl floored it, and the transport lurched forward, racing through the Feral-infested shadows and toward the patch of sunlight where the ship sat waiting. As soon as she reached it, the GMT leaped from the truck and dashed onto the ship, where George waited with the door open for them.

George stared at the battle raging around them, his face pale. "Oh, my God. Are you guys seeing this?"

Owl pushed him aside and sprinted for the cockpit.

"Yep, it's the end of the world," Alex replied. "Unless we get airborne. Then it's just another trip to the surface." She cupped her hands around her mouth and called, "Owl, get us out of here!"

"I'm on it!" Owl shouted back. "Stop bugging me."

The team strapped into their seats, and Alex and George ran to the cockpit, where they joined Owl.

As the startup sequence finished, Owl pulled a lever and the ship lifted off the ground.

They were airborne.

"Oh, my God," George repeated. "We made it. I can't believe we made it."

Owl nodded out the cockpit window toward the vampires still battling below. "What about them?"

"They should be okay," Alex replied. "Now that we're up, they'll disengage. The Ferals should lose interest and focus on whatever drops of blood Chuck left in the transport." She allowed herself a smile. "Thank you. Both of you. If you hadn't gotten the ship running, we would have been screwed."

Owl grinned. "Pleasure's mine. Fixing the ship was the fun part. You guys missed out on the real action. George was a beast with a soldering iron."

George's brow furrowed in concern. "I'm glad we're out of there and all, but what do we do now? It's going to be pitch dark when we get back to Agartha. We gotta figure out how we're going to get past all the Ferals and get inside for the night."

Alex and Owl exchanged a glance, then Alex put a hand on George's shoulder. "I don't know how to break this to you, George, but we're not going back to Agartha. Owl, hand me that radio."

24

CB, Jessica, and Brian stopped a little way before they reached the entrance to the GMT hangar.

The walk through Sparrow's Ridge had gone surprisingly well. In their worker's jumpsuits and hardhats, the badges they'd passed had assumed they were just Ridge residents on their way home from another shift. No one had given them a second look.

Jessica held her arm limply at her side. Dried blood covered much of the arm, but the bleeding had stopped. The shock had started to wear off and she could walk on her own.

Brian stared at the door to the building. "So how do we get in? I'm pretty sure that none of our key cards are going to work."

Jessica looked at CB. "I don't suppose you have Alex's key card, too?"

"Afraid not." He paused a moment. "I hate it when important things are out of my control, but in this case, we don't have a choice. We're going to need a little faith for this one." With that, he walked over to the building and pushed the comm button. "This is Arnold Brickman. I have Jessica Bowen with me, and she needs some medical attention. I'm asking you to open the door."

A moment later, there was a buzz and a click. CB, Jessica, and Brian exchanged a nervous glance, then entered the GMT hangar.

They silently walked through the long hallway that led to the hangar. As they reached it, four men with automatic weapons stepped into their path, blocking them from entering the large, open room.

Beyond the four armed men, CB saw technicians, medical personnel, and maintenance crew. Apparently, word had gotten out that CB had arrived.

He recognized every face, and he knew every one of their names. Many of these people had worked with him for years.

He looked at the four armed men, waiting for one of them to speak.

Finally, one man said in a weak voice, "Colonel Brickman, please put down your weapons. It's over."

CB looked him straight in the eye. "It *is* over, Carl, as I'm sure you know." He spoke loudly enough that everyone in the area could hear him. "No one understands what's really happening better than the people in this room. I'm sure every one of you knows that Resettlement was a complete failure. It cost us some of the best people *New Haven* had. All because of Fleming's ego. And now he's spitting on their memories by denying that their deaths even happened."

He paused, scanning their faces with his eyes, trying to see if anyone would object. No one did, so he continued.

"Look, I don't fault any of you for following Fleming. I followed him myself, for a time. Too long, really. His grand vision pulls you in. It makes you forget about the ugly reality of what he's doing to achieve his goals. But if you look at the results of his actions, rather than listening to his pretty lies, the truth is clear. Every Resettler we sent to the surface was killed in a single night, and Fleming is lying about it."

The faces watching him wore uncomfortable expressions. Many of them looked racked with indecision. CB understood. There was no easy choice for these people. Betray the leader of the city or betray the leader of the GMT. For these patriots, either option would have been unthinkable not long ago.

Still, he was about to ask them to make that very choice.

"I have given everything to this city and its people. I know you have, too. I've trusted you with my life on many missions to the surface. Today, I need you to support me on one more mission. This one will be to save the city of *New Haven* from Fleming. I need you to fight for the very survival of the human race. Will you help me?"

The guards looked at each other, lowering their weapons slightly but not putting them down.

Finally, a voice replied from across the room. "I will help you, CB."

CB blinked hard, trying to place the man. He wore a black outfit, just like those worn by the faceless GMT, but he wasn't wearing a mask.

"Fleming sent me and my team down to Fort Stearns," the man continued. "Only two of us survived the trip. Fleming wouldn't even listen to our report." He turned to the others around him. "Everything CB said is true. We need to take Fleming down."

CB nodded slowly. He remembered the man now, from when he'd been a badge. "Thank you, Beau. And I'm sorry you went through that."

A murmur of agreement went through the room, and the four armed men lowered their weapons.

"What do you need, CB?" one of them asked.

CB smiled and gestured to Brian and Jessica.

"A terminal in the control room and a working login," Brian replied.

"The transport ship," Jessica added. "And someone who knows how to fly it. Also, a few pairs of handcuffs."

Some eyebrows raised at that, but everyone quickly went to work.

A group of technicians led Brian to the control room, practically fighting over whose login he should use.

Jessica followed a bunch of crew members to the ship to explain the plan and what they needed to do to prepare the ship.

CB wished them both luck. He knew if there was any chance of pulling this off, they were going to need all the good fortune they could get.

"What about you, Colonel?" one of the technicians asked. "What are you going to do?"

CB walked to the rarely used door at the end of the hangar and entered a code into the key pad. "I'm going to get an old friend."

AFTER INSTRUCTING the crew on the ship preparations, Jessica made her way to the control room to check in with Brian. He was already deep in the control systems he'd previously hacked, and was checking to make sure everything was ready to go.

"Brian, the transport ship is almost ready to head out. How are things looking on your end?"

Brian kept typing for a moment, before he realized that Jessica was standing there. When he looked up, he processed what she'd just said. "Yep, everything is looking good here." He glanced at her arm. "You sure you're up for this? Maybe we can get someone else to handle it."

She shook her head. "You know as well as I do, there's no one else who can do this. I've felt better, but I can keep it together long enough to take care of business." She reached out and ruffled Brian's hair. "To be honest, we're both a mess right now."

He let out a laugh. "Let's finish this and then we can sleep for a week."

"That sounds like the smartest thing any of us has said for days. I'll see you soon." With that, she made her way back into the hangar proper.

Beau, the former faceless GMT leader, stood next to the transport ship, waiting for her.

"Ready to do this?" she asked, climbing aboard.

"Uh, yeah," he said.

She raised an eyebrow. "That wasn't the most confidence-inspiring answer."

He cleared his throat. "Well, it's just... I should probably mention I've only flown this ship once before. I've only flown *anything* once before. Most of my flight time was in a simulator."

Jessica paused, not sure how to respond to that. Then she shrugged. It was too late to come up with a new plan now. If she survived the day, it would be a miracle. Might as well add flying with an inexperienced pilot to the list of foolish tasks she was undertaking.

Beau settled into the pilot's seat and started the ship as Jessica found her harness and began putting it on.

Two minutes later, the airlock opened and the ship flew into open sky.

FLEMING SAT with his head in his hands, his weary eyes glued to the monitor on his desk. He had set it to show alternating security footage of the five locations the badges and the GMT were currently focusing their efforts. He'd hoped to see his soldiers taking CB, Brian, and Jessica down, but so far all he'd seen was his people fruitlessly searching for the fugitives.

Sarah sat across from him, watching in silence. She'd given up trying to improve his mood. Fleming was losing his mind, and she was beginning to believe it was beyond her powers of persuasion to bring him back. Her only hope was that it was a temporary, stress-induced condition. If they could get through today, take down CB and his friends, and regain control of the increasingly violent protesters, then maybe things would return to normal. Maybe the Fleming she knew would come back to her.

But things seemed to be going from bad to worse. Kurtz had been found bloody and beaten in Sparrow's Ridge. He'd managed to croak out that he'd been attacked by CB before the doctors hauled him off to medical.

Losing one of his two closest advisors hadn't done much to improve Fleming's mood.

"Sir, something is happening in the GMT hangar," a voice reported on the radio. "The airlock is opening."

Fleming instantly sat up straight, his eyes alert and his pupils dilated to a degree that didn't seem normal to Sarah. "CB! He's trying to leave the city. Probably wants to reunite with his vampire allies." He touched the radio. "Get the defense turrets ready. If anything leaves that airlock, I want it blown out of the sky! In the meantime, I want the whole force of the GMT converging on the hangar. Apparently, the workers there still support their traitorous old boss."

"Yes, sir," the voice replied. "Redirecting the GMT to the hangar now."

For a tense minute, a heavy silence hung over the room. Then the voice spoke again.

"Sir, a ship has left the hangar. We're tracking them, but we, um, can't shoot them down."

Fleming's face reddened. "What do you mean you can't shoot them down? Why not?"

There was a pause before the voice responded. "We're not sure, sir. The defensive turrets aren't responding. It's like something overrode our control of the weapons."

Fleming leaped to his feet and kicked his chair, sending it skidding across the room. "Goddamn it! Track the ship. Check its trajectory. I want to know where they're headed, and I want to know it now."

"They appear to be flying alongside us, sir. They're banking wildly, but they're staying close to *New Haven*."

"What? Why would they do that?"

"I don't know, sir. It appears they're moving toward the front of the city."

"The flight deck," Sarah said, her voice tense. "The front of the ship is where the flight deck is located. They're trying to get control of *New Haven*."

Fleming's eyes widened, revealing even more of his bloodshot eyes. "Why would they want to get control of the flight deck?"

She thought a moment. "I don't know. Maybe they want to fly us to Agartha to get help from their friends there."

Fleming looked horrified at the thought. Then he gritted

his teeth. "It doesn't matter. They can't get on the flight deck. It's the most secure spot on the ship. And even if they did somehow manage to take it, there's no way they could hold it. Making a move for the flight deck would be suicide."

———

CB ENTERED the room with the glass walls and strode to the monitor, checking to see if Frank was moving. The vampire appeared to be sleeping, as he usually was when CB arrived.

Ever since Frank had transformed from a Feral to an intelligent vampire, CB had been visiting him daily, bringing him blood bags and at least a few minutes of conversation. It was clear that his century and a half of life as a Feral, mixed with the constant daylight surrounding his metal cage this entire time, had left him mentally scarred, but surprisingly, CB found him to be a kind, soft-spoken man, whose main concern was the well-being of *New Haven*.

During their conversations, CB had begun to wonder if maybe Frank's new, intelligent life was more horrible than his existence as a Feral. Frank was fully aware now, and the fact that *New Haven* was constantly in sunlight gave him a permanent case of daysickness, depriving him of the night vampires needed for their well-being. Frank was in constant pain, and he spent most of his time sleeping.

CB deeply regretted returning Frank to his intelligent form just to prove a point to Fleming, though the fact that Fleming had never once asked about Frank after that initial meeting proved how compartmentalized the leader's mind was; anything that didn't fit his specific worldview got pushed to the back, never to be thought of again.

With the flick of a switch, CB turned on the two-way comm system attached to the camera in Frank's cage.

"Frank, it's time. I need you to wake up."

CB watched on the monitor as the vampire slowly opened his eyes, wincing from the pain of the daysickness.

"Hello, CB. It's good to see you. Thank you for coming."

CB slid a blood pack through the tray, and the vampire took it and drank. As much of a rush as they were in, it only made sense to let Frank feed before they began. CB needed him at his best, and the vampire's mind always seemed a bit sharper after he'd fed.

When he'd finished, Frank passed the empty plastic pouch back through the slot to CB. "Tell me, CB, how's the city today?"

CB took a deep breath. "Honestly, things are not going great. You told me that if the time ever came that the city was in danger of destruction, you'd help me. I'm sorry to tell you, that time has come."

Frank replied with a single word. "Fleming."

"Yes." CB had filled Frank in on the goings-on in the city during their daily visits. He'd told him about the plans for Resettlement, about Fleming murdering the rest of the Council, and the way he was lying to the city. Now he just had to catch him up on the rest. He figured short and sweet would be the best approach.

"Fleming sent three hundred Resettlers to the surface two days ago. As best we can tell, they're all dead, though Fleming won't admit it. I'm a fugitive. The people are protesting in the streets and those protests will most likely turn violent soon. We need to take down Fleming, but he's very well protected."

Frank sighed, and in that sigh, CB heard a century and a half of pain and regret. It was clear that hearing this news about the city he loved and had helped to found was breaking his heart. "I wish I could help, CB. Unfortunately, daylight has a pretty bad effect on vampires."

"That's why we are about to pilot the ship into darkness."

Frank tilted his head in surprise.

"It's never been done, so no one's going to see it coming," CB continued. "You have the strength and speed to get to Fleming. We need to go over some details, but most importantly, I need to know that you are okay with doing this. Fleming is in a secured building and he is protected by a small army. There's no guarantee you'll survive."

Frank thought only a moment before answering. He spoke very clearly, looking right at the camera. "I'm not sure if you noticed, but my current living conditions aren't exactly ideal. Risking my life sounds like a welcome change from this torturous monotony. Besides, I already gave my life up for *New Haven* when I volunteered for the vampire gig. After the pain I've endured, dying to save my city is sort of the best-case scenario." He paused a moment. "Besides, I've had these vampire abilities for a century and a half. I'd really like to see what I can do with them. You get us into darkness, I'll take out Fleming."

"Thank you, Frank."

Frank nodded. Then he tilted his head as if he'd thought of something. "If I succeed in killing Fleming, what happens next?"

It was a question CB had been thinking about a lot the past couple of weeks, so he had an immediate answer. "General Craig will take over until we can hold free elections for a new Council. We'll get it done fast. A return to a normalcy will be important after everything this city's been through."

A faint smile crossed Frank's face. "I meant, what happens to me?"

"Ah, sorry." CB hadn't given much thought to that question.

"I'm not going back into this box, CB. I'd rather walk into the light than endure another day in this hell."

"I have a better idea," CB said. "There is a place on the surface that should be safe for you. It's a long story, but I think it might be a place where you could find some well-deserved peace."

"That sounds incredible. You can tell me more when this is over. For now, all that matters is saving the city. How long do we have until night falls on *New Haven*?"

"My team is working on it as we speak."

JESSICA CHECKED the cable attached to her harness one more time, then she radioed up to Beau in the cockpit. "You holding us steady?"

"Surprisingly, yes I am. We're just above the flight deck and keeping pace with the ship."

"Excellent. You're not a bad pilot, Beau. You should have Owl give you some lessons. Maybe the GMT could use a backup pilot."

"Ha. I think I may have burned my good will with the GMT by joining Fleming's pale imitation of the group."

Jessica smiled. "I think you'll find CB's the forgiving sort. But let's get through this mission first. If we can survive the next hour, something like getting on the GMT is going to be a cakewalk by comparison." She flicked the channel on her radio, bringing Brian in on the conversation. "We're in position, Brian."

"Okay, going in five seconds," Brian answered.

Jessica took a deep breath to steady her nerves, then she

put the oxygen mask over her mouth and hit the button to open the cargo door.

Air rushed out of the ship, and Jessica held on to the hand rail next to the cargo door to steady herself. Thirty feet below, she saw the ship's pilot through the glass surrounding the flight deck. The pilot had six heavily armed guards standing around him. They were all staring up at her in confusion.

"Come on, Brian, do your thing," she muttered. Then she stepped out the cargo door and began lowering herself down toward the control tower.

Though the flight deck was the most well-protected place on *New Haven*, Brian had come up with a rather elegant solution to get them inside with minimal struggle. The fire-suppression system.

Like many vital areas in *New Haven*, fire was one of the primary concerns for the flight deck, and the suppression system had been designed to deal with any blazes in a highly effective manner. The room with the fire would automatically be sealed off, and the oxygen would be sucked out of the room. This would ensure that the fire went out without damage to the vital systems.

When they were in the basement of the control tower, Brian had hacked into the fire-suppression system. It was now under his complete control.

As Jessica watched, the air rushed out of the flight deck and through a vent on top of the tower. The pilot and guards scrambled to get to the oxygen tanks, but since Brian had deactivated the warning lights, by the time they'd figured out what was happening, it was already too late.

She reached the exhaust port on the roof of the tower and waited for the air to stop rushing out. By now, Brian had activated and locked every fire door in the building, which would make getting in a real chore for any badges or GMT members Fleming sent after her.

When the air stopped rushing out of the exhaust vent, Jessica climbed in. A moment later, she popped out a ceiling panel in the control room and dropped onto the flight deck.

She took a quick moment to check her surroundings. The pilot and guards were unconscious. At least, she *hoped* they were only unconscious.

"I'm in, Brian," she said into her radio. "Want to give me a little air?"

"Roger that," he answered.

As the vents closed and the room once again filled with oxygen, Jessica moved around the room, handcuffing the pilot and guards to support posts. So far, none of them had woken up, but she wasn't about to take any chances.

Then she approached the flight controls and took off her oxygen mask. Her hands flew over the instruments as she adjusted the flight path, ignoring the warning bells that chimed in protest to the new direction in which she was sending the ship.

For the first time in its history, *New Haven* was about to enter the darkness.

———

ONCE JESSICA HAD control of the flight deck, Brian let out a whoop of joy. Then he turned his attention to making sure she could keep control of it. He tapped a few commands on the screen, and within moments, he had Fleming's personal communication feed in his left ear.

He listened with delight as Fleming and his team absolutely freaked out, trying to figure out how and why Jessica had taken control of the ship and where she was planning to fly it.

Fleming ordered every badge and faceless GMT member in the city to abandon his latest order of getting into the GMT hangar and to, instead, head for the flight deck.

"Yeah, good luck with that," Brian muttered. Between the flight deck's impressive security and Brian's control of the fire-suppression system, that was going to be no easy task.

Besides, he could pump the air out of any individual room in the control tower. If some badges did get too close, he'd just make them stop breathing.

As he was monitoring the faceless GMT's progress, one of the techs called to him. "Hey, Brian. Something's coming through on the GMT radio channel. You're going to want to hear this."

Brian blinked hard in surprise. He hated unexpected wrinkles in his well-laid-out plans. "Put it through to my headset."

The tech did so, then spoke into the radio. "This is GMT control. Could you say again?"

"Sure thing, GMT control," the voice replied. "This is Captain Alex Goddard. The GMT is incoming."

25

BRIAN CLUTCHED HIS HEADSET. "Is that really you, Alex?"

There was a long pause. "Brian? Damn, man, it's good to hear your voice. I thought Fleming would have killed you by now."

"Not yet, he hasn't," Brian said with a laugh, "though it's not for lack of trying. I thought he *had* killed you. Guess I should have known better."

"What are your coordinates? We just left the surface and we're coming your way. We figured it was time to pay Fleming a visit."

"Sending them now. We'll have the air lock in the GMT hangar open and ready for you. Assuming you get here before Fleming's guys break down the doors."

"Roger that. Owl says we'll be there in twenty minutes." There was a brief pause. "Hey, Brian, are you sure those coordinates are right? Owl says you're pushing pretty hard against the dusk line."

"We're doing more than that," Brian replied. "We are taking *New Haven* into full darkness."

"What?"

On the monitor, he saw a group of faceless GMT members entering the control tower through the basement.

"Look, I'll explain when you get here. For now, I need to concentrate on keeping Jessica alive."

To her credit, Alex didn't question that statement. "Roger that. We're on our way."

As the conversation between Brian and Alex ended, the sun dipped behind the western horizon and darkness crept over New Haven.

All over the city, people stopped what they were doing, and their eyes went to the sky.

Protesters in the Hub lowered their signs and looked toward the darkening horizon, as did the badges, who were supposed to be corralling them.

People working, people drinking, people making love. They all observed the darkness in wonder and fear. Sleeping loved ones were woken to see the spectacle. Most of the city had never experienced a darkened sky, and seeing it now was like watching a second sun appear; it was entirely unexpected and unnatural to them.

After a few moments of collective silence, chaos erupted. Some people screamed. A few fainted. Most scattered, heading back to their homes to be with loved ones. They had no idea if their ship was malfunctioning, or if they were about to be swarmed with vampires. After all, wasn't that why *New Haven* flew in the sun? To keep the vampires away?

As the people scattered, the darkness grew deeper. There were no exterior lights anywhere in *New Haven*. There had never been a need for any. The city plunged into darkness.

In Fleming's office, Sarah watched the scene outside of the window, a sick feeling in her stomach. Never had the city so badly needed their leader to address them and calm their fears. But he was in no condition to do so. He was currently occupied with other concerns.

"Why would they do this?" Fleming asked, as he stared at the monitor on his desk, searching for signs of the fugitives. "CB's an evil traitor, but he's not an idiot. He has a reason."

Sarah answered without taking her eyes off the window. It was difficult to even see the street below, now, but still she stared. "It seems pretty obvious to me. He wanted to sow chaos in the city and prove you're not in control."

Her voice was flat. She'd long since given up trying to calm him. At this point, he was right to panic.

Fleming thought about that for a moment, then shook his head. "I don't think so. This is something else." He tapped his fingers on his desk. "I should know this. I should be able to figure this out."

Finally, Sarah turned away from the window and looked at Fleming. "You don't think this is about Agartha, do you? Is it possible the Agartha vampires have a ship that could reach us?"

At the word *vampires*, Fleming froze, suddenly understanding. "No. Not Agartha." He looked at her, the terror clear in his eyes. "Sarah, they have a vampire on board."

Sarah shook her head slowly. "That's impossible. We've only been in darkness a few minutes."

"You don't understand. There's been a vampire on board the whole time."

Sarah stared at Fleming, her mouth agape, certain he'd truly lost his mind.

Fleming grabbed the radio, clutching it so hard his

fingers turned white. "I need every faceless GMT unit at the Hub immediately."

"Sir, what about the flight deck?"

"Let the badges handle that," he barked. "Get the faceless GMT here now!"

Setting down the radio, he ran to the door and threw it open. The four guards outside looked at him in surprise.

"There is a vampire coming here to kill me," he said in a breathless voice. "I have reinforcements on the way, but until they arrive, it's up to you to protect me. Come wait in here."

The guards looked at each other, fear and confusion on their faces.

"Listen carefully, if the vampire arrives, you have to kill it. Even if it bites me, even if I tell you to stop. No matter what I do or say, keep firing on the vampire until he is dead. Do you understand?"

From their perplexed expressions, it was clear they didn't, but they all nodded.

"Yes, sir," one of them said. "We'll kill the vampire."

THE LIGHT WAS FADING in the room with the steel box.

"Is it time?" Frank asked.

"Almost." As always, waiting was the hardest part for CB. Once he threw open the door to that steel box, things would move quickly. He'd barely have a chance to breathe before this ended, one way or the other. But now, he was left to think about all the ways that this crazy plan could go wrong. A single, lucky headshot from a guard outside the GMT hangar could take Frank down and bring his plan to a screeching halt.

He pushed the thought away. It was much too late to reconsider now. Either the plan would work, and *New Haven* would find peace and balance again, or CB, Jessica, and Brian would die as traitors and the city would be ruled by a madman for the indefinite future.

As the last light faded over the horizon, CB turned on a headlamp he'd brought from the hangar. He opened a wall safe mounted opposite the steel box. Inside was a single key. Then he used the key to open a cabinet next to the monitor. Inside was a red button with a sign above it. "WARNING: BUTTON UNLOCKS STEEL CAGE. DO NOT PROCEED WITHOUT AUTHORIZATION FROM THE CITY COUNCIL."

The way CB figured it, the fact that the Council had been murdered was authorization enough. His hand hovered over the button, but he hesitated, as something in the monitor caught his eye.

Frank was changing.

The change wasn't as obvious as when he'd transformed from a Feral back to his human form, but it was a change, nonetheless.

For the first time since CB had met him, Frank was standing up straight. He looked strong and fresh, his usual pained expression gone.

"I can feel it, CB," Frank said. "It's time."

"Yes. It is." CB took a breath, then punched the button.

He heard a series of hydraulic locks moving. Then the box that Frank had called home for the last one hundred and fifty years slowly split. The two halves separated, and CB stood face to face with Frank for the first time.

The vampire slowly stepped forward, moving toward CB.

In his mind, CB pictured what would happen if Frank

attacked. He knew the vampire would be able to kill him in seconds, and he'd be helpless to stop it from happening.

Instead, Frank extended his hand. CB took it, and the two shook.

"Good to meet you, Colonel Brickman," Frank said with a smile.

"Same here."

The hand shake went on a little too long, and when CB pulled his hand back, Frank seemed reluctant to release it. CB realized this was the first human contact Frank had experienced in a *very* long time. He felt a pang of sorrow at the thought.

"We'd better get moving," he said. "Follow me."

He led Frank through the glass corridor and to the GMT hangar. Frank looked around in wonder as they walked.

"This place was new last time I saw it," Frank said. "We had such dreams for this city."

"Let's take care of Fleming, then we can see about making some of them come true." CB pulled open the door and they walked into the hangar. It felt surreal, leading a vampire into the GMT headquarters.

As they entered the control room, every eye looked up at them. Though no one spoke, it was clear that they all knew that Frank was a vampire.

CB nodded to Brian. "Can we get Frank a headset? We'll want to stay in contact with him as he goes after Fleming."

Brian quickly nodded and grabbed a comm unit off the desk. "Nice to meet you, Frank. We'll be able to talk to each other with this. I can guide you, if needed. Do you, um, know your way around?"

Frank smiled. "Know my way around? I helped build the place." That statement was met with uncomfortable silence from the techs. He slipped the headset over his ear. "That said, I'm not sure how much has changed since my day. A little guidance would be appreciated."

"Okay, great. From what I can see, you should have a pretty clear path to the Hub. Once you get there, things are going to get hairy. There are badges all over the place. You've got twenty outside the building, plus a lot more wandering around the area."

"Piece of cake," Frank replied. And he sounded like he meant it.

"Once you get inside the building, there are six guards on the main floor. Then six more on Fleming's floor. Four guards are in Fleming's office, along with Fleming and a woman named Sarah. I'll walk you through the rest on the way."

"Got it."

When Frank was outfitted and ready, CB led him to the GMT hangar door.

"Be careful, Frank. Fleming is going to be well protected."

"The way I feel right now, I don't think a few guards are going to be a problem." He paused a moment. "CB, I want what we're doing here to bring lasting peace. The people need to know the truth about Fleming. I'm going to make him confess before I kill him."

"You think you can do that?" CB asked.

"I'll get him to talk." He started toward the door, then stopped, turning back to CB. "Thank you for believing in me. After so many years of hopeless insanity, I feel like I finally have a purpose. I won't let you down."

An unexpected rush of emotions went through CB. "No. It's us who should be thanking you. Fleming's always said vampires aren't as dangerous as we claimed. Go prove him wrong."

Frank nodded, then turned back to the door. They could hear badges trying to cut through the lock. "Okay. Let's see what this vampire body can do."

Suddenly, Frank surged forward. He kicked the door, and both the door and the frame broke free of the wall around it, flying backward into the badges working there.

Frank was in motion again before the remaining badges could even react. He took all five of them down before they even fired a shot. Then he sprinted off, heading toward the Hub.

Just then, Alex's voice came through the radio. "We're almost there. Is somebody going to open the airlock, or what?"

"SORRY, ALEX," Brian answered. "Things have been a little crazy. We'll have her open in a moment."

"Roger that," Alex said. "See you soon."

The mood aboard the away ship was tense as they approached their city. Every one of them knew they were walking into a fight. Fleming already believed them dead, and it seemed unlikely that he'd give them a hero's welcome when he found out they weren't.

They all understood that whatever happened tonight, things in *New Haven* would never be the same. Come tomorrow, either they'd be dead, or Fleming's reign would be over.

Owl glanced over at Alex. "Should I do the thing?"

"Yes. Do the thing."

"Sorry, what thing?" George asked.

"It's sort of a tradition," Owl answered. She flicked a switch on her radio, broadcasting her voice to everyone on the ship. "Okay, listen up, everybody. We are approaching

New Haven. A city built on an airship. Population approximately forty thousand."

Patrick's voice interrupted her. "Uh, what the hell, Owl? We don't need to hear a bunch of facts about *New Haven.*"

"Yes, we do," Alex answered, her voice firm. "We need to be reminded of what we're fighting for."

"The city was the last accomplishment of a dying civilization," Owl continued. "In humanity's darkest days, the greatest minds on Earth worked together to launch her. According to the records, one of the most difficult things for them to decide was the name of the ship. Before settling on *New Haven*, the names *Archangel, Sunrider,* and *Pigeon Wing* were all top contenders."

"Wait, *Pigeon Wing*?" Ed asked.

"A lot of lives have been lived on this ship. Generations were born and died without ever setting foot on the surface. She's flown for one hundred and fifty years, held together by the brilliance, hard work, and sheer stubbornness of humans who refused to admit defeat."

"Not to mention, a few replacement parts gathered by the GMT," Wesley added.

"And now she's ruled by a delusional madman," Owl concluded.

Alex set her jaw, her face a mask of determination. "Not for long."

FLEMING SAT BEHIND HIS DESK, his face pale.

All day, he'd been pacing, and Sarah had wished he'd just sit still for a few minutes, but this was almost worse. For the first time, Fleming looked truly afraid.

And all because of an imaginary vampire. She decided to try reasoning with him one last time.

"Sir, even if there is a vampire on the ship, there is no way he could get to you. The faceless GMT is trained to kill vampires. That's their whole job, right? Plus, you have half an army in the Hub. This office is the safest place in the city right now."

A sudden flurry of gunshots came from outside the building. They heard yelling, banging, and then nothing.

Fleming sat up straight, his eyes wild. "What was that? What's going on out there?"

The guards in the room looked at each other, their faces suddenly drawn with worry.

"We'll find out, sir," one of them said, then he began talking into his headset.

There were a few more gunshots, and these sounded like they might be coming from *inside* the building.

Sarah swallowed hard, for the first time wondering if maybe Fleming wasn't crazy. Maybe there really was a vampire aboard *New Haven*.

The guard looked at Fleming. "They're saying something attacked them. They don't know what it was, but it tore through their ranks. It's inside the building."

The guards moved into position, lining up facing the door, their backs to Fleming and Sarah.

Fleming reached into a drawer in his desk and pulled out a pistol. He held it in a two-handed grip, and still the weapon was visibly shaking.

Sarah looked from the door to Fleming and back, waiting to see what would happen next, and afraid she already knew. There was a vampire in the building, and it was coming after them. They were as good as dead.

More gunshots, this time from their floor. The fighting

was happening right outside the office. They heard a series of loud thumps, like something slamming against a wall. Was it furniture? Or bodies?

"What's happening out there?" Fleming asked frantically.

"I don't know," one of the guards replied without turning around. "They've stopped answering."

"Who?"

"Everyone," the guard said, his voice shaking. "Everyone has stopped answering."

To that, Fleming had no reply.

Suddenly, a thunderous crashing sound erupted, and the twin doors to the office were ripped off their hinges. The guards peered through the now open doorway, but there was no one there. It was as if the doors had simply disappeared.

Then one of the doors flew through the opening, slamming into two of the guards, knocking them across the room.

Something rushed in, almost too quick for Sarah's eyes to follow.

And suddenly, a man in a green jumpsuit stood before her. He looked no different from someone she might see walking through the street in Sparrow's Ridge, except for his glowing red eyes.

It was a vampire. A vampire was standing right in front of her.

Fleming began firing immediately, but even at this close range, his aim was way off. The first two shots hit the wall behind the vampire, and the third struck one of the remaining two guards in the neck.

The vampire barely seemed to notice the gunfire. He grabbed the final guard and hurled him through the window. The guard screamed as he tumbled through the air, before he landed on the street below and was quickly silenced.

Then the vampire turned to Fleming. "Hello. You must be Fleming. My name's Frank."

And then the vampire was in motion. He dashed across the room with uncanny speed, ripping the gun from Fleming's hand.

Fleming only had time to shout, "Wait, I need to tell you—"

Then Frank's teeth sank into his neck.

The vampire's eyes closed in ecstasy as he drank. Then, after a few moments, he pulled himself away, gasping with clear physical effort. Fleming crumpled to the floor.

"I hope I did that right," the vampire muttered, Fleming's blood covering his chin.

Sarah's hand went to her mouth, unable to believe what had just happened. Fleming was dead. This vampire had killed him. Something deep inside her refused to believe it, and yet the evidence was right in front of her.

She dropped to her knees, tears filling her eyes.

Then, impossibly, Fleming climbed back to his feet.

Sarah scurried backwards until her back touched one of the fallen guards.

"Ah, good," Frank said. "You're back. I wasn't sure it would work."

Fleming looked just as surprised as Sarah felt. He stared down at his hands in disbelief.

"The people of *New Haven* need to hear what really happened to the City Council in your own words" Frank said. "Can you record audio in here?"

"Of course," Fleming replied.

"Good. Turn on the recording equipment. Now."

Fleming immediately began tapping on his computer screen.

Sarah felt like she couldn't breathe. What the hell was happening? This vampire... it was as if he were controlling Fleming. She put her hand down, intending to use it to push herself to her feet, but her skin touched cold metal. She closed her fingers around it and pulled it toward her.

"Are we recording?" Frank asked.

"Yes," Fleming answered.

"Then I want you to—"

The sound of a gunshot cut off his words.

Sarah held the rifle in a death grip, still pointed at Frank. He lay face down on Fleming's desk, a small black hole in his back where the bullet had gone in. Considering the amount of black, inky blood on the desk, the exit wound had been much larger. Frank slowly slipped to the floor where he crumpled into a motionless heap.

Sarah had done it. She'd killed the vampire. She slowly got to her feet and let the rifle slip from her fingers. "Fleming? Is that still you?"

"Yes," he said slowly, a smile growing across his face. "It's me. But better." He blinked hard. "And hungry."

ALEX STOOD in the GMT control room, watching the security footage over Brian's shoulder. She couldn't believe what she was seeing.

Her reunion with her friends had been short and sweet. The medical staff had gone to work on Chuck as CB quickly gave the rest of the team a high-level overview of how they'd unleashed Frank on Fleming. The GMT had then crowded into the control room to see the plan play out.

Alex had watched on the monitors in real-time, her fingers digging into Brian's shoulder as Frank drank from Fleming. And she'd watched in horror as everything went terribly wrong.

The only person in the control room who didn't hesitate when Sarah shot Frank was CB. He immediately grabbed the radio.

"Jessica, you need to change course. Get us back into the light now! Fleming's been turned."

On another monitor, Alex could see Jessica springing into motion. In mere moments, Alex felt the ship turning.

Brian's security feed made it clear that Fleming felt it, too. He looked up suddenly, then dashed out of his office.

"Oh, shit," Alex said, the realization hitting her. "He's going after Jessica." She turned to CB. "I don't suppose you have another vampire locked away somewhere."

CB's face was stone. "I've got something better. I've got you."

Alex turned to her team. "You hear that? We have one more vampire to kill tonight."

"Good thing we're still dressed for work," Wesley said.

CB opened his mouth, and for a moment Alex thought he was going to give them some of his famous motivation. Instead, he said only one word.

"Go."

JESSICA STOOD on the flight deck, her back pressed against the controls. "So, what you're telling me is, Fleming is on his way to kill me and you don't know how to stop him?"

There was a long pause. Then Brian said, "Yes. I'm sorry,

Jessica." Another pause. "Crap. He's right outside the flight deck."

Jessica tried to steel her nerves. She held a gun she'd taken from one of the unconscious guards, and she'd aimed it at the door. Since Fleming didn't need to breathe, Brian's technique of sucking the air out of a room wouldn't be effective, but she knew a well-placed bullet could be. She just had to keep her cool.

Something heavy smashed into the flight deck's door, and a large dent appeared. The door wouldn't withstand another hit like that.

She glanced over at the controls, double-checking that the auto-pilot was still engaged. They were at least five minutes from daylight, but maybe if she stalled, Fleming would waste enough time killing her for the ship to get back into the sunlight.

She ran across the room to the farthest point from the controls.

Just as she'd predicted, Fleming's next hit ripped the door right off its hinges.

Fleming strode into the room. His usual politician's smile was gone, replaced with an expression of stony anger.

"Fleming," Jessica said. "How have you been?"

"I'm a bit dead, at the moment. A condition that has me avoiding sunlight. I need you to turn the ship around. Now."

"I'd love to help you, Fleming. Seems like you're having a bit of a day and could use a break. But I'm an engineer, not a pilot." She nodded toward the unconscious pilot on the ground. "I guess we'll just have to wait for him to wake up."

Fleming's lip curled in a snarl. "Quit stalling."

"I'm not. I just—"

And then Fleming was in motion. By the time Jessica realized he was moving, he was already across the room and had his hands on her shoulders. He leaned in close, so his dead face was less than an inch from hers.

"If you don't turn this ship around, I will bite you. You will be my eternal slave, and I will make you kill every one of your friends." He paused. "Although it would be my first time, so I might accidently kill you. Could go either way. I would suggest changing course right now, unless you want to find out which horrific way things end for you."

———

ALEX SPRINTED toward the control tower at the front of the ship, cursing the bulky GMT gear that she was wearing. She was still fully decked out from her mission. If she'd only thought to ditch some of the heavier equipment.

Still, she was pulling away from the rest of the team. All of them were in good shape, but none of the others could run like Alex. With every scream of her burning lungs, she reminded herself that her friend Jessica was alone, and that Fleming was coming for her.

Fleming. How many times had Alex wished that she could get him alone in a fight? Now, it looked like she was going to get the chance. Only, Fleming would have such a physical advantage that she had almost no hope of winning. She'd seen the vampires fighting the Ferals at night, when Jaden and his crew rescued the GMT. She'd watched the vampires sparring in Agartha. While a brand-new vampire wouldn't be up to their level of finesse, he'd still have the same speed and strength.

The thought of facing a vampire at night made her shudder.

The thought of saving her friend and punching Fleming in his smug face kept her going.

As she reached the building, she saw that the front doors were smashed in. It looked like Fleming had already been through here. She followed the path of destruction, knowing she was close on his trail. She could hear pounding on metal and crashing coming from up ahead. Fleming was in the building, breaking through all the doors on his way to the flight deck.

As she started up the final set of stairs, she glanced back. The rest of her team was too far behind. She couldn't wait for them. Jessica needed her help now.

She reached the top of the stairs and felt a wave of despair as she saw how Fleming had demolished the heavy metal doors. How could she possibly take down someone so strong?

She stepped onto the flight deck and saw Fleming, his hands on Jessica's shoulders. Jessica's back was to Alex, her body blocking any clear shot Alex might have at Fleming. They were at the front of the room, directly in front of the large glass wall that looked over the expanse beyond the nose of *New Haven*.

"I'm not going to turn the ship," Jessica said coldly. "Do what you have to do."

Something sparked in Alex's mind. She remembered the sparring session she'd watched in Agartha. One moment in particular. When one vampire had thrown the other.

A thought had gone through her mind when she'd seen that: Vampires are subject to the laws of gravity and physics. In the air, a vampire was just as vulnerable as anyone else.

"Bad call," Fleming said. He bared his teeth, preparing to bite.

No more time to think; Alex had to act.

She raised her pistol. "Fleming!"

He turned, and his eyes widened, clearly shocked to see her alive.

She fired four shots so quickly that someone who didn't know might have thought her pistol was an automatic.

Fleming looked down, checking to see if he was hit. When he saw that he wasn't, he smiled. "Maybe the great Alex Goddard isn't—"

He stopped as a loud cracking sound came from behind him. He turned just in time to see the glass shatter outward from the four bullet holes.

The room depressurized and the air rushed out, sucking Fleming and Jessica out with it.

Alex didn't hesitate. She sprinted across the room, half running, half carried by the suction, and dove through the window after them.

The three of them tumbled past the edge of *New Haven* and into the dark void beyond.

Alex maneuvered herself into a dive, trying to cut an aerodynamic line to catch up to the other two. Fleming snarled as he saw her coming. He let go of Jessica and tried to angle himself toward her.

Jessica screamed as she fell. She was spinning wildly, the space between her and Fleming quickly increasing.

Alex glanced at Jessica, silently hoping that she could hold it together for just another moment. Then Alex raised the pistol still clutched in her hand. She took careful aim as the wind rushed by.

Fleming flailed, trying to gain control of his fall. He stared at Alex, the look on his face revealing his complete bafflement at how she'd gotten the better of him and why she'd thrown herself down after him.

Alex held the gun as steady as she could and squeezed

the trigger. The round went straight through Fleming's forehead.

She was pretty sure that he was dead, but pretty sure was not good enough. Not where Fleming was concerned.

She drew her sword and dove toward his suddenly limp body. As she reached him, she swung hard, knowing this would take more force than normal. Her sword bit into his neck, decapitating him.

For a long moment, Alex stared at his severed head falling through the air.

She couldn't believe it. The fight was finally over. Fleming was dead.

Alex allowed herself just another second to stare, then she dove toward Jessica.

The engineer was still spinning wildly, but Alex reached out and caught her arm.

Alex pulled her in and shouted, "Hold on!"

Then she activated her jetpack.

Thank God, she hadn't had time to take off her gear.

The jetpack struggled and coughed under the weight of two people. It held them aloft, but Alex wasn't sure it would be enough to get them back up to *New Haven*.

Then Owl's voice came through her headset. "Need a ride?"

In the distance above, she saw another, smaller ship pulling away from *New Haven*.

"Yes!" she shouted.

Alex and Jessica floated in the dark sky, clutching each other for dear life as they waited for the away ship to arrive.

EPILOGUE

FIREFLY WALKED the corridors of Agartha aimlessly, much as he had every night for the past two weeks.

Jaden, the vampires, and the people of Agartha had all welcomed Firefly and the former Resettlers to the city. The newcomers were provided blood and places to sleep, though some of them had to bunk three to a room due to space constraints.

Despite the warm welcome, it was clear the presence of nearly two hundred new vampires was causing some upheaval in the city. Everything from the supply of blood to the question of what the new vampires were even supposed to do with themselves was up in the air. Jaden and his vampires had a strict routine, but more than doubling their number had thrown off their well-ordered lives.

But to Firefly, the worst of it was being left alone each night with his tortured thoughts. He was having a difficult time grappling with everything that had happened. He'd dedicated his life to keeping humans safe from vampires, and instead he'd gotten an entire settlement killed. Not to mention Robert, whom he'd personally murdered.

And now he had an endless, meaningless life stretched out in front of him, with nothing to fill it but regret.

He sensed two vampires moving in behind him, and he greeted them without looking back. "Hello, Jaden. Hello... is that Natalie?"

"Nicely done," Natalie said. "Got it in one. You must be learning our scents."

"Can we talk to you a minute?" Jaden asked.

"Of course," Firefly answered, the surprise clear in his voice.

Jaden led him to a corridor deep in the interior of the mountain. It was a part of the city Firefly had yet to visit. "I'm sorry I haven't been around much these past two weeks."

"It's all right," Firefly said. "I'm sure you have better things to do than babysit me."

Jaden chuckled. "Indeed. I've been doing some thinking, and I've had a few insights. I spent time grieving, thinking about my friends who died in Denver. But then I suddenly remembered my Shakespeare. 'We few. We happy few. We band of brothers.'"

"Sorry, you lost me. Shake what?"

"Ugh, don't get him started," Natalie groaned. "If you give him the least bit of encouragement, he'll do the entire Saint Crispin's Day speech."

"That was one time," Jaden protested.

"Yes, but we were trying to fight off the second wave. The Battle of Pittsburgh, wasn't it? Not exactly the time for speeches."

Jaden turned back to Firefly. "The point is, I realized you're part of the vampire brotherhood now. We take mentorship very seriously, and it's time we start teaching you what being a vampire truly means. We have a lot of work to do if we want to set things right."

"Set things right?" Firefly asked. "Fleming's dead. Mark and Aaron are dead. Agartha and *New Haven* are safe."

Jaden laughed. "You're still thinking like a human. Yes, the immediate threat is defeated, but what about the larger one? You think this world is as it should be? You think it's meant to be filled with Ferals, too dangerous for humans to even set foot here during the night?" He shook his head at the stupidity of the idea. "Look, Fleming was a fool for moving on such an aggressive timeline, and for just sticking a bunch of humans behind a thirty-foot wall and thinking they'd be fine. But he wasn't wrong about one thing. Agartha and *New Haven* won't last forever."

Firefly nodded slowly. "I guess we should start coming up with a plan."

Jaden burst out laughing again. "Start? What do you think we've been doing these last one hundred and fifty years? We have a plan. We were just missing one element."

"What's that?" Firefly asked.

"You." Jaden reached a door and scanned his keycard. The light next to the door beeped and Jaden turned the handle, looking back at Firefly with a sly smile.

"Wait, what?"

Jaden waved him inside. "Come. See."

Firefly stepped into the large room. The walls were covered with maps, mostly of places he'd never even heard of. Hand-drawn circles and writing covered much of their surface. "What is this place?"

"It's our war room," Jaden said. "It's where our plan is going to come together."

Firefly noticed another man standing on the other side of the room. He greeted Firefly with a nod.

"Ah," Jaden said, "You two haven't met. Firefly, this is Frank. He's a fellow *New Haven* resident. Former resident, anyway. He moved down here to enjoy our less sunny atmosphere."

Firefly sniffed and noticed no human scent coming off this man. Frank was a vampire. "I don't understand. How could a vampire—"

"We'll explain it all," Jaden said. "For now, just know that he's a friend. He helped take down Fleming. Even took a bullet to the chest."

"Missed my heart by an inch," Frank said with a smile.

"It's about time you had some good luck," Jaden pointed out. He turned back to Firefly. "Frank has a role to play in what's to come, too. His knowledge is going to come in handy."

Natalie elbowed Jaden in the ribs. "Quit being so coy. Just tell him."

"Fine." Jaden's face grew more serious. "Firefly, you and your people dedicated yourself to Resettlement. To bringing the humans back to the surface. That fight isn't over. In fact, it's just beginning. We're going to make sure you see it through."

Firefly shook his head. "I still don't understand. Why me? Why us?"

"Because you're the link between humans and vampires," Natalie explained. "I haven't been a human in centuries. And this guy," she cocked her thumb at Jaden, "they literally hadn't invented windmills the last time his heart beat. But your vampires are still connected to the humans."

"It won't be easy, and it won't be quick," Jaden explained, "not even by vampire standards. But I think we have a plan to make it work."

For the first time in two weeks, Firefly felt a spark of hope. After everything he'd been through, every mistake he'd made, maybe there would be a way to truly help the world. Maybe his existence could have a purpose after all.

"What's the plan?"

Jaden and Natalie exchanged a glance.

"Tell him the other part," Natalie said.

Jaden looked at Firefly. "For this all to make sense, you need to understand something. You've heard about the three waves of vampires that destroyed humanity, but there's more to that story. A lot more. There are things that happened during the infestation that humans *can never* know. But as a vampire, you must know them. That's our burden. And it may hold the key to true Resettlement."

"What things?" Firefly asked.

Jaden nodded toward the still-open door. "Shut that. Then I'll tell you the real story of how civilization fell."

Firefly walked to the doorway, his knees shaking ever so slightly, not sure if he wanted to hear what Jaden was about to tell him.

Then he closed the door.

THOUGH IT WAS ONLY six thirty in the morning, the GMT workout facility was already bustling with activity.

Patrick and Ed took turns at the squat rack, trying to outdo each other both in terms of weight lifted and insults hurled.

Wesley was on the sparring mat with Beau, each of them wearing boxing gloves and headgear. While Beau wasn't officially on the team, CB had given him a provisional status while Chuck recovered from his injuries.

On the other side of the room, Owl sweated her way through a set of shoulder presses. Chuck pedaled his exercise bike, his arm still in a sling.

Alex stepped into the facility and took all this in. It was great to see her team working out, but it only reminded her that she wouldn't be able to join them today. She had another mission.

Ed did a double take when he saw her. "Whoa, Captain, you look good!"

She grimaced. Exactly the type of response she'd been hoping to avoid. CB had insisted she dress up today. "Yeah, well, don't get used to it. Tomorrow these heels will be in the closet where they belong, and I'll be back in my combat boots."

She heard a grunt from the corner of the workout area and let out a laugh at what she saw there.

CB stood behind a bench in full dress attire. And below him, Brian McElroy was doing a set of bench presses.

Alex sauntered over, a wide smile on her face.

"One more, Brian. You got this!" CB barked.

Brian let out a massive grunt as he lifted the barbell and its modest set of plates, finally getting them all the way up.

Alex waited in silence while CB helped him guide the bar back onto the rack. Only then did she speak. "Brian McElroy. I'm impressed! When did you start pumping iron?"

Brian's face reddened when he saw her. "Oh, hey, Alex." He glanced at the clock. "About thirty minutes ago. I sort of made a promise to CB. I said if we made it through the Fleming thing, I'd start taking care of myself. I procrastinated for two weeks, but a deal's a deal."

"Good for you," Alex said. "You ready to go, CB?"

CB nodded grimly. Clearly, he wasn't looking forward to

this any more than she was. "Polls open in thirty minutes. We better get moving."

They started to leave the gym, but at the last moment, Alex turned back. "Hey, Brian, you want to meet me at Tankards tonight?"

He tilted his head in surprise. "Sure. What for?"

"A date," she said with a smile.

"Oh!" He suddenly sat up a bit straighter. "Yeah, a date. Let's do it."

"Seven o'clock. Don't be late." With that, she turned and followed CB out the door.

"You just made his year," CB said with a chuckle.

"Good. Maybe he can make my night. I haven't seen much action lately."

CB sighed. "Please don't break him. We need his help to put this ship back together."

"No promises, but I'll try to be gentle." She paused. "Speaking of putting the ship back together, how's Jessica?"

"Good. Excellent, actually. I saw her last night."

"I'm really glad you two found each other, CB," she said.

He smiled. "So am I."

They walked in silence through Sparrow's Ridge. They'd almost reached the edge of the Hub when Alex spoke again.

"So, we save the city, and our reward is more boring meetings?"

"I'm not thrilled about it, either. But try to remember, it's supposed to be an honor."

The two weeks since Fleming's death had gone by in a blur of activity. General Craig had taken control of the city, and his first goal had been to re-establish peace. Through a combination of surveillance footage, eyewitness accounts, and even a video message from Firefly, they'd been able to convince most of Fleming's followers of the truth of Resettlement and what Fleming had done to the City Council.

Surprisingly, Sarah had been one of the keys to making that happen. She'd given an interview that had been broadcast citywide, in which she'd explained the details of exactly how the Council bombing had gone down, and how Fleming had lost his mind in his final days. Everyone knew she was doing it to save her own skin, but at least she was doing it.

Today was Election Day. General Craig had pushed to get the elections set up quickly, and he was even running for a City Council spot himself, albeit reluctantly. And he'd invited CB and Alex to the Hub to help him oversee the voting process, to ensure that everything went smoothly. In reality, that meant spending the day in a board room with a bunch of politicians, as they argued and waited for the election results to roll in. It wasn't a task Alex was looking forward to, but she knew it was important.

"You know," CB said, "maybe you should run for office next time around. Everybody in *New Haven* seems to love you these days."

"Ha. No thanks. The storm drains under Denver were scummy enough. I don't need to wade into politics."

As they reached the door to the Council building, Alex paused. "CB, hang on a second. There's something I need to say."

CB stopped. "Okay, now I'm worried. You're not moving to Agartha, are you?"

She laughed. "No, nothing like that. I just wanted to say thank you. You believed in me when no else did. You gave me my shot and let me join the GMT. Then you let me stay on the team when you probably should have kicked me off. Then you let me lead."

CB looked at her for a long moment before answering. "All I did was give you a chance. You took it, and you gave this city your all. If not for you, a lot more people would be dead. You're the fiercest warrior and the most dedicated person I've ever met. I'm proud to be your friend."

Alex blinked back the tears that sprang to her eyes.

"I don't know what's going to happen next," CB continued. "Fleming stripped this ship to the bones, and it's going to take a hell of a lot of work to get our systems safe and stable again. The GMT is going to be making frequent trips to the surface in the next few months. But today the city gets to decide its own fate."

Alex pulled open the double doors and took a deep breath. "Okay, CB. Let's see what happens next."

The two of them walked side by side through the doors and into *New Haven*'s future.

AUTHORS' NOTE

Dear reader,

Thanks so much for reading these books.

As of this writing, we've been working on the Vampire World Saga for about two years. It seems like we discover new things about Alex and her world with just about every new chapter we write.

It's pretty cool how stories can evolve. In our original outline, Firefly was meant to be the big bad of book three. Things didn't turn out that way. Alex kept wanting to give Firefly a chance, and—as flawed as he is—he refused to give in fully to the dark side. His unexpected resilience made this book so much better.

Our goal with this third novel was to make it like the exciting last half hour of a movie: all action, adventure, and emotional payoffs. We hope you enjoyed the ride.

So, what's next?

As you can probably guess from the ending, we're not done with The Vampire World Saga. True Resettlement is coming, but it will not come easily. There are plenty more secrets to be revealed, and not all of them will be easy for Alex and her team to learn.

The Savage Truth, book four in the Vampire World Saga, comes out April 17th, 2019.

Once again, thank you for reading The Savage Dawn!

Best,

P.T. Hylton and Jonathan Benecke

Printed in Great Britain
by Amazon

28972605R00169